DARK
MAGIC

STEPHEN GRESHAM

P

PINNACLE BOOKS
Kensington Publishing Corp.
http://www.kensingtonbooks.com

PINNACLE BOOKS are published by

Kensington Publishing Corp.
850 Third Avenue
New York, NY 10022

All Kensington Titles, Imprints, and Distributed Lines are available at special quantity discounts for bulk purchases for sales promotions, premiums, fund-raising, and educational or institutional use. Special book excerpts or customized printings can also be created to fit specific needs. For details, write or phone the office of the Kensington special sales manager: Kensington Publishing Corp., 850 Third Avenue, New York, NY 10022, attn: Special Sales Department, Phone: 1-800-221-2647.

Pinnacle and the P logo Reg. U.S. Pat. & TM Off.

First Printing: February 2002
10 9 8 7 6 5 4 3 2 1

Printed in the United States of America

DARK MAGIC

Artie whirled around, hoping the flickering firelight onshore would continue to give off enough illumination for her to see what was out there. But at first she saw nothing except the silvery glint of something sharp and bonelike swimming her way. It reminded her of a shark's fin, and she gasped at the sight of it.

Yet, try as she might, she could not move. Could not escape.

Whatever it was stayed submerged, generating waves and eddies that slammed against her and threatened to pull her under. Artie screamed as hard as she could, calling out for help.

Then something shaggy brushed against her thigh.

She screamed again.

She thrashed about, attempting to fight and then attempting to run, though even as she did so she experienced an overwhelming urge to give in to whatever mysterious force was pressing in upon her.

Hands wrapped around her waist. Hooves bruised her wrists. The right side of her body went numb. She felt half of her face twist and her mouth lock in a rictus. Water began to fill her lungs.

One world opened—a world of dark magic. Another closed. And then blackness devoured everything. . . .

Books by Stephen Gresham

IN THE BLOOD

DARK MAGIC

Published by Pinnacle Books

This is in memory of my mother, Helen Elizabeth Kennedy Gresham (1920–2000), who read my fiction with eyes of love, finding in my work words more naked than flesh, stronger than bone, more resilient than sinew, and more sensitive than nerve. She understood the human forms of dark magic of which I write in this book.

PROLOGUE

If you have a secret self—read this tale. . . .

ONE

You could have heard it on the dark side of the moon.

Anyone who knew how to listen could have.

Willow Fossor knew.

She freed herself from the school bus and in a rush of relief twirled through a chalky-white cloud of dust. As she did so, she could hear the unmistakable clang, clang, clang of Joe Boy's signal off in the distance. Ball-peen hammer against a plowshare hanging by a chain. She could hear it even with her headphones on. She could hear it over the wounded rage of Nirvana's CD, *Nevermind,* and her favorite cut, "Something in the Way." Real music. No Britney Spears or Backstreet Boys or intelligence-assaulting rap for Willow. No brokenhearted down-on-my-luck country-western twang: no Dixie Chicks or Faith Hill or George sleepy-eyed, cowboy-hat-wearing Strait. The only music that touched Willow's soul was either the velvet ferociousness of Nirvana or the spine-clawing, bump-in-the-night sound of Danzig's *Black Aria.*

Witchy music.

Joe Boy's clang meant that someone was crossing on the rope-pull ferry to the spit on the backwater edge of Night Horse Creek, which, in turn, flowed into Night Horse Swamp. She could imagine Joe

Boy—thirteen, same age as she—his round, homely face sweat-glistened, his hair slicked down with possum grease, his mouth open like a carp bottom-feeding, his eyes small and dark like a muskrat's. Not beefcake or gridiron material. But what a swimmer he was—Willow was certain he could swim across the ocean and that his knowledge of the great swamp was encyclopedic. She believed he could even teach the resident critters things they did not know.

When the ferry signal ceased, she took off her headphones and set her jaw against the chant of her peers: "Willow, Willow witch! Ain't she a bitch!"

She hated them. Hated their sweat. Hated their intolerance. But loved their fear. More dust billowed as the black and orange bus—colors that made Willow think of Halloween, her favorite holiday—hissed and squealed and groaned away. Fleshy pink faces hovered at the back window, tongues sticking out, obscene gestures flashing like daggers. When one especially brave boy mooned her, Willow giggled at the sight of his fish-belly-white rear flattened against the glass. And then the ugly world of sound and fury swept from her until it became small enough to swallow.

Willow smiled smugly at the sway she held over her bus mates, none courageous enough to sit by her. She enjoyed a certain power over nearly everyone, in fact, at Homewinds Junior High School, Homewinds, Alabama, where her otherworldliness had spawned insecurity and ignorance among both students and faculty. Twice during the current school year she had been temporarily suspended. Once for allegedly putting a hex on Miss Truckett, the mannish physical education teacher who hated Willow with a passion and who had openly vowed to make her life a nightmare. Instead, Willow had playfully cast the evil eye upon Truckett one day in the lunch room as she hovered hungrily over a plate of lasagna. Five minutes later that same lasagna was spewing steamily into the laps of colleagues unfortunate enough to be sharing her table. Truckett, it seems, had picked up a stomach bug upon the instant. Though nothing supernatural could be proven, Willow was sentenced to a two-day exile from school. And then there was the episode involving Tiffany Wilburn, head cheerleader, a flawless blonde who had whispered some catty hallway remark that Willow overheard. By morning Tiffany's pretty bottom had beaded up in the nastiest rash one could imagine—Old Testament intensity. Accusations were leveled, and, again despite a lack of material evidence against her, Willow enjoyed another two-day respite from the citadel of learning. Permanent suspension was hinted at should she step out of line again. Or should it *appear* that she had stepped out of line again. Willow's mother interceded with threats to enlist the legal aid of the A.C.L.U. to protect her daughter's rights. Things quieted down. For the most part, fear-generated looks that could kill replaced words.

Willow thrilled to the sound of those unspoken, unsayable fears.

And the fear on that bus was as palpable as the dust and the warmth of the late afternoon. It was May. Willow was glad to be alive. She started walking home along the crushed-shell road that bordered Night Horse Swamp, the ancient sanctuary tinderbox dry from several months of drought. Locals blamed the Fossor witches for the dire conditions. Wise swamp watchers knew that a cleansing fire would arrive before summer's end. Willow could imagine the beauty and power of such a conflagration. She could imagine the roar of it and how glorious it would feel to be in the maw of it.

Then last night's dream returned. The yearning

essence of dreams fascinated Willow. Her grandmother Fossor had taught her to revere dreams—"They speak the language of the soul," she had often claimed. For Willow, dreams possessed a stubborn thereness. And this one in particular contained a scene that stirred her with confusing feelings—a vague ache of desire as well as a stab of guilt. In the dream a man (was it really a man or an animal?) was lowering himself/itself upon her, his/its face hidden by a clutch of shadows and this shadow man/animal (a glint of antlers?) was panting hot breath and beyond him/it a voice, one she didn't recognize, was speaking a single word.

Coda.

A word that made Willow think of the panther. For her, the beast was a wild thing of beauty. The nameless, guardian deity of the swamp. Alone, free, and fierce. Things that Willow longed for. But the dream word and the panther and the shadow man/animal were pieces of a puzzle that would not fit together. Thoughts of the dream quickened her steps. She wanted to get home and tell her Aunt Mushka about the dream, wanted someone to listen, wanted to know why a shadowy man/animal might show up in the nightly projections of a girl-not-quite-a-woman.

Willow suddenly stopped walking, closed her eyes, and cupped one breast.

Her nipple hardened. That vaguely delicious ache again. She rocked gently to and fro locked in some forbidden lullaby. But quickly she blinked back to reality and dropped her hand from her breast. She thought of her mother who had recently bought her a new outfit from the Gap—short black skirt and mauve-colored, close-fitting top with spaghetti straps—to help her blend in at school. Willow, however, liked her long dresses—today's was crimson, the color she liked best—and she liked not wearing makeup, though getting ready for school often meant dodging her mother's ironic request (how many mothers actually *want* their daughters to wear makeup?) to touch up her lips and cheeks with some color or take a swipe at her with a mascara brush. And Willow positively loved not wearing underwear or pantyhose—no panties or bra. Wearing nothing beneath her bulky dress made her feel bold and dangerous and *unbridled*. . . . She liked that word. Besides, her breasts were still small and perky—what was the point of a bra? Her mother insisted she wear one, but her Aunt Gretta sided with her: "A healthy girl like yourself doesn't need one. Let yourself be natural."

Natural. Another good word.

And Willow liked wearing sandals, even in winter, and she liked jewelry—handmade by her Aunt Arietta: her bracelet of astrological signs, her bloodstone ring, and, most of all, the amulet she wore on a chain around her neck. Aunt Mushka had given it to her the week she got her period—"This is to celebrate life and the coming of womanhood. Your flower has bloomed," she was told. On a metal disk the rayed sun enclosed an eye lined in flames. On the reverse of the amulet, these words:

SOL OMNIPOTENS
TECUM LUCESCO

And Willow didn't mind perfume as long as it was from Aunt Mushka's arsenal of herbal scents mixed with honeysuckle and extract of kudzu—the latter smelled unmistakably like grape Kool-Aid. And Willow liked her long black hair, today still plaited in a herringbone design created to mark Walpurgisnacht on April 30 and then Beltane on May 1, a wiccan sabbat to celebrate the setting free of one's spirit from the hold of winter. Willow loved the annual observance when she and her mother and aunts would gather under Night Horse Oak and circle the massive tree and garland themselves and create an altar to the Goddess and light candles and censer and recite words of praise and joy and eat oatmeal cakes and vanilla ice cream and drink cups (Willow was allowed just one) of Mushka's lusty brew of ginger ale, fruit juices, lots of honey, and a cup of alcohol. And there was much laughter and then the soul-arresting reverie of a bonfire.

She hurried on, buoyed by the memory, a memory dampened by the fact that her Grandmother Fossor had passed a few months ago and could only join them in spirit. Willow missed her grandmother. Missed her great wisdom and vast strength.

Coda.

But there was that word again—a word she hesitated to say aloud.

Was it a word to call out into the Otherworld?

Who or what might respond to that word?

Her grandmother had hinted at the danger of such words.

Dark magic.

"But, Grandmother, a witch must be free to speak," Willow had contended.

To which the wise blood had replied, "Do not call yourself a witch. A true witch does not. If someone asks, say simply that you follow the Old Ways." And it was true that the Fossor women were not witches in the popular sense: they did not worship Satan or sacrifice animals or have some coven that performed bizarre sexual rites—and they did not go door to door soliciting new members. They did not ride brooms or shepherd a flock of goats, though Aunt Mushka had a weird blue-gray cat named Rosebud that some might label a witch's "familiar."

The Fossors were simply a family that revered Nature and their secret selves.

And they followed one rule: And if it harmed no one, do what you will.

But Willow knew that if she were truly to follow that rule, she wouldn't be attending public school. Why couldn't she be home-schooled as her mother and her aunts were by Grandmother Fossor? She knew, of course. She knew that her mother didn't want her always to be a societal outcast. "You must keep one foot in the real world!"

Mother, I don't belong!

A car was approaching as Willow embraced a fantasy of leaving school behind completely: snotty girls, mean boys, suspicious teachers, intolerant administrators. And she had no friends, though a few misguided souls had tried to be—probably because they thought it would be cool to be friends with a witch. Like being in a television sitcom or an MTV video. Willow believed she didn't need them. She had Joe Boy and her aunts, and she had her father despite the fact that he and her mother had divorced several years ago and Willow had chosen to go by her mother's maiden name, Fossor, rather than Scarpia.

It was a pickup truck and not a car. It was roostertailing dust and it sounded like some huge beast clearing its throat. Willow had a pretty good idea who it was, and wisdom dictated that she dodge off into the thick cover at the edge of the swamp. But she smiled to herself. And chose not to. The pickup was black and shiny and filled to overflowing, cab and haul space, with teenage boys clad in baseball caps and unbuttoned shirts. And they would be carrying at least one gun and two cases of beer. When the pickup swung around a bend and sped toward Willow, she held her breath. And as the vehicle rushed past, the rough gaze of the boys raked across her; whoops and predatory cries trailed away from her before another sound: that of a slewing skid like glass shattering. And a screeching turnaround. Willow giggled and stepped off the road into some tall sedge grass before positioning herself a hundred feet or so from the shoulder and yet remaining in plain sight.

Coda.

Thinking of the word made her feel strong. Untouchable. Like the panther.

The pickup pulled directly into view, idling like the grumble of a bull gator. Shouts and whistles resolved into a few distinguishable lines: "Suck my dick, witchy girl!" and "Drink my jizz!" and "Hey, can you turn Ben's pecker into a nightcrawler?" One boy chucked a huge wad of chewing tobacco at her, but it fell harmlessly into the thicket. Redneck drawls spun off tongues as naturally and crudely as could be; words like "fuck" and "pussy" filled the air.

A pack of animals lacking beauty.

That was Willow's thought. These boys were just that: *boys.* They had no real wilderness in them—no manly wilderness, such as Willow craved, such as she had felt in the shadowy entity from her dream. She knew what these boys wanted. She could smell the stench of their dammed-up sexual desires. She could read their minds—their masturbatory fantasies as bright as fresh blood or the sunrise. She smiled and waved. And they growled eagerly in response. She felt powerful. Then something playful seized her, and in the next instant she seductively lifted her long skirt up past her waist and waggled her bottom from side to side. The bird's nest—as she liked to think of it—between her legs was there for the mongrels to see. A tiny pink bird was hiding in it—something these boys would *never* see or touch or know.

A delighted shock slammed into the boys. The hoots of surprise were deafening. Rebel yells rang out as if they were charging up a hill to run the Yankees once and for all out of Dixie. Doors slammed and bodies poured from the pickup. A revolver was fired off as harmlessly as a premature ejaculation. Willow laughed. Then she ran. Laughing triumphantly. Loving who she was. Feeling like a creature no human could ever catch. Feeling like the panther of Night Horse Swamp.

She sank into the landscape far beyond the reach of the boys.

Into a realm where one fell into mystery and walked in fable.

A place of constant change.

A thunderstorm was edging closer pushing a dead silence ahead of it. Willow could hear that silence, *feel* it, just as she could feel the drop in barometric pressure and taste on her tongue the promise of lightning. Then she found her bearings and smiled once more as the barks of the boys faded, a sure sign that they had given up the witch-hunt in favor of cold beers and profanity-laced bravado. She stood at the edge of a coffee-colored pool where tall cypresses were mirrored at her feet. She took off her backpack and slipped her satchel from her shoulder. She kicked off her sandals.

She belonged here. And being here was magic.

Yet, she yearned for transcendence.

Her heart floated on the primeval landscape of purple bladderwort and climbing heath and swamp haw and mistletoe festooned high in the cypresses, her soul rode upon the constant flux of water and vegetation and unseen creatures. Here was a world never the same from one day to the next. With sacred attentiveness, she watched a pair of anhingas cavorting nearby, their feathers shimmering black, their bills as sharp as spears. She watched them so intensely that she imagined at any moment she would levitate or leave her body completely and ghost through the air.

And look down and see the panther.

That creature, the last of the Florida panthers introduced years ago to the Night Horse Swamp by Darryl Crowfoot, a game warden and member of the Bushyeye tribe, as part of a program to help increase numbers of the endangered species. But the program had failed: poachers, disease, and the habitat all legislated against success. In despair, Crowfoot started drinking heavily, built a houseboat, lived on it in the swamp, then disappeared, joining other legendary figures such as J.R. Mercy and Sabbath Choker and his sisters as Night Horse denizens never accounted for.

Willow blinked and the magnificent birds vanished.

Not took flight. Vanished.

Quite suddenly, nothing about the swamp seemed familiar. She felt lost. She wanted her mother and the warm circle of her aunts. *Coda.* The word skittered through her mind like a large rat. Her father had taught her enough Italian that she knew the word meant "tail," but she also knew that it essentially meant anything serving as a concluding part— a "coda" to what, though? It was a mystery. And it was a word she was dying to speak aloud.

Glancing down at the reflection of herself in the backwater pool, her breath caught.

Who was this girl returning her gaze?

Continuing to be arrested by the reflection, she forced a thin smile and spoke softly and cautiously.

"Coda," she said and grasped the amulet around her neck.

At first, she did not notice the response of the swamp, for she felt the need to empty herself, to rid herself of everything that could not belong to her: the backpack (with history, biology, and English texts and handouts and notebooks), her satchel (with lip gloss, a cutesy dragonfly barrette, and a lavender case for tampons), her sandals, and, finally, her long dress, which she tugged over her head. She tossed everything except her amulet and ring into the pool and watched until every item sank. Free and powerful was what she felt—a naked body could generate more magic than a clothed body. Every witch knew that.

A wind from nowhere played with her hair and caressed her body.

Just as she was ready to wade into the pool, she eyed a dead branch, slightly longer than a yardstick, and decided to use it as a "stang" to steady herself. She guessed that it was either sweet gum or dogwood. She picked it up. And that's when she began to hear frogs croaking and birds chirping excitedly and to notice water moccasins slithering toward her. A gator bellowed; she sensed its approach. Gas bubbles from decaying swamp peat rippled the surface of the pool.

And one thing more: the panther.

She, too, was responding to the call.

Shivering delightedly, Willow began to wade out into the tepid water. This was the hour for magic, and yet she did not want to wait a single second for whatever was about to transpire. In the back of her mind, in a hot cell of memory, she could hear her Grandmother Fossor guiding her: "Patience. Magic requires patience," she would say. "Try it gently. Wait for what wants to come."

Willow closed her eyes and nodded.

She held on to the stang tightly.

She imagined herself and the panther as one, sharing a hungry heart. Then she was ready.

"Coda!" she shouted. "Coda!"

She opened her eyes and knew that every living creature in the swamp was aware of her, and in that moment she began to experience what every follower of the Old Ways longs for: *waking up*.

Becoming.

Opening like a flower.

And as the storm drew closer she imagined sugary flashes of green lightning. Real storm and surreal storm and strange creatures near enough to reach out and touch.

Then the magic took hold.

The stang squirmed to life as a reptile, dropped into the pool, and slithered away. Fear pumped through Willow's veins. Her blood sang. Something was rushing toward her out of the everywhere. She knew she was going to be attacked, but her cry was not in fear.

"Coda!"

She began to breathe the air of a different planet.

An urge to fight seized her. Then an urge to run. And yet even more powerfully, an urge to embrace whatever was out there, its hot, panting, animal breath licking at her skin even from a distance. Antler points drawing blood. It was all a terrifying, gorgeous dream she could not wake from.

It was like dreaming past dark.

Dreaming on as the beast attacked.

Dark magic.

Surrendering in the blood.

Before silence fell upon the scene like a lid closing on a coffin.

And the thunder rolled.

TWO

What did Dvorak know about witches?

As Tina Fossor switched on her computer, she listened one notch more closely to the allegretto section of Dvorak's symphonic poem, "The Noon Witch"—one of her favorite pieces of classical music despite its negative depiction of witches. All she knew was that Dvorak had apparently been inspired by the familiar, scary figure from Bohemian folklore—the Noon Witch, a child-stealing menace. Clarinets and bassoons ushered in the malevolent motif as a caricature of a witch materialized in Tina's thoughts, and then in the andante sostenuto, announced through shivering, muted strings, the old crone demanded of a frightened mother: "Give me your child!" Clutching that child to her bosom, the mother ran, escaping from the dark threat before collapsing and crushing the child to death. The music told the story.

Tina cringed.

Why, she wondered, must death and evil dominate images of witches?

Child stealing? How absurd.

She thought of Willow, and in the next instant glanced at her clock radio. Her daughter would be home from school shortly. Earlier in the day Tina had made a vow to herself that she would work harder to develop a better mother-daughter relationship with Willow—to try to understand what darkness in the blood made things so difficult between them. They loved each other. Beyond doubt they did. But what—deeper than love—was missing?

She sighed and heard thunder, closer now, and hoped Willow would beat the storm. Lightning crackled over the swamp. *We need the rain,* she told herself. Maybe this was the Goddess responding to Aunt Mushka's rain chant a few days ago. But if no rain accompanied the thunder and lightning, might not one of the fiery strokes ignite the dry swamp? That rested in the hands of the Goddess. No point in speculating.

The face of the panther suddenly held Tina's attention.

Such a beautiful creature. And her sister Gretta's color photo of her served well as a screen saver. Tina imagined the big cat seeking shelter from the approaching storm—all that primitive female strength and power and knowledge. Raw, gorgeous instinct. The image winked off the screen as Tina punched up her Web site to check the afternoon's e-mail requests.

She smiled at the darkly fanciful logo of www.spellscast.com.

Her baby. Her creation. And an increasingly profitable one at that. Purple dominated the Web site. It was Tina's color: purple, for those who sought increased spiritual awareness. The home page was a doorway of standing stones, two vertical and one horizontal forming the top of the entranceway. A lighted candle in the center of that entranceway. Black lettering against a purple backdrop. Instinctively, Tina reached for her kudzu dolly, the vines woven to a make St. Bridget's Cross, and rubbed it gently. A charm that never left her computer, it was designed to ward off computer hackers and spirits that might invade the microchip soul of the machine. Tina didn't really understand computers, but she understood charms. This one worked. Better yet, her loyal customers believed it worked. They bought dozens of them along with amulets and magic rings and all manner of "witchy" software available on line.

The magic of the Old Ways, reduced to trinkets, meant dollar signs.

But casting spells was at the heart of Tina's corporate identity. And, by the looks of her e-mail folder, today was registering high demand: fourteen requests in the past twenty-four hours. Depending upon the nature of the spell desired, customers would pay from $29.95 all the way up into the hundreds of dollars. First in line was "Velma" communicating in cyberspace from Saddle Rock, Kansas. Tina smiled. She wondered whether Velma's neighbors in Saddle Rock knew that she had resorted to witchcraft to help solve whatever problem was plaguing her.

Tina knew, of course, what it would likely center on: love.

And, more so, *need*.

All we love is need.

But even as Velma's hesitant request materialized on the screen, Tina let her attention wander. Because she had heard Joe Boy's signal earlier, she had one ear cocked, any moment expecting her doorbell to ring. She assumed that someone—a brave housewife from Homewinds probably—was about to call on her, perhaps to ask her to cast a spell on the blond hussy who had her hooks into the woman's husband, or perhaps one or more "church ladies" on a holier-than-thou mission to save Tina's soul from the clutches of Satan.

Joe Boy's signal had also reminded her of last night's dream.

An unsettling one. In it, she was somewhere deep

within the swamp, and Joe Boy was pleading with
her—pleading with her to kill him. She had woken
from the dream in a cool sweat, confused and borderline terrified. She had thought instantly of her
mother: *she would know what it means. I miss her wisdom.* Joe Boy was such a precious guy. His affection
for Willow so obvious. Was there some symbolic im-
port to the dream? Or did it literally presage some
dark unfolding of events? Perhaps Aunt Mushka
could offer a reading of it.

Velma was waiting on the screen. There was no
time to ponder the mystery of dreams. Tina had to
turn to what she did best: casting spells. Exercising
her magical powers. Intuitive powers at least. She
had to listen to her customers, connect with them
psychically—embrace their souls—and assure them
that their wish could come true. Velma's e-mail ram-
bled. She spoke of having lost her husband of thirty
years and of the crushing loneliness she had experienced, of how she had tried and failed to make a
life of widowhood, of how friends and even an Internet dating service had been unable to find her
a new companion. She thought she needed another
level of help, though she quickly added, as many
customers did, that she had never dabbled in the
occult or spiritualism or witchcraft. But a friend of
a friend had mentioned www.spellscast.com. Maybe
Tina's service was worth a try. She hoped that Tina
could cast a spell for her. She wrote out her request
in one simple sentence: "Bring a nice man into my
life."

Warmth flooded Tina's throat.

Velma's words summed up the hopes of so many
women, and so many of those same women were
disappointed. Yes, a "nice man" would be comfortable. Secure. A companion. A friend. Yet, Tina
doubted whether those attributes were what women
really longed for. Wasn't there, in a hidden cell of

the most secret chamber of every woman's heart, a desire for something other than a "nice man?"

Fallen angel.

That's what Tina believed every woman's secret self wanted. Someone *dangerous*. She herself had known two such darkly irresistible creatures: her father and her ex-husband. Her father, Michael Thomas Fossor, a classical musician who ended up teaching music at a small, liberal arts college in Birmingham, Alabama, had been as restless as a Beethoven scherzo. He had lived a sweeping, up-tempo, excruciatingly frustrating life sucking at the marrow of existence to extract every drop. And had never been satisfied. Sitting on his knee as a child was, for Tina, like being too close to a raging fire. But she had loved the sensation. She had been annealed by it. Then leukemia had seized the man's body, plunging him into a private hell before the transition known as death took him, leaving only his shadowy presence in her life.

John Scarpia was another such passion-possessed soul. A dark lover who had swept Tina off her feet, he taught her about sex and more. She gave him all that she had to give, then anguished over why it was never enough. Until one day she realized that men who are fallen angels don't want intimacy— they want to hear the sound of a heart tearing like rotted cloth. They don't want growing; they want burning. They don't need love; they need lightning. So Tina had given him his freedom, and perhaps because John Scarpia adored his daughter, Willow, he stayed in the Night Horse area, operating a derelict fish camp, replete with bait shop and rundown cabins and canoes for rent. But, mostly, John Scarpia drank and chased women, many of whom were gladly caught and less gladly tossed aside when he had grown tired of them.

Any other fallen angels out there for me? Tina wondered, dismissing the foolishness of wishing for still another destructive creature in her life. Unconsciously, she brushed her fingertips over her stomach. Sexual desire webbed its way into her blood, into her thoughts. At thirty-five she wasn't ready to give up a part of life that she had always enjoyed so much. Yet, Homewinds, Alabama, hardly offered a meaty selection of unattached, sexually attractive men. There was, however, a married man who set fires of lust ablaze in her: Glen Favors, a George Clooney look-alike who doubled as a deputy sheriff for Catlin County and as a construction remodeler. He had helped her sister, Gretta, build her cabin. But beyond the fact that he was married was another problem: Gretta was madly in love with the guy.

Of course, I could cast a spell. I could turn him my way possibly.

That's not what she wanted. She wanted a stranger to come into her life because *he* wanted to.

What we are searching for is searching for us.

The thought emerged, passing in a heartbeat.

Thunder, lightning, and then the first, tentative, heavy drops of rain. Tina could hear them hitting her roof and thumping against her deck, which overlooked Night Horse Creek. It was a pleasant, natural sound. Tina cupped it momentarily to her ear before the maternal instinct in her intruded.

Does Willow have her umbrella?

Well, she's a big girl now. She has to learn to take care of herself.

The Goddess helps those who help themselves.

It was time to concentrate on Velma. Start the magic.

She studied Velma's message, zeroing in on her request. Then she closed her eyes, anticipating the warm rush of magical intuition. She waited for the words to come. For the syntax of spell that always wrote itself—no, *blazed* itself—across her thoughts.

But it would not come.

Tina ratcheted up her concentration.

Nothing.

She opened her eyes and, confused, glanced at her clock: 4:32 P.M.

Her magic had stopped flowing.

And it was the cold, draining shock of almost having had a car accident. She couldn't breathe. She felt disoriented. Her comfortable home office seemed suddenly unfamiliar. *Willow.* Her daughter's name ghosted into her thoughts, then dissolved. Thunder boomed unexpectedly close. Tina gave a start, stifled a scream.

Her computer winked off. And there was a momentary silence.

Followed by a noise from someone on the deck.

A man clearing his throat.

"I can't let you stay here."

Tina, her arms folded against her breasts, looked down at the man who was squatting, his eyes drawn to the windblown sheets of rain and to the swamp beyond. He seemed oddly comfortable and so at home with himself that Tina almost felt that he belonged on her deck more so than she did. After coming out and finding him there seemingly oblivious to his trespass, she had told him he couldn't take refuge on her deck. She had demanded to know what he wanted, and when he hadn't responded immediately, she threatened to call the police and felt somewhat foolish for doing so. Nothing whatsoever about the man suggested that he might do her harm.

And yet. . . .

"Did you hear me? I said that I can't let you stay here. You have to move on."

"I understand," he said.

Then he cleared his throat.

His voice was gentle, though firm. It sounded tired, yet hopeful. It was the voice of a man constantly on the road. A voice soaked with dust. The voice of a storyteller.

"A woman can't be too careful," Tina added, and realized that her words didn't sound like her. "Common sense dictates—"

His eyes swung toward her—blue eyes, the bluest eyes, bluer than Paul Newman's or Sinatra's—and a warm, crooked smile spread, barely concealing bad teeth. His hair was long and blond, shoulder-length and wet, dripping down upon a ragged, fading jean jacket. He wore blue jeans with a split across one thigh. Boots that looked as if they had walked a million miles. He seemed deliberately to keep his hands hidden.

"Sure, you're right. I do know that. I was just hoping to keep my guitar dry. And I saw what a marvelous view you have of the swamp." Then he paused and seemed to look into each individual raindrop as it fell. "There's something holy about a thunderstorm, isn't there?"

Tina shivered. Not because she was cold, but because she was not in control of the situation and she prided herself in being strong and in control and holding her own in conversation with any man. And one thing more. He was right. There *was* something holy about a thunderstorm. She had heard her mother say almost those exact words a dozen times. She relaxed ever so slightly and noticed a flat-top guitar next to him along with a dingy, tattered duffel bag nestled close like a sleeping pet.

"I don't mean to be inhospitable," she said.

"Oh, I know that. I do. The world is getting to be a mean place. It has terrors in it." He folded out of his squat and stood as the rain slackened. "Even

a spot as beautiful as this one. I'd been thinking I'd
be sent to a spot like this one day."

"Sent?"

"Yes, ma'am."

"By whom?"

"Maybe you could call it the winds of fate. Or
maybe beauty led me here."

"Beauty?"

"Yes, because beauty is a going-home to an adventure in an unknown land."

"Very poetic. That's a nice line. What does it
come from?"

He had looked away before she had responded.
He was gazing at the island where her sister lived
and beyond, into the rain-glistened swamp, seeing
into it as if it were a place he had not seen before,
yet somehow knew existed. Without glancing back
at her, he said, "It comes from thinking about
beauty and home and keeping the unknown always
beyond you."

Tina caught herself. This was foolish, conversing
with a stranger. What about him had tempted her
to drop her guard? With his hands stuffed into his
pockets, he said, "I'm Willis Shepherd—go by
'Shep.' I think of myself as a troubadour. I write
songs and sing them. Sing old folk songs from the
sixties, too." He cleared his throat again, and the
next line he spoke put Tina into a brief, anticipatory
trance—just exactly what she sought for with her
clients: "I am myself," he added, "a song the dark
powers sing." Then he smiled as if to acknowledge
the melodramatic observation.

And suddenly they were looking into each other's
eyes, and she heard herself, as if she were speaking
from another room, say, "I'm Cavatina Fossor. I live
here and run a business out of my home, and my
two sisters and my Aunt Mushka live here, too. Allegretta lives there—in that cabin on the island—it's

called 'Pan Island'—and Aunt Mushka and my other sister, Arietta, live next door. I have a daughter, Willow.''

His eyes appeared to twinkle like the first tentative stars of evening; it was as if a secret association had been claimed.

"Cavatina. There's one in Beethoven, isn't there? Are you a fan of the string quartets, too?"

She nodded. And told him more. About her father naming his daughters after musical movements and about her mother schooling her daughters in the Old Ways and then about her Internet business: casting spells for people in need. When the gushing of words ceased, she experienced a wave of embarrassment that staggered her. But the stranger seemed to find nothing unusual about her being so forthcoming. He seemed, in fact, to expect it.

"I wonder," he said, "if you'd allow me to sit inside a minute. Maybe we could have a cup of tea. I'd guess you have herbal tea around."

Tina was shaking her head before she could prompt her words.

"No, I'd rather you didn't. My daughter will be home any moment, and I have work to finish." *Why did the magic stop?* And she imagined Velma back in Saddle Rock, Kansas, suspended in air waiting for her request to be granted. "You may stay out here on the deck, but only until the rain ends."

Afraid that he would talk her out of her position, she slipped back inside. A screened door separated them. She went to her computer and sat and stared at the darkened monitor. She did not, however, turn on the machine, because she was listening, listening to the breathing of her stranger. *Not my stranger.* Twice he cleared his throat. Then he began to talk, his voice seemingly disembodied and almost ghostly. He talked of being on the road. He talked of loving his solitude and living the questions rather than searching frantically for answers.

His voice nearly put Tina into a trance.

And she found herself regretting that she had not allowed him to come inside. All he apparently wanted was to get in out of the rain and have a cup of tea. Almost mechanically, she went to her kitchen and brewed tea—Chinese green tea—and poured two cups of it and put the cups on saucers and heard the light rain falling and felt warm inside.

She was smiling and feeling like her old self again when she called out for the stranger to come in and join her for tea. But the only response she received was the sound of the rain. And when she pushed out onto the deck she discovered that her stranger had departed.

THREE

"Glen?"

Gretta Fossor had caught just the barest whiff of Old Spice. Or imagined that she had. And had sensed that he must be there, concealing himself at the edge of the cabin or near the door being careful that no one would see him. He would be soaked from the sudden thunderstorm, and she would pull him near her hearth fire and warm him with cups of black coffee and her embrace.

And she would thank him, as always, that he had taken such a risk to come.

And he would thank her and tell her, as always, that she made the risk much more than worthwhile.

"Glen? Is that you? Are you there?"

She opened her cabin door and smelled rain and the ghostly fragrance of ozone left by lightning. But the Old Spice had evaporated or perhaps it hadn't been there at all—she had only wished it there. Aftermath gusts of wind blew sprinkles into her face. She shivered and blinked hard. The surface of Night Horse Creek was a dull, heavy gray as if the thunderstorm had painted it thickly as it brushed across the swamp.

He wasn't there.

Holding in her disappointment, she turned and glanced around at her cabin, a simple abode of two rooms where everything belonged, where everything—from her table and two chairs to her hearth where a firepot smouldered—had a function. Everything fit into the slots of her life: things necessary to live or necessary for basic comfort. The first room was her living room and kitchen; the second was her bedroom, replete with a cot and a water closet and a crude shower stall. She was pleased that Glen had honored her request that they not make love in the cabin; more so, she was pleased that he had not pressed her to explain, because she wasn't certain that she could have, except to say that for her, intimacy belonged somewhere else.

Because Glen belonged somewhere else.

He haunted the two rooms—he haunted her life—but he lived somewhere else, *with* someone else.

As Gretta drifted out from the rear of the cabin, she instantly smelled the panther—pungent, wild, an earthy femaleness. Then, immediately, she ducked back inside to get her camera. Perhaps the relenting of the rain had caused the panther, her brute neighbor, to issue forth from her cover to see what was stirring. Perhaps she was hungry.

From Gretta's vantage point, she could look deep into the swamp, deeper than almost anyone else; in fact, she prided herself on having the right eyes to do so. The panther was rarely sighted, and yet, having the right eyes, she had seen the creature many times. Had photographed her many times. Long and precious hours, camera ready, Gretta had perched on a deer stand she had erected between two tall pines just off the North Fork run of the swamp and watched and waited. She had opened herself to the inscrutable possibilities of the swamp and, especially, to the beauty of the panther. Patience. Patience, she had come to believe, was the key to bliss.

Bliss.

Such a lovely word, soothing and soft as a baby's breath.

In those hours on the deer stand bliss had come to her like a ghostly bird fluttering near yet never touching her, never landing on her shoulder, never even singing songs without words. Being in its presence she had experienced such joy, such pleasure that she came to believe that the winged spirit had escaped the Otherworld and had sought her out. She alone. For she had described the phenomenon to her mother and her sisters and her aunt and though they had smiled and shaken their heads as if they *sensed* what she spoke of, nothing quite like it had come into their lives.

It was as if a light had shone upon her soul.

A light with no known source.

But if bliss had made itself a presence to her, her sentry deep in the swamp had also frightened her with an awareness of something quite different. Opposite of bliss, in fact. A dark, brooding, unseeable force—as arresting as a serpent's hiss—a force that her mother often referred to as "the Terror." And Gretta's awareness of this force convinced her that the Terror was not something her mother had concocted years ago to keep her daughters from wandering into the swamp alone. Oddly, this indefinable fear generated by the dark force heightened her sensation of bliss.

Bliss had made her feel whole and complete. A surrogate for physical intimacy.

And it remained so until the day she decided to tear down the old cabin—the original one built on Pan Island by Sam Choker or Brother Owen or perhaps by Darryl Crowfoot (no one seemed to recall which)—and to build a new one. She knew she would need help with the project. And that's how Glen Favors entered her life.

His good looks troubled her momentarily because

she hadn't felt a burning attraction to anyone since
high school where she had learned the bitter truth
that homely girls like herself had best put aside
thoughts of luring a handsome boy to them. Of
course, her two sisters had always been able to virtually take their pick of males. Tina, three years
older than she, had fashioned herself into a beauty;
Arietta—"Artie"—was, at five years her junior, a
naturally lovely young woman, though she always behaved as if her beauty were an annoyance. Like a
chipped fingernail.

Off duty one weekend from his job as a deputy
sheriff, Favors accepted a ride in her small boat out
to her island where he gave every indication that
he was enchanted with her plan. It seemed to Gretta
as if he felt she had transported him to some magical isle from which he could not return as the same
person. He told her that he truly admired her for
shunning society as she did, for living by herself in
the long-abandoned cabin—for adjusting to the
rhythm of nature instead of people. And she had
hoped that he wasn't making fun of her. Along with
finding out about Favors's skills as a carpenter, she
had gathered that he was in his mid-twenties, a few
years younger than Artie and significantly younger
than herself—*how* significantly became a point of
debate in Gretta's thoughts after that first day of
working together to raze her former home. She also
learned that he was married, no children, and that
his wife, Robbie, a slightly built redhead, worked at
Good Ole Gals, a restaurant not far from John Scarpia's fish camp. After the first few days Gretta and
Favors had worked together, she had, in fact, made
a special trip to the restaurant on a spying mission,
returning uncomfortably pleased to discover that
Robbie was no beauty herself—merely girlishly cute.

Yet, Gretta had harbored no illusions: Favors had
stirred something deep within her, but besides the

fact that he was committed elsewhere (and, most likely, *not* interested in her), she had no room for him—or any other man—in her life. A man wasn't *necessary* just as a computer or a microwave or a television or a new dress or a jillion other things weren't necessary. She could live without them. It was late afternoon on the fourth day she and Favors had been hard at work on framing the new cabin that she asked herself: *yes, but when have I ever felt so good about myself?*

This man opens up an undiscovered world of bliss for me.

Yes, bliss. Her favorite word. A bliss different from the bliss she felt out wading in the currents of Nature, yet somehow related to that sensation. At the end of that fourth day, she had been sawing a two-by-four and had paused to wipe her brow when she was caught by Favors's stare and by his hand being raised to her hair.

"Is that sawdust or stardust?" he had teased.

And she had laughed at his goofy line. But not at the touch of his fingers to her hair. Not at the rush of warmth she had experienced, tiny bolts of sexual energy that crackled in the pit of her stomach. And lower. In that moment something changed. The dynamic of Favors as someone being paid to help her and she as the customer who wanted to be involved in the construction of her new abode dissolved. It wasn't a touch or a moment that could be taken back.

And she suspected that both of them knew it.

In the days following that moment the air was different, the sky was different, and Gretta found herself doing something she almost never did: checking her appearance before Favors arrived each morning. She looked forward to his smile, to his smell, to everything about his presence. She shaped her day around him, preparing lunches and snacks for them to eat together. And he responded ever more appreciatively to her efforts, and they would drift into stimulating conversations after their respites, and the boundaries of their emotional and intellectual lives began to blur, then reformed before coalescing.

"What is your magic?" he asked her one glorious noon hour. "I mean, as a follower of the Old Ways, as you say you are, doesn't that mean you have developed some personal form of magic?"

"I have," she said. But she hesitated. To confide further would be to invite him to explore with her the country of her soul. To know her secret self.

"Would you demonstrate it for me?"

Yes, for you.

"You'll probably scoff at it," she said.

But his eyes told her he wouldn't. So she took him to the far end of the island where a firepot burned over a small flame and explained that each daily flame she built had a different type of wood as its foundation: some days oak, some days cypress or gum or dogwood or pine. Each flame produced a different smoke.

"And when I breathe in just a little of the smoke, I can . . . I can see images, psychic images of anyone I choose to concentrate upon as long as I have deep, emotional attachment to them."

She studied his reaction for signs of disbelief. Found none.

"I believe you," he said, not asking for more. "That's a real gift. It fits you. Your love of family. Your closeness to Nature. The green colors you always wear. You're like something elemental. Something I need to be close to."

And she had intended to explain that her green clothing empowered her to be a protector of Nature. She had wanted, at that moment, to say any number of things. But she did not say them. Instead, a realization had swept through her like a sudden gust of wind.

I am in love with this man.

The first man, other than her father, that she had loved.

Before he had gone home for the day she had given him a glass of her Aunt Mushka's honeyed wine, and he had kissed her on the lips, there in the shell of the new cabin, and she had trembled as if freezing or in abject terror. She could feel his desire for her. Breathless, he had whispered, "My God." And he had touched her cheek. "Oh, Gretta, I'm not a bad man. Don't think that I am. But I want you."

And she him.

On the day that the cabin was finished—several days behind schedule—she invited him on a boat ride into the swamp; she poled down North Fork to where it opened into a lake of sorts covered with water lilies, and there she pointed out a derelict, gray-washed houseboat that virtually no one else knew about. A private place. And she could see, much to her delight, that Favors understood the implication of her attention to the vessel. They boarded it, and he took her in his arms.

"Do you want to come back here tomorrow?" he asked.

"Yes," she said, "more than I've wanted anything in a long, long time."

Bliss. And anxiety. And more bliss anticipating what was to come. Gretta returned to the houseboat late that night and swept it clean and put a new sheet and pillow on the one small bed and then lay on that bed and imagined the weight of Favors's body upon hers.

At the bow of the boat she knelt and whispered an invocation:

"Goddess, give our hearts wings to fly above guilt. *Amor. Veni. Cito.*"

Early the next morning she talked Tina into giving her a ride to the Wal-Mart in Homewinds where her shopping list turned to mush in her sweaty palms. Careful not to let Tina see her purchases, she bought a tube of lipstick ("Thirsty Red"), though she was thoroughly bewildered by the number of shades, and she bought a generic spray cologne, but when the hour of decision arrived, she applied neither the lipstick nor the cologne. She also bought a bag of black licorice twists because Favors liked them and a roll of breath mints, spending far too many minutes trying to choose between peppermint and wintergreen. And then the lace panties.

Her throat burned as she fingered a dozen pairs.

She wanted to try them on but was too embarrassed to. And the colors—she had gone with her mind set on black, then red, then white. Dizzied by the indecision, she opted for a shade resembling a ripe apricot just as she spotted Tina lurking two aisles away. Later, after she had bathed and fixed a simple lunch for the afternoon tryst, she tossed the panties on her bed and just stared at them. And, finally, when the time had threatened to get away from her, she slipped them on. They felt wrong. Much too brief. Much too silky. And then everything began to feel wrong.

Things got better when she poled over to the spit to get Favors.

He looked magnificent to her. No indication in his eyes that he knew she was wearing sexy, apricot-colored panties beneath her long, green dress.

"Thank you for this," he said.

And her head swam and she feared she had become someone else. She couldn't remember what the two of them had talked about in their many animated conversations. Would he notice that she was suddenly a different woman?

She could feel his eyes on her as she poled them to the houseboat on a lovely, sunny afternoon with the swamp crouched and hushed, neutral to their moral trespass. It was something she knew she needed: this man's attention, this man's desire. But she was anxious. She thought about the first and only time she had had sex—with Billy Rayburn the summer she turned eighteen—and how she had essentially asked him to have sex with her because she saw it as one of those natural experiences she needed to have. As natural as menstruation or the emergence of breasts. She hadn't enjoyed it. Neither had Billy Rayburn, or so she assumed, despite his declarations to the contrary. It had been an eagerly passionless event, painful and clumsy and anything but romantic.

Once on the boat, Gretta felt more relaxed. She and Favors had journeyed to the center of a new universe, uninhabited, a cosmos shot through with the beauty of two people who needed each other. Feeling like Eve, she surrendered to the arms of her Adam, and then she led him inside to the small bed with its clean sheet. They sat on the edge of the bed, and the first fingers of alarm pressed into her flesh when she saw his hesitation. A curious holding back. Then a sting of words she had not expected.

"Aren't you going to ask about Robbie?"

Her only response was to shake her head, not to indicate that she had not planned to ask about his wife, but rather because his question thoughtlessly broke the spell. And she could feel her body react as if racing ahead of her consciousness. It began with the sensation that her heart had hiccupped, the natural rhythm of systole and diastole completely disrupted. Then a sudden headache and the initial waves of nausea.

"I'm sorry," he followed quickly. "Gretta, I'm sorry. That was stupid. Please forget I said that."

She shivered and let him hold her, but she knew there would be no lovemaking.

Not that day.

They journeyed to the houseboat again three days later, and this time Favors carried her to the small bed and kissed her softly again and again and helped her slip her green dress over her head, and he told her that the apricot panties were lovely. She saw the appreciation in his eyes. Desire, too. There were few words. Gretta released herself gradually to his touch. He kissed her shoulders and her breasts and stomach, and then his face was between her thighs, and she felt as if she were lifting free of her body, attached only to each pleasure spot as his lips roamed, then lingered, and his hands moved gently yet passionately.

Light-years from Billy Rayburn.

Bliss. Sexual. Throbbing. Pulsing. Warm. Moist. Bliss.

The dark magic of love.

Then he was deep inside her and she was deep inside the womb of her need.

Only swamp creatures heard their murmurings and exclamations of pleasure and satisfaction. Later, Gretta could not even recall what they had talked about afterward—their childhoods, perhaps. Or maybe their talk remained in the microcosm they had created there on the derelict houseboat moored far beyond the civilization of Homewinds, Alabama.

Gretta silently thanked the Goddess for letting what happened happen.

They made love twice more before it was time to go.

"I'll never forget this," said Favors. "You. What you have given me. So much that I've been needing."

And in his handsome features Gretta read a language without a future; it was, instead, a language only of now. The moment. His presence was one of wanting and loving; in this man she believed she had found a force, a spirit, antithetical to whatever mysterious, dark, and elemental power nested at the heart of Night Horse Swamp.

They met on the average of once a month from that point on. Favors bought a small skiff from John Scarpia and kept it hidden so that he could visit her without her having to use her boat, thus helping to ensure that their meetings would be secret. And gradually whatever guilt they suffered from was sloughed off like the old skin of a water moccasin; but now, as Gretta scanned the tangle of swamp vegetation for signs of the panther, she could feel a curious fear rising within her. It seemed to emanate from the island itself like condensation from a morning's dew. And it seemed, otherwise, a fear with no source, no name.

It caused her to chase back into the cabin.

And the fear sharpened as she anticipated what she dreaded she might see. Her breath caught as she slammed into the front room and crouched at her hearth and reached out to touch the rim of her firepot.

Smokeless. Cold. Dead.

"No, damn it, no," she cried.

She thrust her fingers into the ashes and gasped at the realization that her magic had somehow, incredibly, been snuffed out. Tears, not of sadness, but rather of abject terror, squeezed from the corners of her eyes.

"Glen!"

The magic that kept her connected to him psychically with silken strands of love and concern had dissipated. She held her breath and pushed her face over the firepot in a desperate attempt to catch even the most diaphanous image of him. But there was nothing, and to Gretta it could mean only one thing: the man she loved was in danger.

She was in her boat and poling as hard as she could, destination: Tina's. She could phone or perhaps even borrow Tina's car—fear made it difficult to think clearly. *Glen, my darling, what has happened?* Less than halfway from her island to Tina's landing she thought she heard the cry of the panther, and when she glanced down at the surface of the water she saw an image of Willow, her niece.

Naked. Her face a mix of fear and delight. Then it was as if the girl had no face at all. Only featureless flesh. But then the image disappeared like a silver fish shimmering out of sight.

Arms aching, Gretta poled harder as cold drops of rain fell upon her.

FOUR

"Aunt Muska, I think you ought to bake 'misfortune' cookies sometime," said Arietta, raising her voice over the funky sounds of a Peter Gabriel CD. "I mean, why should cookies *always* have good associations? You know what I'm saying? Instead of a little ribbon of paper with 'You're in for a special treat,' why not one that says, 'Some bad shit is gonna happen to you soon'?"

Mushka chuckled and shook her head at the words flung at her from the next room. She continued sweeping out her small kitchen with her pine-needle broom while keeping one eye on the various pots of herbs and one of moon-blessed water steeping on the stove top and another eye on her oven from which the aroma of warm cookie dough was escaping. And if she had had other eyes, she would have been glancing out her kitchen window at Night Horse Creek and would have seen Gretta hurrying her boat away from Pan Island. She might even have noticed that Rosebud, her blue-gray cat, sleeping atop the VCR in the next room, was, by degrees, slipping off, having exhausted herself during the morning hours catching a chipmunk and leaving the bloodied carcass on the back steps as some kind of sacrificial offering or as payment for room and board.

"Arietta, wherever do you get some of your ideas?

Cookies, bad?" Mushka didn't care for Arietta's
choice in music—Gabriel's pieces were too dithery
and throbbing and downright weird. What Mushka
favored was Gypsy music. Give her the plaintive vio-
lin singing that filled czardas over freaky geeky
sounds any day. But then, differences in musical
tastes were only part of an extensive litany of con-
trasts between her and her niece and roommate,
Arietta, a lovely, shapely blonde who, even as they
were carrying on a conversation, was standing naked
before an easel upon which the talented young
woman had an inchoate charcoal drawing. Mushka
tried not to scan her body for evidence of new pier-
cings—as of yesterday there was a ring in one nos-
tril, three in each ear, one in an eyebrow, and one
in her navel—and tattoos—spiders being the domi-
nant motif of the latter, including one such creature
on her left breast and another on her right buttock.
And Mushka dared not ask the subject of the drawing.

"Or what about his one?" Arietta—who liked to
call herself "Artie"—continued, her face tilted up
in a reflective pose making the seductive gap between her front teeth all the more evident. " 'Get
ready for a serious case of diarrhea tonight.' Do you
see how that one continues the theme of the first
one?"

Gabriel's bongos thumped to an end quite suddenly, leaving Arietta's words to wing wildly around
like a bird trapped inside the rooms.

"I do," Mushka followed, "but cookies should
never have anything but good thoughts clinging to
every crumb. They ought to have kindness baked
right in them. Just like this batch of oatmeal cookies
for Willow—they've got my heart in them."

Arietta grunted.

"You sound like a Pillsbury commercial or a
greeting card. Honestly, Mushka, have you ever had

a bad thought—I mean, a truly negative thought in your entire life?"

The older woman paused to lean on her broom.

"Well, once back in high school we were studying Shakespeare's *Macbeth,* and I told our teacher—Miss Whatever-her-name-was—that I liked the witches because they tricked Macbeth and he had it coming. Miss Whatever said that Shakespeare didn't mean for us to like the witches because they were supernatural agents and friends with the devil. She made me look foolish in class, and I thought she was mean as a snake to do that. So. There. I've had at least one."

Rosebud finished sliding off the VCR, hitting the floor with a soft plop, then glaring at the two humans as if certain of complicity on their part. Arietta laughed, and to Mushka the sound was the rustle of fallen leaves touched by the wind.

"That's it," said Arietta. "I like it. *Macbeth's* witches—more ingredients for your cookies: eye of newt and toe of frog, wool of bat and tongue of dog."

"Oh, stop," Mushka cried. "Next you'll have me slicing and dicing up Rosebud for this evening's stew."

"Yum," said Arietta, licking her luscious lips. "Mother would say that'd give you bad dreams, I bet. Hey, it's getting cold in here, don't you think?" And with that she put on a white dressing gown— white her color, the color Mushka associated with spiritual purity just as she associated blue, *her* favorite color, with healing.

Bad dreams.

Yes, Mushka had had one. The sudden thunderstorm reminded her of it. And, yes, her sister, the wise mother of three unusual daughters each committed to the Old Ways, had known about dreams— about the dangers of dreaming past dark.

"A might chilly, yes. A cup of honeyed tea would warm you. Would go well with fresh-baked cookies."

"No, thanks," said Arietta. "I need to finish this drawing. Gotta stir up my magic and see what vision is waiting to come."

Weary because the dream had woken her and not allowed her to go back to sleep the night before, Mushka sat down at the kitchen table and gazed at Arietta, who was in some ways a little girl in a woman's magnificent body. With magic in her right hand. Artistic magic. She seemed merely to need no more than to give her right hand free rein on a canvas or a piece of wood or a glob of clay and some kind of indescribable intensity arose and an impressive drawing, painting, carving, or clay figurine emerged. And that completed product would cast a spell over any viewer of it.

To Mushka, Arietta, this strange, remarkably gifted child-inside-a-woman was a thing of *energy*, an elemental energy—almost a fifth element, rubbing shoulders with earth, water, air, and fire. Arietta, the creature who loved storms and flux and change, who knew that life at its central fire is sensuality. That living is bleeding and shaping and creating.

Mushka blinked. The sharp pain in her forehead had returned, chipping away at her concentration. She reached up to loosen her blue headband scarf, but the pain did not relent. After the cookies were out of the oven, after Willow had visited as she always did at the end of the school day and Arietta had flitted off to do whatever the promptings of her true self demanded, Mushka promised herself that she would tend to that pain. Her magic was healing and reading auras, and so it would only be a matter of settling into a ritualistic meditation and touching her fingertips to the pain—and that unwanted visitor would soon leave.

"I believe the storm has put me some on edge,"

she announced, though she knew she was mostly talking to herself, for she could see that Arietta was floating in a bubble of artistry and thus likely oblivious to all else.

The dream. The thunderstorm. And now, Willow was late. And Willow was *never* late. She considered calling Tina, then thought better of it, reasoning that somehow the call would spark something in their long-running mother-daughter feud. *Leave bad enough alone.* So she reached for her *Tarot of Marseilles* deck and began to shuffle it aimlessly, hoping her intuition would stop pulling her down such a dark and anxiety producing alley.

Three cuts of the Major Arcana.

Then a one-card deal: top card.

Le Jugement. Card XX.

"Judgment," she murmured to herself. And the trumpeting angel on the card caused her to think one thought: *Last Judgment.* Spiritual resurrection. The trumpet in her thoughts was even louder and more upsetting than the Peter Gabriel CD had been, and there was no way to turn down the volume. She felt her eyes begin to tear; the pain in her forehead pressed down harder.

Willow, where are you, my dear?

"Aunt Mushka? Hey, Gypsy lady, did you hear what I said?"

It was Arietta again.

"No, child. I'd wandered off. Sorry."

"What I said was, 'Have you ever made love with a woman?' "

Mushka blinked hard several times.

"Good heavenly days," she said. "Where did that one come from?"

Now seated on a stool in front of her drawing, Arietta smiled like a cat. "Just curious. Well . . . have you?"

"No, no, no," said Mushka. "Not that I have anything 'gainst folks who, you know, prefer their . . . *intimacy* that way, but it's not for me. No, never has been. It's fine for others—that's what a follower of the Old Ways should believe. If it harms none, do what you want. But I've never felt inclined that way. No."

Which was not true. Not exactly.

There had been a woman years ago. From Romania. She had come with her family after Hitler had torn Europe apart. Mushka had met her in Montgomery at a Red Cross function. Marievna. Yes, that was her name.

I was eighteen.

Marievna flickered in her thoughts. Memory reached like a hand into darkness, but all that it could touch was the image of Marievna's face—pale, a high forehead much too shiny and small lips and a small chin. But those eyes. Dark, beautiful eyes and exquisite eyebrows. Not plucked. And a longish, thin nose. Aquiline. A smile that made all the parts of her face even lovelier than the whole. Mushka had adored the young woman's broken English and the courage it took for her to try to adjust to life in the South.

Marievna's hands combined strength and gentleness. She had shaken hands with Mushka, and the eagerness for friendship and connection had raced between them. Mushka had wanted to kiss the young woman's lips, and the desire itself had been staggering. Shame and guilt had flooded Mushka's consciousness. She had no idea whether Marievna had reacted similarly to her. And she never found out either, for within the year the young woman died of pneumonia, the result of her weak constitution and an unusually wet and cold Alabama winter.

"I think I'd like to try it," said Arietta. "Life is about trying different things. I mean, how else can we really discover who we are?"

"You have some particular lady in mind?" said Mushka.

"Sure, maybe. Several women around are attractive that way. Gladys Michaels, for example."

"Gladys, the woman who owns Good Ole Gals? Why, baby, she's old enough to be your mother."

"What difference does that make? She's a strikingly handsome woman, and she's been divorced for years, and I've caught her checking me out. All I'm saying is that it would be interesting to explore, you know, other directions sexually. Not many men are good lovers—wouldn't you agree?"

Mushka pushed up from the table to check on her cookies and turn down the heat under one of her pots of herbs. Rosebud threaded in and out of her legs, threatening to make her trip. And there was still no sign of Willow. She was a good thirty minutes late.

"Can't say as I have a world of experience to draw on there."

"What about Sam Choker? I've heard that ole Sam and one Betty Lou Fossor were a hot item years ago. Steamed up the whole area."

Mushka laughed out loud.

"I 'spect we tried. Least, our bodies were willing and eager, if you know what I mean."

"So, what happened? I mean, why'd you let him get away?"

Why indeed?

Mushka had, over the years, often asked herself that question. Back in the days that she was Betty Lou Fossor, back before she committed wholly to the Old Ways, having been convinced to do so by her younger sister, Anna, and back before she took on the persona of "Mushka," an east European Gypsy healer woman clad in bandanna and gold loop earrings and every shade of blue she could acquire. Back before she gained the power to read auras. Yes, a time before Sam became the unofficial keeper of the Night Horse Swamp and had aspirations of becoming a lawyer. She and Sam had been passionate lovers and had dreamed of building a mansion near the swamp and raising a houseful of kids, a huge vegetable garden, and a menagerie of critters, both domestic and wild.

"I couldn't hang on to him hard enough."

"Another woman catch his eye?"

"No. Well, maybe, yes. I think he fell in love with the swamp and her dark magic and he decided he wanted to marry her more'n he wanted to marry me. Something like that."

"Men are worthless, aren't they?"

"Most. But there might could be a good one out there somewhere. What I'm sayin' is, donchoo go givin' up tryin'. Not till you're as old as me."

As she leaned down and lifted a sheet of cookies from the oven, she heard Arietta exclaim, "It's the panther. I see her. But I thought this was going in another direction."

"Do you see the panther?"

"No, I mean, my drawing. It's like she was there all along, hiding deep in the lines, and now she's chosen to make herself seen. I've been drawing the panther and didn't realize it."

"You know, the strangest thing . . ." said Muska, but she didn't finish because she could see that Arietta had a piece of charcoal in hand and was concentrating fiercely on the drawing. At any moment she would put that charcoal to work and magic would result.

I saw the panther in my dream.

And she had seen something even more terrifying.

Sitting down again after putting the cookies aside to cool, Mushka lifted a hand to her forehead where the pain was stabbing for attention. The dream had been so real, so lucid in its narrative, beginning with a boat ride deep into the swamp with Joe Boy, the kind of journey they often took to retrieve mistletoe from high in the cypress trees. And that's what they had been doing when the narrative turned very dark. Joe Boy, being the best climber of tall cypress she had ever seen, was almost out of view in one particular tree, almost into the clouds it seemed, as Mushka waited in the boat below.

When the long pole she was holding turned suddenly into a huge snake and slithered away from her scream and other snakes joined it as strange words whispered through Mushka's thoughts and she could feel the air around her warm. Delight and fear swept through her at the same time. And where the snakes had gathered, rolling and twisting into a mating ball, a whirlpool sucked them beneath the surface, and there, in the midst of that eddy, a dark shape arose.

During the dream, Mushka had seen the creature clearly.

Now she could remember no details of it except for the feel of its hot breath and the rasp of its panting and a suggestion of antlers. But was it seeking to harm her? That, she did not know. Letting the memory of the dream slip away, she concentrated and murmured a brief invocation to the Goddess to allow her powers of healing to chase away her headache.

She waited. Pressed her fingers more firmly to her forehead.

Then felt chills race through her body as she began to realize that her magic wasn't working. A sharp cry pulled her from her self-absorption.

It was Arietta.

She was babbling hysterically and grasping her right hand.

"Mushka, it's gone dead. It won't work—I can't *make it work!*"

Shutting her eyes tightly, Mushka called upon her ability to see human auras, the phenomena often serving as clues to a person's physical or mental afflictions. But when she opened them again and stared at Arietta, she saw no aura.

And the young woman's cry of panic sounded like that of a wounded animal.

FIVE

It was her first cigarette in months. But Tina felt she needed it, needed something more than herbal tea to calm her nerves. There was still no sign of Willow—she was over an hour late—and as the sun was breaking through the aftermath clouds of the thunderstorm and glazing the surface of Night Horse Creek, Tina sensed that something alarmingly unusual was taking shape.

It wasn't just Willow's lateness—it was a host of other indications: her dream in which Joe Boy pleaded for her to kill him; the surprise thunderstorm; the sudden appearance of the man who called himself "Shep"; the diminishment of her magic; and now Gretta's frantic desire to use her phone. Standing on her deck and staring out at the creek and at Pan Island, Tina tried to puzzle it through.

Mother would know.

Without her, Tina believed the Fossor witches no longer had a center.

Her passing had turned everything upside down and inside out.

Locked in that thought, at first Tina wasn't fully aware when her sister, Gretta, slammed through the door, relief coursing through her voice.

"He's fine. I was wrong. I got him on his cell

phone—and he's fine. Glen's fine. Oh, I thank the Goddess he's all right."

Tina stubbed out her cigarette and was startled to find Gretta throwing her arms around her. Just minutes earlier her sister had raced up from the shore madly requesting that Tina let her use her phone to call Glen Favors because she feared that portents signaled danger for him.

Gretta's firepot had mysteriously ceased to burn. She, too, had lost contact with her magic.

As Tina held her, she whispered, "Gretta, let's go back inside." Then she gently pushed away from her and added, "There are some things I need to tell you, and then we have to go to Mushka's to see if Willow might have stopped in to see her before coming home. She's late, and I'm worried."

Gretta, her face flushed and pink, nodded.

"I'm sorry," she said. "I was so wrapped up in my concern for Glen. You probably think I'm a fool. But the storm and the firepot—all I could imagine was that something horrible had happened. That he'd been severely injured on the job. Or a car accident."

Tina smiled as she shook her head.

"I don't think you're foolish. And it's been an unsettling afternoon for me, too."

When both were sitting on the living room couch, Tina began to recount her experiences beginning with the storm, her loss of magic, and ending with the encounter with the stranger seeking shelter. She also mentioned the nightmare and Joe Boy's deeply troubling request. But mostly she centered on Willow.

"Does this sound like an overly protective mom?"

Gretta pressed the back of Tina's hand. "Not at all. In fact, I must have been, subconsciously, thinking about Willow, too. On my way over, when I happened to glance down into the water, I saw a fleeting image of her. Maybe I picked up on your projections about her. But, hey, she'll probably come bouncing in here any second. Could be she stopped at her father's place to dodge the rain."

"That's a thought. Sure, that's likely it. Why don't you go on over to Mushka's while I call John? I'll join you in a second."

John Scarpia sounded annoyed that his ex-wife had called, and, no, he hadn't seen Willow, but, no, he didn't think the National Guard needed to be alerted simply because she was a little late. Biting back a rise of anger, Tina slammed down the receiver. She was walking briskly between her house and Mushka's when a voice reined her in.

"Hey, it's me. Here I am. Joe Boy. Right here."

She turned, and her first look at the young man startled her. His eyes were large and his face sweaty, and he was standing awkwardly, uncertainly, nervously—it seemed as if he had just been dropped into an unfamiliar territory and needed to make contact with someone, anyone. It also appeared as if he might suddenly tip to one side and fall to the ground, his balance having been thrown off so completely.

"What is it? What's wrong?"

He held out his pale hands in a helpless gesture. To Tina, the hands oddly resembled flippers. And when he spoke again, his words sent chills through her.

"Willow. My friend, Willow. She was in my head. Now she's gone out of it."

"Joe Boy—what is it? What are you saying? Where's Willow? She's late. Where did you see her?"

The young man winced as she rushed to him and grabbed his wrists as if fearing he might flee before he could elaborate on his peculiar remarks. He couldn't immediately focus to meet her eyes, but once he had managed to, his words came out slowly and deliberately.

"I saw her in my head before the storm."

"But, honey, where is she now? Do you know?"

He nodded.

"Tell me, please . . . because I'm worried. She's late, and she's just never late. Did you take her across on the ferry?"

Turning to glance down at the shore of the spit where the makeshift ferry, a flat vessel no longer or wider than an automobile, was tied up, the young man shook his head.

"Joe Boy, honey, you're scaring me now. Look at me and tell me where Willow is. If you know, you need to tell me so I'll stop worrying about her."

His mouth worked and his lips, slack and unresponsive, were like dough being kneaded by invisible hands. Tina, impatient, frightened, forced herself to wait until Joe Boy took several deep breaths and then said, "I saw Willow in my head. Then she walked out of it."

"And where did she go?"

He frowned, obviously not able to find the right words to answer Tina's frantic questioning. Spittle formed on his lips, and then with an exaggerated shrug of his shoulders he added, "She's gone inside the world."

Pulling loose from Tina's grip, he lurched down the ferry as she called after him. But he moved with surprising quickness pausing only to rap the plowshare, the signal for a crossing, before boarding and launching. Tina watched, and from seemingly out of nowhere she recalled something that the man called Shep had said: *I am myself a song the dark powers sing.*

And she thought about her dream in which Joe Boy had begged her to kill him.

And she wondered whether dark powers were, indeed, singing many songs.

Hers included.

Once inside her aunt's home, Tina was met by an older woman's face crumpled with concern as if it were a paper sack.

"Have you seen Willow?" said Tina.

Mushka, her bottom lip quivering almost comically, shook her head.

"We've got trouble, doncha know?" she said.

They went into the small living room where Tina saw that Artie was sitting on the floor in front of her easel whimpering as Gretta examined her right wrist.

"What's happened?" said Tina.

It was a pooling of narratives as they gathered near Artie. Tina told hers again, but mostly she listened and studied her sisters and her aunt and let her intuition hook firmly into the words and the facial expressions. Questions were given voice. She had never seen these women so frightened, so unnerved. Fear was a common ground for their sharing. Even more significantly to Tina, what the four of them had experienced pointed directly to one paradigm: the magic had stopped.

And no one knew why.

But of one thing Tina was certain, and this she announced to the others:

"We have to find Willow. I feel that all of this somehow involves her. We have to find her now."

It was approaching midnight when the four women met again in Mushka's living room where, ill at ease, they stood beyond a circle of candles placed in the center of the room. Tina couldn't stop trembling as she listened to Gretta tell the others that the sheriff's deputy, Glen Favors, was giving Willow's situation top priority despite the fact that the girl could not yet be declared a missing person. For her part, Tina had chased about trying as best she could to stay calm and yet by late evening failing to because she had turned up no trace of Willow. Classmates and teachers had been called, and the route home Willow always took had been combed carefully. And although Tina knew she was racing ahead of herself, she could not keep from projecting that her daughter had possibly met with harm. High school boys emerged as suspects. However, Tina continued to hold two specific men in mind as potentially guilty parties: her ex-husband and the drifter.

But why John?

She could blame John Scarpia for destroying their marriage, yes, but hurting Willow? No, that had never occurred. For him to do something that shocking was almost beyond imagining, and yet Tina couldn't erase her negative feelings because despite having lived with the man, she had to admit that there was still much she did not know about him. And as for the drifter, wasn't he a much more likely suspect?

Suddenly, as Tina was pondering the motivations of the two men she had been thinking of, she realized that Gretta was directing a question at her. She blinked her sister into focus.

"I'm sorry. What did you say?"

"I said that Glen was wondering whether you and Willow had had a fight or whether she's ever been inclined to run away from home. Thousands of kids do every year. Teenage girls included."

Tina shook her head emphatically.

"No. No, that's just not—no, she wouldn't do that. You know she wouldn't."

"Well, he also said that nobody else has seen the homeless guy or drifter you talked with on your deck. In other words, there's not much to go on right now. Glen's doing everything he can."

"What about Joe Boy? Has anyone tried to talk some more with him?" said Tina.

It was Artie who responded. "He doesn't know anything either. A flash of something. His intuition probably. He won't be much help unless Willow has trekked off into the swamp and got herself lost. There's nothing Joe Boy couldn't find back in there."

"Lost?" Tina was incredulous. "You know how well Willow knows the swamp. I seriously doubt that would happen."

"What, then?" said Artie. "I want to know what made my hand go numb. There's still no feeling in it. And what about our magic? Each one of us has had her personal magic shut down. What's going on? Something beyond the disappearance of Willow, I can tell you that."

Tina could find no way into Artie's beautiful face, a face made even more beautiful bathed in candle-light, and it was, in part, that beauty and the indifference it harbored that helped fire Tina's anger.

"Artie, goddamn you, how can you be concerned with our magic when my daughter is missing? So what if you can't draw your silly pictures? My daughter is what matters here."

And with that, all four women began to raise their voices at once until, surprisingly, it was Mushka's that won the moment.

"Stop it, girls! Stop it right now!" And when it was apparent she held the floor, she continued. "We can't do no good if we're fighting each other. I have a much better way for us to help Willow—and maybe get our magic back, too."

Tina could feel her anger easing somewhat. Dear old Mushka. She was obviously frightened to the bone, and while she was normally anything but the

kind of woman who could inspire confidence, she
was suddenly, in the eyes of Tina at least, a woman
who was succeeding in asserting her humanity.
Mushka loved Willow—Tina knew that—and she
loved her grown nieces and did not want to see
them at each other's throats. And so tensions relented as Mushka swept the area beyond the candles
clean with her pine-needle broom and then asked
Artie to place a block of wood in the center of those
candles. Next, from a small, tarnished silver chest
she took an athame—a black-handled, double-edge
dagger that had once belonged to Anna Fossor—
and she directed Tina to stab it into the block of
wood.

It felt good to Tina to do so.

The reassurance of old rituals. Something vital.
Something to be trusted in.

"Now," said Mushka, "we'll recite a charm to protect Willow from evil, and if the Goddess is listening,
perhaps she'll give us back our magic."

From a glass-front bookcase, the older woman reverently lifted a large black book, its cover foxed and
dog-eared. Tina recognized it immediately and felt
a jab of apprehension. It was her mother's "Book
of Shadows," the record that every follower of the
Old Ways keeps to record all of what she has learned
regarding Nature, the casting of spells, incantations,
rituals, and potions. Seeing the familiar book reminded Tina that she planned that summer to give
Willow a book of blank pages that would become
her own Book of Shadows. Tina watched as Mushka
opened the sacred tome, but it was Gretta who interrupted the ritual.

"You know what tradition says about this." Gretta
was staring at Mushka, not in anger but rather with
anxious concern. "When a follower of the Old Ways
passes, her Book of Shadows should be destroyed.

You shouldn't have it in your possession. It will breed dark magic."

Mushka was struggling with her emotions; tears threatened. She nodded at Gretta and said, "Yes, child, I do know that, but I believe we might could use your mother's wisdom. We'll borrow her words tonight in memory of her. She would have wanted us to try to help Willow."

"I think it's allowable," said Tina, though her thoughts were in a swirl. She hardly knew what to think. She distrusted her own judgment. "Perhaps it will demonstrate our rededication to the God-dess."

Gretta lowered her eyes as if to acquiesce. Artie maintained a stony silence, her face expressionless, her body tensed. Mushka glanced around the circle, then took a deep breath and began reading out a simple charm:

"Goddess, tip the horn of the moon tonight,
And pour the essence of that heavenly light
Down upon the one in our thoughts."

And then, as was customary at the closing of every Fossor charm, the old woman whispered, "Blessed be." And the other three women echoed that ex-pression.

"Take hands," Mushka followed, "and walk coun-terclockwise."

They did.

A dozen trips around the inner circle of candles. Then they released one another, and Tina had the uncomfortable feeling that when they did so the bond that had always united them had curiously been broken.

Artie reached down and picked up Rosebud, who had wandered into the circle.

"I felt nothing," she said.

"Maybe Tina's right," said Gretta, pitching her comments Artie's way. "Maybe you're too concerned about yourself, about your own magic. Mother always said that the person practicing the ritual or spell or charm determines its success. I think you feel nothing because you don't care about anyone else but yourself."

Artie's eyes blazed.

"You're one to talk. All you give a shit about is Deputy Favors and if he still wants to fuck you. You're as selfish as anybody else, Gretta. So go fuck yourself."

Tina moved quickly to put herself between her sisters. She could feel it happening—the sloughing of concern for one another, the fear of what their lives would be like if their magic never returned.

"Come on, you two," she said. "Think about Willow. Please."

Gretta was staring into Tina's face. She was frustrated and hurt and not a little frightened.

"Why do you have to keep saying that?" she said. "Why, Tina, do you assume that the rest of us aren't thinking of Willow? Just because you see yourself as Mother Earth—well, maybe if you tried to understand your own daughter instead of sucking money out of your computer we wouldn't be wondering where she is. Maybe if you loved *her* more and dollar bills less—"

Tina's hand met Gretta's cheek like the sudden crack of a whip.

"I love my daughter!" she shouted. "Don't ever suggest to me I don't. You—you have no idea what it's like to worry about a child. Damn you. *Damn you!*"

Gretta fell away to one side, and Tina, instantly regretting her action, dropped her face into her hands, and knew that something beyond the night had entered their tiny family, bent upon destroying it.

The candles flickered. Tina could hear Rosebud purring raggedly as Artie held the creature to her breasts, and she could hear Mushka's tear-laced voice offering soothing words to Gretta. And out in the swamp a wild bird cried and darkness claimed the world as its prisoner.

SIX

You get so you can smell the sun rising.

You get so you can almost make it through the night in your nice little bed that Miss Billie Ruth and Mr. Buck set up for you in the tiny back bedroom of their mobile home. But you don't make it through the night in that nice little bed because you can sleep better in Mr. Buck's overstuffed chair. His rocker recliner. You can curl up in it just before dawn and start to smell all those roasty hot smells of the sun warming the swamp and turning on the grow lamp for everything rooted in the mucky soil. In Mr. Buck's chair, you can smell Mr. Buck. He smells like dust and grease and tobacco and Miller Lite beer. You know that Miss Billie Ruth does not approve of Mr. Buck smoking a pipe and sneaking beers, but you figure she lets him because, well, probably because she loves him.

Sort of the way she loves you. Only different.

"Joe Boy." That's your name to the world. But not to Miss Billie Ruth, who calls you Joseph even when Mr. Buck—whose real name is Simeon—tells her over and over again that you'd rather be called Joe Boy. You think about saying you don't mind it when Miss Billie Ruth calls you Joseph because she says it in a way that makes it seem like it's really your name. She says it the way you imagine your mama would say it, only Miss Billie Ruth is not your mama and Mr. Buck is not your daddy. They are Miss Billie Ruth Private and Mr. Buck Private. Their full names. You don't have a full name, or it's lost or forgotten, and so when you came to live with Miss Billie Ruth and Mr. Buck, they gave you their name: Private. Joe Boy Private or Joseph Private. They gave you their name like they gave you shoes and jeans and T-shirts and a nice little bed, though you would rather sleep in Mr. Buck's chair that smells like him. You can sleep better snuggled up in that smell. It's an even better smell than the one the sun brings with it when it warms up the swamp and all the world is glad to see that great and bright light.

Sometimes you curl up in Mr. Buck's chair and think about your real parents and why they gave you up, and you guess it's because you're ugly or "learning disabled" or smell bad or a thousand other reasons you would not understand in a thousand years. So you stop thinking about that and smell the sun coming up and thank the stars that wink to life over the swamp each night that Miss Billie Ruth and Mr. Buck have given you a home. You like it. It's close to the swamp. It's close to the rope-pull ferry.

You figure that Miss Billie Ruth and Mr. Buck love you.

"Love" is a word that gets tangled up in your mind the way fishing line can if you're not careful with it. Love is sometimes a big word and sometimes a small word, and you need to think about when to use it. Just the other day when Miss Billie Ruth had fixed you fresh cornbread and a glass of chocolate milk—which is what you have every night before you go to bed—you said to her, "I love you," only you said it with your mouth full. That didn't seem to matter to Miss Billie Ruth because she smiled so hard her face looked like a spiderweb of happy wrinkles. But then she touched your hand and broke down and cried some, and you told yourself to watch out about saying that word "love." Sometimes it makes people happy. Sometimes sad. Sometimes both.

And Miss Billie Ruth had hugged you and, through her tears, said, "I pray for you, Joseph. I pray for you every day because I don't know what will happen to you when me and Mr. Simeon are gone."

"Pray." That's another word that can cut you. It's right there with "God." God comes up many times on Sunday morning when Miss Billie Ruth reads the Bible to you so that, in her words, you won't "become a heathen"—whatever that is. God, you are told, is bigger than the swamp and the sky and the sun all put together. God apparently made the swamp. Only you know that the job isn't finished because you see how the swamp changes each day. Not the same swamp on Monday that you get on Friday. You are learning the days of the week, and sometimes you can say them in order. You know that on Sunday Miss Billie Ruth reads the Bible and won't let you operate the rope-pull ferry even though folks might want to go across to the spit or come from the spit to the landing. Every Sunday of every month it's that way. The months of the year are tougher to learn than the days of the week because they take longer to come around. About thirty days if you're watching.

Miss Billie Ruth likes words and she likes embroidery. Can do both at times, especially when you see her on the couch with her embroidery wearing her glasses on a chain Mr. Buck gave her, and she's watching *Wheel of Fortune* and guessing the puzzle, which is something you will never, *ever* be able to do. If they had a show on identifying raccoon tracks or the scat of deer or the hooting of one of several kinds of owls, you would win first prize and an all-expenses-paid trip to some place far from Home-winds. Not that you would care to go. The swamp has all the world you need.

Mr. Buck also fiddles around with words. He's retired. He fills his time working on his old pulp-wooder's truck, crawling in under the hood or jacking it up so he can slide under it and look at its belly. He tells you about its parts. Each part is a different word. You remember the words but not always the parts. Some parts have two names: fuel pump, for example. Or master cylinder. Some just one: carburetor comes to mind. Other words fly into the world when Mr. Buck tries to get his old truck started. Words Miss Billie Ruth does not approve of, according to Mr. Buck. Just the other day he poked a key into that little slot by the steering wheel and that old truck made a sound like a wounded gator but it wouldn't come on to life and Mr. Buck said, "You no good son of a bitch. You cocksucking bastard." Then he grinned at you through his anger and said, "Donchoo go sayin' them kinda words, Joe Boy. They'll make your teeth fall out. And donchoo let on to Miss Billie Ruth that I said 'em neither. Y'hear?"

You did like he said. Mostly.

But then when you were pulling the ferry over to the spit later that day you saw a bluejay fussing at some smaller birds and you said, "You no good son of a bitch. You cocksucking bastard." And you waited. And you pressed your tongue against your front teeth and nothing happened. Your teeth did not fall out. So it goes to show you about words that you can just never tell.

Which leads you to not say much. It's safer that way.

"Willow."

Curled up in Mr. Buck's chair just before the sun sneaks over the swamp, her name comes into your

head and so you whisper it out loud. And there's
another word with it, only it's bouncing around like
those rubber balls they have in Miss Morgan
McGary's special-ed class at school. You will have to
wait until that word stops bouncing before you can
pick it up and look it over and see how dangerous
it is.

Willow is your friend. You like her because you
can be with her and not have to say many words.
You are afraid about Willow. Willow's mother is
afraid about Willow. And Miss Billie Ruth and Mr.
Buck say that no one knows where Willow is. But
you do. And you try to tell them that you do.

"She's gone inside the world," you say.

But they shake their heads and ask questions and
look puzzled so you give up on words.

You don't know why she has gone inside the
world.

All you know is that it's dark there.

And you are not welcome.

You have breakfast while Miss Billie Ruth and Mr.
Buck sleep.

You like to eat slices of bread but just a certain
way. First, you eat the crusts all the way around.
Then you take what's left and ball it up and run a
little water from the faucet on the bread ball so it's
watery and in a way juicy. You eat two of those, take
a big swig of chocolate milk right from the carton,
knowing Miss Billie Ruth would pitch a fit if she saw
you doing it, and you slip out the front door in your
bare feet, long shorts, and T-shirt, and you brush
your hand through your hair and it still has some
possum grease in it from the day before. So you're
fine.

And you can smell the sun as the first light steals
through the woods and over the landing, and you

can smell Willow, too. Kudzu blossoms and honeysuckle. Women, you have come to understand, like to smell good. Miss Billie Ruth likes to smell like coconut butter. Miss Morgan McGary at school smells like several kinds of flowers swirled around together. And Miss Artie—she smells like heaven. Like she's Eve and was never tossed out of the Garden of Eden but got to stay there and perfume herself with the best-smelling stuff in Paradise. You remember Miss Billie Ruth talking about Adam and Eve and the Garden of Eden and the serpent—who's really the devil—and something called the Tree of Life, though you've never seen one in the swamp.

You can't, in fact, imagine a more glorious place than the swamp.

Not anywhere.

In the Garden of Eden the serpent—which you have learned is another word for a snake—could talk. That's something you've never seen either, though cottonmouths will hiss like fire and an old swamp diamondback rattler will chill you to the bone with its rat-tat-tat-tat-tat. Anyway, you remember that the trouble began when the serpent talked Eve into eating an apple. You don't see how that was a problem. Apples are good. You eat lots of them and nothing bad happens to you unless you eat green crab apples. What Eve should have been careful about was eating poisonous berries. Such as holly berries or nandina berries. You just have to learn what stuff you can eat and what you can't.

Miss Billie Ruth says the stories in the Bible are just stories. Meaning serpents can't really talk unless the devil "possesses" them. But stories have "messages" and only a preacher knows all the messages, though Miss Billie Ruth knows her share. Miss Morgan McGary knows stories, too, or at least she can read lots of stories, which is what she does at school.

You don't mind sitting quietly and listening to stories. Rebbie can't sit still long enough to listen unless he takes a big purple pill. Shemoka doesn't listen well either because she's too busy fluttering her fingers like butterflies. Sometimes she gets to fluttering them so hard that sweat trickles down her pretty, black face. You don't mind being at school too much because every so often you get to see Willow. One day you followed the scent of her perfume down some halls until you ended up in her room. It made other kids laugh at her. Willow didn't mind. Later she told you, "I don't give a shit what those kids think."

Those kids wouldn't last long in the swamp. You know that.

So you don't give a shit about them either.

"Shit" is another funny word. A bad word mostly. But Willow claims it makes her feel good to say it. So that makes it extra funny. You know you shouldn't say it in front of Miss McGary because one day you did and her face turned red and you thought she was going to laugh but then she got upset at you. She asked you one day what you thought about the unusually warm spring and you said, "I don't give a shit about it."

So you see every day how it's best to keep quiet or not use many words.

Once outside, you survey the morning.

You think about which day of the week it is. Wednesday. And that means school later. You go to school afternoons on Mondays, Wednesdays, and Fridays. Mr. Buck picks you up from school at 3:30 sharp. You tried riding the bus home with Willow, but the other kids made fun of you and Willow had to knock a few of them in the mouth and so the bus driver complained and the people who run the school asked that you not ride the bus again.

So you didn't.

And you missed sitting with Willow on the bus.

You think it's warm. Moccasins will be up early sunning themselves. Egrets and anhingas will be out searching for food. So will gators back deep in the swamp. You go down to your ferry and sit and let the sun warm your back and you think about Willow. You are troubled some. Troubled a whole lot, to tell the truth.

Here's the problem: you don't believe Willow would have gone inside the world on her own. Someone or some *thing* must have called her there or chased her there or grabbed her and taken her there. She's there. You know she is. But what confuses you is this: when somebody goes inside the world, where exactly are they?

In the swamp somewhere? Behind the moon?

You just don't know.

And that word bouncing around in your head is back, still bouncing but not as much. You can pretty much see it, though the letters won't hold still. You try to sneak a peek at it in the corner of your eye. It doesn't work. Might as well stop trying and go for a swim. You know that the word has something to do with Willow and Willow is your friend and Willow is maybe in trouble—her mother and about everyone else thinks so, too, and maybe she is because it's dark inside the world.

And it smells like death there.

Suddenly you just got to get away from everything—from thoughts of Willow and darkness and death and people being upset about where she is—and you run to the end of the ferry and you jump headfirst into the backwater of Night Horse Creek.

And you're not Joe Boy no more.

The water is colder than you expected it to be. In June it will be warmer. You torpedo deeper and your body feels terrific as your hands become like flippers. Your feet, too. You know what's coming and you welcome it. A transformation. In the water, you have not really stopped being Joe Boy or stopped being human. But while you're in the water, whoever Joe Boy is curls inside something else.

Your other being.

A creature. A water beast. Like an otter or a muskrat or a very strange fish.

You don't try to figure it out. And you don't go around telling anyone about this other being. You don't tell Miss Billie Ruth or Mr. Buck or Miss McGary or any of the Fossor witches, except that once you tried to tell Willow. She listened and said, "That sounds very weird, Joe Boy."

You feel like you could live underwater. You can hold your breath forever. And you probably wouldn't go hungry because you could eat crawdads and minnows but not moss or duckweed. Definitely not duckweed. But you wonder how everyone else would feel if you gave in to this other being and moved out of the mobile home where Miss Billie Ruth and Mr. Buck made you a place. Made you a home. You are a boy—"young man," according to Miss McGary—and there are some things about being a boy you really like. Such as operating the rope-pull ferry and eating Miss Billie Ruth's cornbread and some days going to school. You like being Willow's friend. Who knows? Maybe she wouldn't want to be your friend if you lived in the water. You wouldn't want that to happen.

You think about one thing more.

And it makes your heart swell and you have to jet to the surface and take a boy breath. You glance across the backwater to the spit where it rises like a shoulder and there you see two houses, one in which Willow and her mama live and the other in which Aunt Mushka and Artie live.

"Artie."

You whisper her name and your body tingles. Your lips quiver.

You think about Artie a lot. You know what she is doing right this moment. You know what you want to do only you know you shouldn't. You figure it's like Mr. Buck hiding bottles of Miller Lite in that tank of water behind the toilet—he just can't help himself. You just can't help yourself. You've got to go get yourself an eyeful of Artie.

Because she fills your soul.

You start swimming toward the spit. You like Willow and you like Artie. But something is different. First off, you can talk to Willow or be near Willow and it doesn't make your mouth go dry as dust and doesn't make your palms sweaty.

There are other differences.

You feel the strangest one stirring in your shorts.

You are supposed to know all about such things because the health teacher, Miss Rennie Lou Pleasance, taught your class of slow learners and handicappers about human reproduction. You knew some of it just from scratching around in the swamp and keeping your eyes open. You didn't know all the names of the body parts. You had seen a used condom once floating in Night Horse Creek and you stuck it on the end of the little hammer you bang out the crossing signal with—Miss Billie Ruth made you take it off and glared at you like you should have known better. What you knew is that a condom wasn't something animals needed. You just never saw a muskrat or raccoon using one. So the whole business of sex was somehow obviously different with people. Very different. It involved love and marriage and respect for another person's "needs"—a word that blows through you like the wind.

When you think about "needs," you think about Artie.

You think about how her body affects yours.

You can't help yourself, so you swim right over to the spit and go to the screened-in back porch and situate yourself where you can look in at one corner without being seen and you haven't even laid eyes on her but already your mouth is dry, your palms are sweaty, and your dinkle doo is as stiff as a pussy willow stalk.

You reach down and touch it as it strains against your shorts.

It feels very good to touch it.

You don't mean to, but you giggle. You have to keep one hand over your mouth. You have no idea why you are tickled, though maybe it's because your dinkle doo seems to have a mind of its own. "Dinkle doo" is not what it's really called. That's just Mr. Buck's name for it—"Joe Boy, don't let chiggers bite your dinkle doo 'cause you'll need it when you're a man." He doesn't say things like that in front of Miss Billie Ruth.

Now you see her.

She is the most beautiful creature on earth. Her eyes are closed and she is sitting with her knees ritched out to the sides and her hands on her thighs and she is concentrating and saying something softly and she is rocking to and fro ever so slightly.

And she is naked. Not wearing a stitch of clothing.

Your eyes cannot see enough of her. It's like trying to eat a lot of something you like to eat—cornbread, maybe, or chocolate cake—all in one gulp. You can hurt yourself. Choke to death. Peeping at Artie is dangerous like that. You blink away the initial shock—it's *always* a shock, though a pleasant one—of seeing her and you grit your teeth and you try to concentrate as hard as Artie's concentrating, only you are trying to concentrate on the wonders of her body.

And there are many.

Her hair the color of dawn. Her eyelids. Her lips. Her chin. Her shoulders. And you suddenly realize that as you dive deeper into the magnificent realm of her body that you are holding your breath as well as your dinkle doo and so you release a small bird whistle and then you drink in her breasts. You take a long drink. The sight of her nipples clears your sinus cavities.

Then you study the ring in her navel.

And the spider tattoos.

Then you take another breath, release another whistle, and lower your eyes between her legs and you are biting the edges of your tongue until you're pretty certain they have started to bleed and you are squeezing your dinkle doo like mad and then you—

"Joe Boy!"

You fall back almost dead away in surprise and let go of your dinkle doo.

You have been caught. First time it's happened. Your face is on fire. You cannot scramble away fast enough.

"Wait!" you hear her cry, and even though it seems foolish to do so, you stop in your tracks. Artie has covered herself and she is smiling as she rounds the corner of the porch. "Joe Boy, come inside for a minute."

You hesitate.

Then she says, "It's okay. I'm not upset with you. I'm flattered, in fact."

Your mouth has fallen open, but you can't think of a single word to say. She reaches out for you. "Come on back inside with me. I want you to do something for me."

You follow. You feel as light as nothing at all. On the porch Artie smiles at you again. She keeps her body modestly hidden, but then she says, "I want you to touch something for me."

You can't be certain she said what you think she said. You begin to imagine that the skin on your face is fiery pink and maybe giving off smoke. You hope it isn't. You hope you won't faint away dead.

Not before you've done as she's asked.

You also hope this doesn't fit Miss Billie Ruth's definition of sinful.

Artie hunkers down closer to you and the warmth and sexiness of her body staggers you and you have to close your eyes and you keep them closed until you feel her hand on your shoulder jostling you as if to awaken you. When you open your eyes you see that she has thrust her right arm out toward you.

"I want you to touch my wrist," she says. "My magic," she continues, though it sounds as if she might be about to cry, "is gone. There's something . . . oh, I don't know what's happened. Touch it, please. Touch me, Joe Boy."

So you do.

Not a gentle touch. You sort of lose control and grab her wrist hard and you want to pull her down to you and kiss her maybe. Or something. You are just not sure what you want to do. And then blackness mushrooms in your mind. It's scary.

And that word is in there again. The word that stays close to the word "Willow." You can see it white against the blackness of your thoughts and you can see it falling like an oak leaf and drops down from your mind into your mouth and you gulp and then you say it clear as day.

"Coda."

SEVEN

It felt like violation. Or trespass at the least.

Her daughter's room was achingly familiar and yet ineffably different, and Tina couldn't shake the feeling that she shouldn't be there. Did a mother have a right to stroll through her daughter's room? Of course she did. But under these circumstances—everything felt wrong and, more so, everything seemed so impersonal; everything became a potential clue for tracing the whereabouts of her daughter.

Willow was missing.

Now, late afternoon, missing for forty-eight hours.

Tina fought a tentative rush of emotion surging up from her chest. She calmed herself through a deep breath, and in glancing around the room she tried to recall whether it had ever seemed so empty to her, empty and barren. It had the feel of a cell for a nun or some other religious person or a New Ager seeking absolute solitude surrounded by only the bare necessities. Even the walls had nothing on them save for one poster centered over Willow's bed. It was an elaborate drawing in Victorian style of one angel clasping another around the neck sharing what seemed almost a passionless kiss. The angel doing the holding appeared to be female, but the other might well have been sexless.

Tina studied the drawing. She did not know what

it alluded to. More importantly, she found nothing in it to suggest where her daughter might be.

Missing. Willow was missing. It was a situation Tina could not, regardless of how hard she tried, grasp. So she had gone about looking for her methodically, in good motherly fashion, and yet in a daze. Sleepwalking. A zombie. Mother zombie. She had put together dozens of flyers with a xerox of Willow's latest photo on it, and she had tacked them up everywhere in town and made extras for others to distribute. She had prompted every law enforcement official she could—the equivalent of APBs had been sent out. In another day or so a news crew from a Montgomery television station was scheduled to interview her.

But while virtually everyone was helpful and encouraging, almost to a person they believed that Willow had simply run away. Seeing her as a wild girl—as one of the Fossor witches—they had no difficulty believing she might fly the coop. A witchy girl, they assumed, would be attracted to a big or at least an exotic city—maybe Atlanta or New Orleans or New York or even Salem, Massachusetts. Or the golden realm of witch-friendly California could well be her destination. She could lose herself and be a new person in Los Angeles or, better yet, San Francisco.

Tina, however, was not convinced.

Not at all.

But where is she?

She sat down on her daughter's bed, which had not been slept in for two nights, and she imagined that at any moment Willow would come slinking in, somewhat shocked and dismayed that her mother would be in her room snooping. And Tina imagined that she would stand up and go to her daughter and embrace her as she had never embraced her before. Never mind the anguish that had been generated. Never mind anything except the fact that her daughter was home.

Tina Fossor sat on her daughter's bed and waited.

And the angels on the wall remained locked in their passionless kiss.

And Willow did not return for her embrace.

It was peaceful and serene out on her deck, a state so in contrast with the chaos of her emotions. In one of the deck chairs she had bought only that spring, she sat and gazed at Night Horse Creek and Pan Island and the swamp beyond. The landscape tugged at her. It was as if it had something to say to her, but she did not know its language or was too mentally exhausted to make the effort to listen closely and to comprehend. She had learned that the most intense form of anxiety did not give one extra energy; rather it depleted one's energy, vampiring it off as if blood were literally being sucked from one's body.

Tina's magic remained out of reach.

And wasn't it odd, she speculated to herself, that her magic had ceased the same afternoon Willow disappeared? As a follower of the Old Ways, she knew that could not simply be a coincidence. But the larger, mythical, transcendent pattern of things escaped her, forcing her to concentrate instead on mundane tasks that required no special knowledge or sensitivity.

The truncation of her magical abilities had led her, temporarily at least, to shut down www.-spellscast.com. She hated to take such a drastic measure, but felt she had no choice. She posted an explanation on her site: "family matters" prevented her from responding to all current requests for spells or purchases of items for sale. It was tempting to post a more involved message elaborating upon

Willow's disappearance and perhaps even a cryptic allusion to her own loss of magic. In the end she resisted the temptation. The matter of Willow was too personal, too intimate. For the first time in many, many months she found, in fact, that she did not even want to think about her Web site or any aspect of her business.

She wanted to focus on Willow.

Her mind, however, strayed, and quite suddenly, as she scanned the outline of Gretta's cabin on Pan Island, she began to cry. Her chest heaved and the tears flowed freely. She pressed her fingers into her eyes and rocked into the thralls of her crying.

Not all of the tears had Willow as their source.

Many were provoked by sisterhood. Because Tina feared her slapping of Gretta the other night had severed the bonds of sisterhood. She and Gretta had not spoken since. There was silence between her and Artie as well. Poor, dear Aunt Mushka, a worried hen, had tried on a couple of occasions to talk with Tina, assuage her concerns, and plead with her to apologize to Gretta or make some other peaceful overture.

Tina wasn't certain why she couldn't.

Mother would be angered.

In all the years that Anna Fossor had nurtured and orchestrated the lives of her daughters she had eloquently championed the Old Ways as the best possible lifestyle, and into her daughters she had succeeded in planting and cultivating the seeds of a reverence for Nature, and those seeds had taken root and flourished. But above all she had emphasized that at the heart of the Fossors was the unassailable unity of family.

Sisterhood.

To be a follower of the Old Ways in contemporary America and, especially, in the South, demanded that the three women bind themselves to each other with a silken, yet steely web of trust and loyalty and respect. Let not jealousy or envy or ill thoughts of any kind persist such that the bond of sisterhood might be threatened.

But Anna Fossor was only present now in spirit.

A spirit choosing not to manifest itself or herself as peacemaker or wisdom giver.

She was not even appearing in Tina's dreams, few as they were because of so many sleepless hours.

Tina dried her tears and sighed and chided herself for sitting. She needed to be doing more to find Willow—what that "more" might entail, she did not know. But as was often the rule in the last day or so her thoughts turned to the drifter who called himself Shep. She longed to see him again and talk with him just in case he had seen Willow or perhaps even intuited something about her. He somehow represented the inscrutable possibilities of all strangers. He intrigued her, if for no other reason than that her reading of him was virtually blank. She had no idea whether he might be a child molester on the move or a guardian angel. Could he have been a stalker of Willow? Or was he possibly in tune with—to echo Joe Boy's curious remark— the world into which Willow had gone? Apparently Tina had been the only person in the Homewinds area to have seen and conversed with him.

She found that strange. Very much so.

It was time to search again. Whenever Tina got a gnawing sensation in her stomach, she had to stop what she was doing and retrace the route that Willow took daily from the point at which the bus released her to the moment she entered the house. Slipping on her sneakers, Tina decided to walk the weedy trail along the arm of the spit instead of signaling for Joe Boy to take her across on the rope-pull ferry. It was a warm late afternoon. Tina tugged gently at the back of her blouse as she walked, for she could feel perspiration beading up between her shoulders. Despite the heat, the walk raised her spirits—it provided her with the illusion that she was doing something, searching, scouring, and maybe on the verge of finding her daughter or some clue to where she was.

She pressed along the edge of the swamp, then cut deeper into it, pausing several times because she was struck by its elemental, yet forbidding beauty. Could Willow be somewhere in the swamp? Could she have gotten lost? Glen Favors had already led one search party through the area in which Tina was looking. Boats had been used. Even a pair of bloodhounds. But nothing had come of the search.

Missing without a trace.

But the Night Horse Swamp was a formidably large place, a massive labyrinth in which someone could remain lost—or remain hidden—for a very long time without ever being discovered. Tina knew that one of the best trackers around would probably not be of any use. Darryl Crowfoot could not keep himself sober for any stretch of time; otherwise, if his whereabouts were known, he might be able to lead a search team into areas no else knew about. Except perhaps Willow.

She knows the swamp.

So does Joe Boy.

Tina believed that a symbiosis between the swamp and her young daughter existed, and it meant that the possibility of Willow ever getting lost in this primitive world was remote. It was the same way with Joe Boy. He, too, possessed an inner map of the swamp that almost no other cartographer had, and yet when he had been asked to help search for Willow, he had been reluctant, participating only after Tina had begged him to.

Was the young man deliberately withholding something about Willow?

It seemed improbable that he would do so. "Willow!"

Wading into a small pool of coffee-colored water and leaning against a knobby-kneed cypress, Tina called out as she had hundreds of times in the last two days, and as had been the consistent pattern, the only voice that returned was her own.

The canoes were tied up and waiting to be rented. They were scarred and weathered, and like everything else at her ex-husband's fish camp, cabins, and bait shop, they had been neglected so long that Tina figured they would be shocked if given attention. Once upon a time, she had loved those canoes. Loved gliding over the darkly crystalline waters of Night Horse Creek as her husband, her fallen angel, manned a paddle, handling it with something resembling an unfolding of sexual passion—steady, attentive to details, building to a sustained rhythm.

It was nearing dark as Tina pushed her way up from the canoes to the rear of the bait shop. She smiled to herself at the sight of a lone figure in a rocking chair, a man half hidden by the encroachment of shadows.

"Hey, Pa-Po. It's me—Tina."

She waved. The man, bedecked in coveralls and a baseball cap, did not move a muscle, nor did he say anything. His name was Petto. He was John Scarpia's father, and he was mute. But to Tina he would always be one of the sweetest human beings she had ever known. As she approached, his bad eyes must have pieced out her visage—for she knew his hearing was poor—and the beginnings of a smile were flickering at the corners of his mouth.

"Pa-Po, I'm back again. Still looking for Willow. Any chance you've seen her?"

She knew there wasn't. His dark eyes followed her

as she drew very near, and as she leaned down to
embrace him, she heard a warm chuckle that
seemed to come from his chest. She pulled close to
his face and those same dark eyes danced. She
kissed him on the nose, and his smile widened. She
studied what still held fast as handsome, Italianate
features.

"You old dog—you'll always be the sexiest man
on the planet. Do you know that?"

He nodded and held his smile and worked his
lips and chuckled. Tina patted his cheek.

"Pa-Po, is John around?"

The old man—his resemblance to his son remarkable—tilted his head toward the row of cabins. Tina
hugged him good-bye and set out to find her ex-
husband. As twilight was beginning to deepen, she
slowed at the sight of a young and quite beautiful
woman standing at the porch railing of one of the
cabins, her eyes drawn to the dark backwaters of
Night Horse Creek. To Tina, it was a curiously romantic image—young woman, perhaps a newly-
wed—waiting for her man to join her. There would
be dinner and, no doubt, a late-night canoe ride
and then a return to the cabin for intimacy to hold
sway.

From her vantage point she could see John Scarpia striding toward that same cabin, his gait firm
and energetic, loaded with animal sensuality. Tina
was about to call out to him, but she stopped herself
when she saw the way he was smiling at the young
woman. Then he was up the steps in a bound, and
the young woman, mindful of being discreet,
backed into a shadowy corner of the porch. Tina
could hear soft laughter and hushed words.
Numbed, she watched as her ex-husband gently
spun the young woman around so that he was behind her, his arms around her waist. More soft
laughter. Then his hands sliding up over the young

woman's breasts. And Tina looked away just as the young woman swung her face around for a passionate kiss.

Good Ole Gals was virtually empty.

Tina sat in a booth as far away from the front door as she could get. Steam from a hot cup of tea spun up in front of her eyes. Her sister Artie was there, too, at the other end of the restaurant that specialized in fried catfish and southern-style hush puppies. The place smelled of grease and smoke and stale beer, but on weekends, especially summers, business boomed. Though she tried not to stare, Tina couldn't keep from watching Artie—who had made a point of ignoring her—and the questionable group stuffed into the booth with her. There was Gladys Michaels, an attractive older woman and one of the owners of Good Ole Gals, but there were also two young men and a young woman, each younger even than Artie. What the three most had in common was their pallor. Skin almost chalky white; hair black and spiked, world-weary faces highlighted with dark makeup. Dark clothing, mostly leather. Tina shook her head at what appeared to her to be caricatures of vampiric figures. What did Willow call such creatures? Goths? They were ludicrous.

Tina looked down at her tea.

She was waiting for Glen Favors to join her. It was nearing 10:00 and he would be off duty. He had someplace else he needed to be, but had agreed to meet Tina briefly because she had been so insistent. Yet as she waited, she knew there wasn't much he could do. Perhaps she just needed for a man—any man—to listen to her. Images of John Scarpia and his attractive young friend flickered in her thoughts. She had headed home without interrupting him to ask whether he might have heard from Willow. At home she had checked for phone messages; she had checked her e-mail and chatted a bit with Aunt Mushka. She had tried to eat something but was not hungry, and then decided that she needed to speak with Favors again.

Banging out the ferry signal, she had waited for Joe Boy to take her across to where her new Honda was parked in a car port that Simeon Private had built. Aunt Mushka's ancient Ford Maverick was parked there, too. On the ferry ride—a distance of less than a hundred yards—she sensed that Joe Boy was nervous. She hoped to deflect his nervousness by updating him on her various efforts to find Willow; then, when she fell silent, Joe Boy paused at the rope pull and said, "Willow smells like honeysuckle and kudzu blossoms."

He was right, of course. Tina envied Joe Boy's interface with the world. So elemental. Primitive. Real. For him, just being in the world was magic enough.

"Hey, there. You look a million miles away."

Startled, Tina glanced up and the reverie of being with Joe Boy on the ferry was suddenly gone. The handsome man standing by her booth was smiling. His sympathy for her was everywhere in his expression. She was warmed by it.

"Thanks, Glen, for coming."

He sat down with her, his hands clasped together and resting patiently on the table as she began at once to ask questions, to speculate on any possible lead concerning her missing daughter. She raised the issue of the drifter again and of any recent reports about child molesters or sexual deviants in the area. She was reaching and she knew it. Favors listened. Said what he could. Mostly, he allowed her to bleed off some of her anxiety.

"What next?" she asked when she had exhausted all and more of what she had intended to say.

"Hope for a breakthrough. Frankly, I think she'll get in touch with you. She'll run out of money or get scared or, most likely, homesick. There's a pattern to these things."

"I still can't believe she'd run away. It doesn't sound like her."

But Tina wasn't exactly sure what did sound like Willow.

I don't know my own daughter.

Then Favors began to talk about the Internet, about situations he knew of in which a girl or a young woman had developed a relationship with a stranger via cyberspace and had left home to be with him.

"Was she part of any chat rooms? Was she into that kind of thing?"

Favors pressed hard until Tina had to revolt against the direction of his probings.

"No!" she cried. "She wasn't into the Internet! She was into magic!"

Her frustration broke like an egg. Favors seemed to know he had gone too far, and he apologized. Tina returned the apology and added, "I'm at a loss to know what to do."

"I'll do everything I can," he assured her.

And Tina knew that there was no more to it than that. She had never felt so helpless in her life as Favors rose to go.

"Tina," he said, "I know your sisters and your Aunt Mushka are real upset. Gretta, she's—well, she cares about you and Willow. God knows she does. Don't doubt that. Please."

Words from a man in love.

"I know," Tina whispered, nodding her head.

"Gretta's different from any other woman I've ever known." And this time his words seemed directed to some inner listener. Then he squeezed the back of her hand. "You Fossor women are a breed apart."

"I'll take that as a compliment."

"It's meant that way. But, you, I've got to say this: sometimes I get scared thinking about what might happen to all of you. Your system of belief, the way you live your life—down this neck of the woods it seems like it makes you a target."

Tina watched him go. Watched him pause to say something to his wife, Robbie, who was on the night shift. Under different circumstances she would have felt sorry for Robbie, the cheated-upon wife. But the darkness surrounding Willow's disappearance crowded out all the rest of the humanity and compassion she had to offer the world.

EIGHT

Something passed by.

Gretta remained shaken to the core, almost unable to move as she stared into the wooded area at the north end of the island, her island—Pan Island—where she had seen . . . *something*. It was nearing twilight and the sun, low and still burning brightly in what she always viewed as its daily majesty, had to battle through the tallest trees of the swamp to knife its rays into the island. The day continued warm and humid and Gretta could smell herself.

And she could smell what had passed.

An animal? A man? Something elemental? Or merely something her imagination had peopled the air with? She did not know and not knowing frightened her all the more. She couldn't help staring as she stood; small pines and a scattering of hardwoods—mostly sweet gum and dogwood—held her eye. A green thicket roped among the trees. Briar vines vaulted up several of the hardwoods to create a delicate curtain that made visibility even more difficult. Yet, she had seen something. Sensed its presence. There could be no mistaking it.

Willow had been missing for just over seventy-two hours. Gretta had started keeping track. Hours sounded better than days, and days would sound better than weeks, she reasoned. She had come from her cabin to try a small burning in hopes that her magic had returned. It was a ritual she repeated each day, some days two or three times. That night she would meet Favors on the houseboat. In gathering and piling up an assortment of sweet-gum twigs, she had been pulled three ways: nervous anticipation for her magic to return, worry about Willow and, finally, desire to see Favors.

She had hunkered down near the twigs and set them on fire and had leaned over the first fingers of smoke after whispering an invocation for the Goddess to return her powers. Using both hands she fanned the tentative wisps of smoke into her face. She breathed. She coughed twice. She pressed her fingertips against her temples and concentrated upon Willow.

Then upon Favors.

But saw nothing except a sickly yellow pulse of light.

No visions. No magic.

Her once rich connection with the Old Ways, with the promise of magic the Goddess held out to true believers, had been broken. She sat down hard and rocked back and forth, her face buried in her hands, and she sobbed. Connections broken. There had been more than one. She knew that if she touched her cheek in a certain way she could still feel where Tina had slapped her. It was there faintly like a not very obvious birthmark. Like sunburn.

Sisterhood.

What had happened?

She loved her sisters.

Now there was pain and silence and distrust among them. And she felt that she could no more forgive Tina than she could swallow a burning twig of sweet gum. She wanted an answer to questions she could not articulate. She wanted to be in Favors's arms, and, more so, she wanted to *belong* there.

As her tears relented and the sun lowered, she had felt it. Instinctively, she had glanced at the wooded area. Movement. Yes, probably a small animal foraging or perhaps a deer that had swum across the creek. Yes, she saw a gleam of antlers. She stood up. She shaded her eyes with her hand and then felt the presence of something, and the initial feeling it generated was one of peace or, more precisely, awe. Something transcendent.

Holy.

She held her breath and kept herself perfectly still so as not to frighten the creature. But she sensed that no ordinary animal could send off such vibrations. It was moving as if indifferent or unaware that she was watching. It possessed bulk and yet an indistinct form or shape. It was dark colored, like a shadow. Gretta let her eyes adjust, for she knew that she had the right eyes for seeing the natural world, and she held her gaze with the concentration of a marksman zeroing in on his target.

And that's when the creature looked her way.

She heard herself give out a silly, girlish gasp, a half shriek, and then she lost the angle of those dark, brooding, beastly eyes—then quickly upon the moment a slight rustle. She might have seen fur, something shaggy, a glint of more antlers, an impossible number and arrangement of antlers, and the thud of sharp hooves upon the floor of the woods. She could smell its hot, panting breath.

And then it was gone. Vanished. Dissolved. Perfectly blended into the cover.

Bliss and horror filled Gretta's veins.

Was this what she had experienced deep in the swamp perched on her deer stand? It frightened her to think that what she thought existed so far from the eye of man might suddenly be quite near. On her island. Where it had never been before.

She closed her eyes, believing she had seen "the Terror."

And she shuddered.

Mother would know what it means.

The night sounds of the swamp closed in on Gretta as she waited on the deck of the houseboat, her lantern burning ineffectually from a hook on a post. Favors was late. She needed desperately to have him hold her, but she needed equally to hear her mother's reassuring voice explaining why the Terror—if that, indeed, was what she had seen—was suddenly so bold as to be wandering on Pan Island. And she feared that if she stared too intensely into the darkness that those cold, beastly eyes would emerge from nowhere and stare back at her.

Having been onboard only a few minutes, she had heard, somewhere in the heart of the swamp, the cry of the panther, and it had ripped across her senses like the scream of a woman in anguish. She had gone and sat on the bed—*their* bed—and she had fussed with her hair and thought about what she might do to give Favors more sexual pleasure than before. *Will he,* she wondered, *grow tired of me? I have no imagination.* She had brought along a small cooler with ice and two cans of beer—cheap, "lite" beer—because she knew he sometimes drank beer at the end of a day.

It was more than relief, more than sexual anticipation that swept through her when she saw his boat coming up the run. Saw his lantern and heard him deliver his version of a swamp "holler"—his comic signal of approach. It brought a smile to her lips because Glen Favors could never be a swamper. He

knew it, too. But all that mattered to Gretta was that
he was who he was—her friend and lover. And tonight he would allow her to forget about the anguish brought on by the damage to sisterhood, by
the sickening sense of loss surrounding Willow, and
by the frightening sighting of the mysterious creature on Pan Island.

Laughing at her eagerness, Favors gave in as she
pulled him onboard and dragged him to the bed
where she began to undress him as she kissed him
passionately. She wanted their passion to take her
beyond guilt and fear, to take her into a world in-
habited only by them.

"Let me feel all the desire you have," she whispered to him.

Afterward, nestled so close that she felt as if she
were beneath his flesh, she admitted to herself that
it was his hands that turned her on the most. Skilled
hands. Carpenter's hands. Hands that could build
things. Hands that could hold her, caress her. Hands
that fit over her breasts warmly. Hands that could
cup her bottom and drive their bodies deeper into
each other. Hands that might keep all the darkness
of her hours at bay.

She thought of those hands wielding the revolver
he always brought along. She wondered, but had
never asked, whether he had ever been forced to
shoot someone. Had he ever killed another person?
Lying against him so closely, she heard him ever so
hesitantly clear his throat.

"I want to promise you something," he said.

Giddied by his words, she pressed up to survey
his face in the lantern light.

"What? That you'll love me until the moon falls
out of the sky?"

He chuckled, and then she felt embarrassed because she sensed he wasn't going to deliver one of
his comically romantic statements.

"It's about Willow," he said.

"Yes?"

She could feel herself tense.

"Gretta, I promise you that I'll find her. I know how upset you are. I know how much you care for her. I've promised Tina, too, but . . . that's different."

And she was about to say something—something about what she had experienced that afternoon on Pan Island and how, quite suddenly, she vaguely connected it with Willow, but he shushed her before she could speak. He pressed his lips close to her forehead and whispered, "I hear someone."

He slipped from her arms and into his clothes making hardly any noise. In the lantern light that accentuated shadows, she watched him pick up his revolver and creep from the bedroom. She had no clear idea how much time passed, perhaps no more than a minute, before he returned and she moved into his arms.

"It's okay," he said. "Whoever it was is gone."

Minutes later they dressed and went out onto the deck of the houseboat and stared into the darkness of the swamp and listened for something beyond the usual swamp sounds, and Gretta pressed herself against this man she loved and told herself that, for him, she would do anything.

She would even give up the Old Ways if he asked her to.

He meant that much to her. She would find a way to keep always this close.

"Are you sure it wasn't some varmint?" she asked. "A possum or a coon maybe?"

"Yes, I'm sure." Then he cocked his head to one side. "Listen. Do you hear that?"

She sucked in her breath.

"No," she said, "I can't hear anything that isn't always out there."

But another half dozen heartbeats and she heard it.

Somewhere far off, the plucking and strumming of a guitar.

NINE

Aunt Mushka couldn't remember ever feeling so cold in May.

Absently she petted Rosebud and sipped at lukewarm tea and considered spiking it with some alcohol—didn't matter what kind. Needed something to warm her insides. Being without her magic was the source of it, she had concluded, the source of her being so cold. That and her dreams.

"Kitty puss, I feel old," she murmured. "And I ache all over and I can't do nothing about it, it seems. I hurt around my heart, too."

The cat looked up, and Mushka could almost imagine that she was commiserating with her. But Nature had been kind to creatures such as Rosebud—no heartbreak over shattered relationships with loved ones. To animals, life was moment-to-moment futurity; they lived more in the now than humans possibly could.

Mushka was envious. The pain in the depths of her emotional center was eating away at her like a cancer. Willow was still missing, and the Fossor sisters were as disconnected as distant stars. And Mushka believed that only one person knew the secret to bringing them together again.

Anna.

But as the old woman sat and let her thoughts float to the surface, she realized that she had always

rather feared her younger sister—feared her wisdom, her know-how, and her willingness to traffic
in darkness. Anna Fossor could, it seemed, dance
with terrifying spirits and dangerous entities and be
neither harmed nor seduced.

And she was a poetess of dreams. Knew their me-
ter and rhyme scheme. Beat time with their meta-
phors, similes, and images. Found intimacy with
their symbols. So it was then that Mushka longed to
hear what Anna might have said about last night's
dream, a nightmarish narrative about a secret area
of Night Horse Swamp and the lingering impression
that it somehow related to Willow's disappearance.

Mushka closed her eyes. Rosebud began to purr.
Memory reeled in the magic theater of the old
woman's mind, and she was there again, in the john
boat with Anna and a stranger—on their way to "the
Pulse." Years ago.

The stranger's name was Sister Golden Hair. She
was a member of the Bushyeye tribe, a small settle-
ment of which lived in the bowels of the swamp.
Anna knew her and trusted her. On a hot morning
one July, she had asked Sister Golden Hair—whose
blond hair was an aberration among her black-
haired fellow tribesmen—to guide her and Mushka
to the genius loci of the swamp, a place few if any
whites had ever seen.

Mushka remembered how excited Anna had been
to be on the journey, and she also recalled how
quiet and expressionless Sister Golden Hair had
been as she poled the john boat, eyeing the various
runs with an uncanny expertise. At her feet she had
tied a young raccoon. Mushka had assumed it was
a pet.

"What is so special about where we're going?"
she had asked Anna along the way.

Anna had smiled in her polite yet condescending
way. "It's a place never touched by the seasons. It's

a place where the swamp has turned upon itself . . .
where it . . . feeds upon itself, or so I've been told.
A place of dark magic."

"Does it have a name?"

"It has a Bushyeye name, but they wish for it not
to be spoken by a white person. I've translated it as
'the Pulse'—the mysterious heart of an unseen life
force."

"Sounds like we ought to be nurses rather than
witches," Mushka had mused.

And Anna's response had been melodramatically
serious. "But it's not like anything you know. You
can't prepare yourself for it."

One other point about the journey Mushka recalled was that Sister Golden Hair would not allow
any trail markings to be made—if one were to return to this mysterious realm, one had to do so by
tracing the route on one's heart. Most curious of
all, when they finally reached the spot, Mushka realized that both she and Anna had lost consciousness for a short period of time—as if the strange
area had hypnotized them.

Experiencing the Pulse was not something
Mushka would ever forget.

It was, indeed, a place that appeared to be locked
in the grayness of perpetual winter, a stagnant pool
of ashen-colored water and decaying vegetation and
fog-shrouded, stunted trees, the totality of the area
not larger than a tennis court. Yet it dominated the
landscape. And the mid-nineties temperature
dropped at least twenty degrees as they approached.
At the center of the Pulse what appeared to be the
shoulder of a sandbar rose less than a foot above
the water.

Sister Golden Hair guided the john boat to that
tiny spit of firmament. Then she turned to Mushka
and Anna, her face implacably expressionless. She
hesitated momentarily as if to ask the two women

whether they really needed to see more. Anna said something to her in the Bushyeye language. The woman then lifted the raccoon from the boat and placed it on the grayish sandbar, and before poling quickly away she appeared to genuflect. Mushka had glanced at Anna, but her sister was totally enraptured by the scene.

They watched from thirty or forty feet away as the raccoon sniffed around and the swamp grew silent. No birds or insects sang out. No breeze stirred. The air smelled faintly of rotted flesh or perhaps blood. The low fog was all that moved until something happened that caused Mushka not to believe her own eyes.

The Pulse convulsed and swallowed the raccoon.

Not like quicksand. But rather as a huge beast might. Like a sea monster. In one breathtaking gulp, the raccoon disappeared without so much as a struggle.

Sister Golden Hair rattled off a remark directed mostly at Mushka. "What did she say? Anna, good lands, what just happened?"

Her sister, still obviously astounded by the display, carefully chose her words. "She said . . . she said that you have now seen the god of the swamp feed upon its own."

Where the sloping ridge of the spit gave way to a spilling over of Night Horse Creek, Mushka waded in the ankle-deep water. It was pleasantly warm. She appreciated the warmth because remembering her dream had chilled her. She had dreamed that she had returned to the Pulse. She had dreamed that Willow was there, but she could not see Willow's facial features—eyes, nose, mouth—and yet she knew it was Willow. And she knew that the Pulse waited to be fed.

She was awakened by her own screaming.

Now Mushka wanted nothing more than to visit a spot that she felt would bring her solace. Another few minutes found her standing under a magnificent water oak—Night Horse Oak—a tree easily over a hundred years old, its roots anchored to the most solid land surrounding the swamp. And there Mushka knelt beside a St. Bridget's Cross that Artie had carved from a broken limb of the extraordinary tree.

It was Anna Fossor's grave.

"Blessed be, sister," Mushka whispered. "May your spirit rest easy in the Otherworld. Blessed be." Then she hesitated and plucked at a few stems of rye grass growing atop the grave. "Anna, we all need your wisdom and heart. Things have gone to shadow and dark magic."

She choked back the welling of her emotions and began as calmly as she could to narrate the events, as she knew them, surrounding the disappearance of Willow and its aftermath. She included a description of her dream and details of the nightmarish visit to the Pulse. And when she had finished, she waited for the spirit of her sister to walk into the day and speak to her.

But it did not.

Mushka thought about her sister's death. Heart failure was ruled. But what could have caused such a strong, dynamic woman to suffer such a demise? It was beyond mystery.

Anna's magic was so strong.

Mushka believed that her sister's life was one every woman might profitably emulate. It was Anna who always maintained that women's lives were either much too limited or much too secretive. Women had wilderness in them, and they should embrace it. They should fill up on the adventuresomeness that lies deep in their souls like the peat at the bottom of the swamp. Women should transcend all their losses and hardships when certainties fade. They should more than merely survive, they should prevail by tapping inner reserves of power and strength.

Following the Old Ways, Anna Fossor maintained, could free a woman to be heroic.

To be a hero to herself.

"Hey, can I join you?"

Surprised to hear another voice, Mushka jolted out of her graveside reverie. It was Artie, stepping toward her like a delicate fawn—innocent and lovely, yet bereft because her magic had departed. She was wearing her right arm in a sling.

"Oh, my, that would be good 'n fine," said Mushka. "I was just talking at your mother."

Artie raised her long dress slightly to sit down beside her aunt.

"Does she have any answers?" she asked.

Mushka smiled shyly. "Patience. If she would speak to us, I think she would tell us to have patience. Time and the Goddess will give us answers."

Artie shook her head.

"I want to believe that," she said. "But why has the Goddess forsaken us? And how much time do we have before the darkness takes an even firmer hold on our lives?"

Hours later, Mushka continued to have no answer for Artie. They had talked a while longer, then returned to the house where they shared a simple supper of fruit and banana bread. When Artie left for another evening with her newfound friends who gathered at Good Ole Gals, Mushka decided to visit Miss Billie Ruth Private. She had ridden over on the ferry, exchanging a few words with an unusually quiet Joe Boy. Swamp topics were mostly what they gravitated to—the low water level, the effects of the drought. No references to Willow.

Billie Ruth Private was as wise as a witch though she called herself a Christian. Mushka saw her as one who loved almost beyond the reach of belief. She understood people and had reverence for Nature. She tolerated Simeon—loved him for certain. Would have been lonely without him, but she accepted what came her way. It was pleasant for Mushka to talk with another woman about recipes and sewing and all matter of domestic business. The subject of Willow, however, did come up, though in terms of Joe Boy missing her and being out of kilter without her around.

"He's at a loss," Billie Ruth explained.

"We all are," said Mushka.

"What on earth could've happened to her?"

Mushka had no reassuring response for Billie Ruth's question. And so, late evening, she bade Billie Ruth good night and asked Joe Boy to ferry her across to the spit. The moon was waxing, and the backwaters of Night Horse Creek smelled sweet and alive. Things were growing even as they crossed the dark, moon-splashed waters.

"You need to go after mistletoe?" Joe Boy asked halfway across.

"Oh, one of these days it wouldn't hurt none to," said Mushka. She was aware that Joe Boy was nudging her some. His precise intent escaped her. She assumed, of course, it might be related to Willow. "I can always use more mistletoe. Should be a good crowd of it high in the cypresses these days."

"I can take you anyplace in the swamp you need to go." Joe Boy's eyes were wide and dark and expectant.

Mushka decided to take a chance. "You think Willow's in there somewhere? In the swamp?"

Joe Boy closed up. In the moon's spotlight, she

could see that he was thinking hard to himself. He didn't answer, but as they reached the landing of the spit, a word blazed into Mushka's thoughts—a word she suspected came from Joe Boy.

Coda.

The word meant nothing to Mushka. But she took it as if it were a gift that Joe Boy had secreted to her, wanting no one else to know that she had it.

And by the time Mushka reached her kitchen and began making herself a cup of mild, specially brewed, sleep-inducing tea, she knew that Willow was somewhere in the swamp, moving and animated.

But not necessarily alive.

TEN

Nature was their curriculum.

The swamp was their classroom.

The image rushed into Tina's thoughts of her mother walking and talking along the edge of the swamp, her three young daughters in tow, like a mother quail and her chicks, and the grammar of Nature was attended to at every moment. Plants were identified as were animal tracks and the songs of birds and the bark of trees and the taste of the wind.

The magic (Anna Fossor spelled it "magick") of witchcraft—the Old Ways—was sprinkled over those moments like sugar. And Tina and her sisters were preached to warmly, sensitively, about the flow of Divinity in Nature—it flowed like Night Horse Creek through their lives and through the world, and what one had to do was find how to live in harmony with Nature.

Succeeding meant that one could live in harmony with one's self.

Tina needed that. Had it as a child.

Where did I lose it?

Her mother often said, "Invoke the Goddess to help you help yourself."

Tina had been trying to. But her invocations seemed to be falling on deaf ears.

The Goddess was not listening.

Yet, as she stood by her car on the dusty road that wound close to the swamp, she had convinced herself to be hopeful. She had received a promising lead on the whereabouts of Willow, and she knew she had to pursue it. Standing in the noonday sun wasn't too much to endure if it meant securing even the smallest bit of information about her daughter.

The young man had introduced himself as Emil Sinclair. He went to Homewinds High School. A sophomore there. Tina had never heard of him. But his phone call late last night had rattled her world.

"I can tell you something about Willow," he had said.

She had heard a puzzling conflict in his voice, and when she had pressed for details he had deflected her, insisting that she meet him where the school bus routinely made a stop after school. Tina knew the spot—it was where Willow got off each afternoon.

Waiting became torturous.

The call, she admitted to herself, might be a prank. There had been nearly a dozen calls, some of them sympathetic, but many of them cruel and obscene. But something in Emil Sinclair's voice suggested this call was possibly different. For in his voice she heard a young man who had feelings for her daughter.

Or am I misreading him?

She hadn't informed Favors or anyone else about the call. She would pursue this on her own. A mother seeking her daughter with or without the aid of the Goddess. Motherhood was an aspect of the Goddess, she reminded herself. Blessed be.

Sinclair was twenty minutes late by the time he roared up on his motorbike wearing no helmet. The young man had long blond hair and bore a striking resemblance to the actor Brad Pitt. Tina was surprised by how sober and polite he was and by the way he walked up to her immediately and apologized for being tardy. Called her "ma'am" and expressed what seemed a genuine sadness that Willow was missing.

"I saw her the day she disappeared," he said.

"Tell me everything you can."

It wasn't much, and yet Tina found that his words burned in her throat, a good burning, the kind that engenders optimism. The afternoon that Willow should have come home Emil Sinclair was riding in the back of a pickup with a group of his friends—"rowdies," he called them—" . . . but we wouldn't have hurt her," he added. "I wouldn't have let that happen." He showed her exactly where they had seen her and then seemed embarrassed to relate the moment that Willow had lifted her dress to shock them.

"She headed on into the swamp after that, is what I'm guessing, ma'am."

He stayed at Tina's side as she scoured the area. She thanked him for sharing what he knew, though there was one question she couldn't resist asking: "Why did you take so long to tell what you knew?"

He shrugged. "I kept thinking she would turn up. She's so different . . . she's not like other girls I know. I'm sorry. I know I should have said something sooner." Then he told her that it was his lunch hour and he had to get back to school.

Tina sensed that he was hesitating as if he wanted to say more. "What is it?" she said.

"Oh, it's just that . . . Willow, she had a lot of courage, you know. Must not be easy being a witch and all. I . . . I admired her. I wish I could have known her better."

Tina smiled. She touched his shoulder. "When she comes home—when we find her perhaps you can strike up a friendship with her. She's a good girl. She'd be a good friend, but, yes, she's different.

A follower of the Old Ways is almost always an out-sider. It makes you tough. Problem is, it can make it very difficult to trust anyone who doesn't share your philosophy of life."

When the young man had roared away, Tina con-tinued her canvass of the area, slipping out of her shoes and rolling up her pants' legs to wade into the shallow backwaters of the swamp, her eyes comb-ing every inch at her feet for clues. Her search wasn't systematic; in fact, if anything she opened herself to an intuitive feel for what might have at-tracted Willow deeper into the swamp.

The panther watched her from a prairie head.

A chill fanned upward from Tina's stomach when she caught sight of the lovely creature some fifty yards away, a distance the big cat must have found comfort in. Tina met the eyes of her watcher for no more than a few seconds before the panther, always aware that the smell of humans meant potential danger, slipped off into the sedge grass like a ma-gician completing a sleight-of-hand trick.

Have you seen my Willow? Tina wanted to shout to it.

But the panther was seemingly much like the rest of the swamp—indifferent. And Tina could recall her mother quoting Thoreau: "Nature puts no ques-tion and answers none which we mortals ask."

So it was the task of humankind to adjust to the world of Nature, not the other way around. Despon-dent, Tina waded on, an aimless meander back in among pools where the trunks of old and rotted cypresses stood clinging to their pasts, their knobby knees gray and wrinkled. She was concentrating upon bringing Willow's face to mind when she heard it.

She stood as still as she possibly could and lis-tened.

Yes, a guitar and a man's voice.

Singing an old swamp song she had heard long ago.

"All I want in this creation
Is a pretty little wife and a big plantation.
All I want to make me happy
Is two little boys to call me pappy."

She liked the voice. But then, as if the singer, who was out of her sight, sensed her presence and did not want an audience, the song ended without another verse. Emptied of what had been the early afternoon's surge of hope, Tina began to retrace her way to her car.

ELEVEN

It had been a wild-goose chase.

Driving back from Columbus, both of them realized how desperate they had become—Tina especially. She was grasping for every straw, and she was angry with her ex-husband for wasting her time. Why she couldn't admit that at least he was trying escaped her. It simply wasn't possible. She knew she would always hate him for abandoning her and Willow.

Scarpia must have felt her anger, for when he broke the silence of the monotonous drive, he said, "I suppose you blame me for this. I suppose, in fact, you think it's my fault that Willow's missing. Go ahead and say it. But you're wrong, and I don't give a fuck what you think. I really thought we would find her or I wouldn't have dragged you along."

Tina started to come back at him with claws, accusing him of being self-centered and more concerned about whether he might be to blame than about whether they found their daughter. But instead she sighed. Then glanced at him and said, "No, we had to check it out. We needed to see for ourselves that it wasn't her."

The drive over had been quite different. They had actually been civilized to each other. For the most part, they had talked about Willow, and Scarpia had iterated what a guy he knew from Columbus, Georgia—just across the Alabama line—had told him after having seen the poster with Willow's photo: that only the day before he had seen a girl who was a dead ringer for Willow. She was part of a teen prostitution ring operating out of a seedy motel near Fort Benning.

"Couldn't be Willow," Tina had maintained.

Scarpia agreed, but he had been won over by the guy's certainty.

"I couldn't live with myself," Scarpia had said, "if I didn't follow up on this."

Tina had relented. Yes, of course. You had to look wherever a finger pointed. But it was impossible for her to see her daughter mixed up in anything like prostitution. So they had driven to the area, and Tina's heart had crawled into her throat.

Scarpia tried to remain calm. "The guy said late morning the pimp has the girls in that Laundromat. Let's go in separately and try to raise a red flag. I'll go in first. Apparently there are three girls—a new one just joined them, is what he said."

Tina felt sick.

But she followed Scarpia's plan, entering the grungy facility a minute or so after he had. The roar of washers and dryers was almost deafening. The cloying aroma of detergent and Clorox stung her nostrils. She wandered around as if lost until she entered a long, more narrow section at the rear where she saw her ex-husband talking with an elderly black man, his face blue black and shiny like new leather gloves. Pretending to be checking for an empty washer, Tina edged close enough to overhear the man. At first, however, she couldn't make out what he was saying. Then she noticed the back of the heads of three girls. One of them suddenly stood; she was black with a good figure filling a red, knit top, and tight skirt. Hoping to see their faces,

Tina moved behind Scarpia, excused herself, then turned slightly.

The black man was grinning at the well-built black girl; Tina heard him say to Scarpia, "Ain't she got pretty titties?"

Tina felt a flush of something like humiliation. Deflecting it, she angled to where she could get a good look at the other two girls.

And was stunned by what she saw.

One was a milky blonde with a bad complexion, but the other, while not especially attractive, had black hair like Willow. In fact, other than being a few years older than her daughter, the girl could have been her twin.

Tina caught Scarpia's eye. He had seen her, too.

Then he said something dismissive to the black man and turned and walked away. The girl with black hair saw that Tina was staring at her and snapped, "Go fuck yourself, bitch!" Feeling like matter out of place, Tina hurried from the area and practically ran back to the car. She could not hold back tears—of relief? Of sadness? Of what?

She could not be certain.

Scarpia got in the car and pulled away in silence.

As they neared Homewinds, Tina decided to tell him about Emil Sinclair and what she had come to believe about Willow and the swamp. And she mentioned the drifter named Shep and that she was convinced she had heard him playing and singing. Her implication was clear: the drifter might well be connected with Willow's disappearance.

"You're way off on that one," said Scarpia. "I've met that guy at the fish camp and talked with him. Even suggested where he could get a singing gig maybe. He's no serial killer or child molester, if that's what you're thinking."

"How can you know that for sure?"

"Hey, you don't have to be a goddamned witch

to get a sense about people. That guy's harmless. What I'm beginning to think in all this is that you poisoned Willow with all your weird, fucking ideas—worshiping Nature and casting spells—all that shit sent her off the deep end probably. There's no better one to blame on this but you, Tina—you and your whole messed-up family."

"You're a bastard!" she hissed.

"Maybe so, but I'm not the one who filled my daughter's head with all that witchy shit."

"No, that's just it," said Tina. "You haven't been around to be any kind of influence on her. Too busy chasing anything in a skirt. Why can't you think of somebody other than yourself for once? When are going to stop being led around by your dick? You're getting a little old for that, aren't you?"

She knew he wanted to pull the car over onto the shoulder and hit her.

But he didn't do it. He drove on in silence as the anger in the car dissolved like a fogged-over window.

He sighed heavily after another mile and said, "So what do you want me to do? For Chrissake, what in the hell do you want me to do, Tina?"

She was trembling too much from the afterthralls of anger to speak immediately. She let the silence surround his words, and then, in a tone she had always reserved for her most serious requests, she said, "I want you to go into the swamp after her. And not come out till you find her."

TWELVE

"Don't pay any attention to them."

Gladys Michaels touched Artie's cheek and then caressed it as she talked low, her voice as soothing as the night air spilling over from the swamp. Patches of grayish mist hugged the ground near Night Horse Oak where they were sitting around a fire not far from the grave of Anna Fossor. Two young men and a young woman were cackling as they smoked marijuana and played with a camcorder. They wanted Artie to do a striptease for them, which they, in turn, were going to record for posterity. She had dismissed their request. Her dislike for them—she couldn't even recall their names—was growing, and she had sought refuge in the company of Michaels.

"I'm just so on edge these days," said Artie, forcing a smile.

"It's understandable," said Michaels. "The thing with your niece—if she's not on the road, then it looks bleak."

"Don't say that. I can't let myself think that. This has really torn us apart, you know—my sisters and me—and losing our magic. I think that's why I keep coming out here to Mother's grave. I keep thinking I'll see an answer or that the magic will return."

Michaels pulled Artie closer. "I shouldn't have suggested that your niece . . . that there's been violence. I'm sorry. And I shouldn't have let them tag along."

She gestured toward the laughing threesome, each dressed in black, each pale as the moon waxing near full above them.

Head on Michaels's shoulder, Artie whispered, "You're like a mother to me. And more. Your warmth. And the way you understand the creative in me—how I've got to reconnect with it or I'll go crazy."

They held each other and rocked softly, making themselves oblivious to the inane chatter and laughter of the others, and oblivious as well to the sounds of the swamp. Of hidden things stirring and moving and watching.

"But you have to be careful," said Michaels. "Someone's back in town who could be a threat to you and your sisters."

"Who is it?"

"Have you ever heard of David Sinclair?"

"No."

"There's a kid who works for me as a busboy and dishwasher—Emil Sinclair, a good boy. But he has an older brother who lives in Atlanta where he's creating a hate network. He took over a neo-Nazi group in Soldier called 'the Torch of Dawn.' Pure, unadulterated racists. Now I've heard he has a new wrinkle. He hunts witches."

Artie squirmed in the older woman's arms. She and her sisters had seen plenty of folk, mostly from the local churches, who did not approve of them or their beliefs. The Fossors had experienced vandalism and threats and rumors of violence, so Michaels's news wasn't surprising.

"They come and go," said Artie. "Nobody's burned or hanged one of us yet."

"This guy may be different—a real psycho. Just promise me this: you'll be very careful. In fact, what

I'd really like is for you to come stay with me. Living with your aunt is not safe."

Artie looked into the woman's eyes and saw love there. Saw an affectionate friend who wanted to be her protector. Surrendering to those eyes, she angled her head and raised her lips and the two women kissed warmly, deeply.

And the night tore open with shrieks and maniacal screechings.

"Whoa, check this out! Woman on woman! Mama Gladys has got her a piece of witchy ass."

Michaels tried to stop them, yelled at them, but they pushed her aside and shoved the camcorder into Artie's face. In a fake, movie voice-over, one of the young men said:

"Forget about Blair Witch, we give you the Fossor Witch. In the flesh."

While the young woman trained the camcorder on Artie, the two young men began tearing at her clothes. With her left hand, Artie swung at them and screamed. Michaels fought with them, too, giving Artie a chance to pull away and dash to the campfire.

She yanked a burning stick from it and held them at bay. "You stupid bastards! Leave me alone!"

But they continued their assault, laughing gleefully and grabbing while the camera ran, recording every moment. Michaels kicked one of the young men in the back of the leg and he feigned being seriously hurt, his action generating even more laughter.

Tossing down the stick, Artie sought the one safe zone where she believed no one would follow: she splashed into Night Horse Creek.

"Artie, no, please," cried Michaels. "Please, they're stopping. See, it's okay now."

Artie, trembling, staring at the fire-blazed faces, shook her head. "Get out! All of you! Do you hear

me? Get away from my mother's grave! Get away
from me!"

"Artie, I'll take you to my place. Please, sweetheart," Michaels coaxed.

"No. Don't say anything. Just go. I don't want to
go home with you. I want to be alone. I need to be
alone."

Minutes later, they were gone. First, the camcorder trio, high on pot, but unwilling to pursue Artie
into the water, then Michaels, who walked away re-
luctantly, repeating her offer to take Artie home
with her.

Waist deep in Night Horse Creek, Artie watched
their shadows trail off. She was crying and hating
herself for crying. And she wanted Michaels, and
yet she was also afraid of her or perhaps afraid of
what leaving her family would mean.

Most of all, she wanted her magic back.

She was wet and starting to feel cold.

And then she sensed that she was not alone.

It smelled like an animal.

Artie whirled around, hoping that the flickering
firelight on shore would continue to give off enough
illumination for her to see what was out there. But
at first she saw nothing except the silvery glint of
something sharp and bonelike swimming her way.
It reminded her of a shark's fin, and she gasped at
the sight of it.

Yet, try as she might, she could not move.

Could not escape.

Whatever it was stayed submerged, generating
waves and eddies that slammed against her and
threatened to pull her under.

Artie screamed as hard as she could, calling out
for help, desperately wanting Michaels and the others to still be in earshot.

Then something shaggy brushed against her thigh.

She screamed again.

She thrashed about, attempting to fight and then attempting to run, though even as she did she also experienced an overwhelming urge to give in to whatever mysterious force was pressing in upon her.

The thing surfaced behind her. She could feel its hot, panting, animal breath on her back. And it was all like a dream, a confusing, terrifying, beautiful dream. She had dreamed past dark into the night with the almost full moon looking down upon her.

Coda.

The word fire-branded across her thoughts from nowhere.

She wheeled around to face the creature, but before she could turn herself completely, she was yanked beneath the surface, and for a few seconds she was aware that she was being pulled in opposite directions.

Hands wrapped around her waist.

Hooves bruised her wrists.

The right side of her body went numb.

She felt that half of her face twist and her mouth lock in a rictus.

Water began to fill her lungs.

One world opened—a world of dark magic. Another closed.

And then blackness devoured everything.

THIRTEEN

You're pretty sure she didn't know who saved her.

But you think about it. You have a lot to think about now.

You had watched her go to Night Horse Oak with the four of them, and you did not like any of them. The ones with the camera especially. They wanted to hurt her. Hurt your Arietta. Or at least make a fool of her.

You know what a "fool" is. Mr. Buck told you all about it. Warned you about people wanting to make fun of you because you are "slow." Another curious word. That slow meant slow in the head and not slow at running—not slow at swimming because you definitely are not. But people do things. Mean things, according to Mr. Buck. Try to make people look like a fool.

They wanted Arietta to take off her clothes while they took a picture of her. Naked witch. The woman didn't want them to, and you didn't want them to, and you almost charged in there and started hitting them and calling them all the names Mr. Buck has taught you not to say.

You saw them kiss. Arietta and the older woman.

It made something cold as ice slide down your backbone, and you don't know why except that you don't want *anybody* kissing Arietta—your sweet Artie.

Especially on the lips. Unless it is you. That would be fine. That is what you want.

You want more.

That's what you have to think about. Because of what you did.

Back in your nice little bed you felt the pull of the moon. You came home wet and Miss Billie Ruth got after you for taking a late-night swim. She did not know about Artie and Night Horse Oak and how Artie almost drowned.

You saved her.

It will be your secret.

You get to thinking about secrets. About how powerful they are. A secret is something you keep, and sometimes you have one and you don't really know how you got it. You just do. Sometimes you just decide: I have a secret. So you do. You saved Artie. That is your secret. That is the good part of your secret.

There is more.

You were in your nice little bed thinking about it and your teeth started chattering, but not because you were cold. No. You figure your teeth were chattering because you were afraid. Very afraid.

Of what pulled Artie under the water.

An animal maybe. By the smell of it. By the size of it.

A mystery animal. A secret animal. You had sensed it before. Have for several months, but you do not know what it was. You just know that it wanted to kill Artie. Or scare her mostly. And it did.

When you swam out to save her, it let go—did not try to fight. You know it could have. Then you got Artie back on shore and built up the fire some and dragged her over close to it and she was more than just asleep but not dead. You put your ear down to her heart and you could hear it beating. That made you feel good. You sat there and waited for her to wake up. Then you saw what had happened to her face. Twisted around the mouth. You got scared.

But you could not leave.

Because you wanted to touch her. Touch her broken face. Touch her other places, too. Her breasts. You wanted to. You wanted to lay your head between her breasts. Your dinkle doo got hard as you watched her. You felt bad about that. Almost sinful. But you remembered how she had asked you to touch her wrist. You had. You couldn't make it better.

You wanted to get on top of her and do sinful things.

You got fire in your throat just thinking about it. You thought maybe it was wrong. You thought maybe Miss Billie Ruth would tell you you were going to hell, the place in the Bible you don't never want to go, but you will if you sin.

Sin.

You get turned upside down by that word. Sinful. Miss Billie Ruth says everybody is sinful. But you can't imagine that Willow is. Or Artie. You get to thinking that the mystery creature that attacked Artie is what is sinful. You get to thinking maybe it came from hell.

But you know better. You know it's a swamp creature. And older than the sun.

Older than sin.

You ran away from Artie because the fire inside you spread. From a distance you watched to make sure she finally woke up. She did. She coughed and spit up water and felt her head and her face, and you could tell she was cold. But you were not.

Your thoughts burned. You got confused and scared. And you felt the moon tugging at you and so you went home and then you couldn't sleep in your nice little bed and you couldn't sleep in Mr. Buck's chair.

So you went out to the ferry and sat and looked at the moon.

You got to thinking you needed to leave.

Just go into the swamp until your thoughts stopped burning

You were sitting there deciding whether to take some leftover cornbread with you when the stranger with the guitar came up as quietly as any night creature you've ever known. He is called Shep, he said, and you said you are called Joe Boy, and he said that he saw what you did. And he wanted to know one thing:

"Tell me about what attacked the young woman."

You couldn't say much.

You thought the man called Shep looked kind of like the man called Jesus in a picture Miss Billie Ruth has on the living room wall if Jesus had blond hair. Son of God. In the picture the man called Jesus is carrying sort of a lantern and standing at a door knocking, and Miss Billie Ruth says that one day you'll hear the man called Jesus knocking at your heart.

You haven't yet. Son of God. Savior. Here to save man from his sins.

Hasn't saved *you*.

It's hard for you to imagine that you would ever need to be saved.

You saved Artie, and the man called Shep didn't ask about her. He asked about the mystery animal. He wanted to know all about it, but you didn't know about it really. All you know is that you wanted to touch Artie and it made your whole body start burning inside and now you feel the moon tugging and so you need to go.

Into the swamp.

"I have to go into the swamp," you said to the man called Shep.

He plucked a couple of times at his guitar. He let you touch it. And then he said, "I'm going back there myself. Going in there to listen to its dark songs."

There was a path of moonlight glazed across the backwater.

The man called Shep stood up and then he did something like nothing else you've ever seen: he walked right across the water to the spit, keeping always on that path of moonlight. And then he disappeared on the other side.

You decided to follow.

You couldn't do it the way he did.

Like magic.

Like a story about the man called Jesus walking on water.

So you swam instead, hands and legs becoming like flippers. You became another creature. Not Joe Boy. And you thought maybe you'd find out how Willow went inside the world. And you thought about Artie and you hoped she was all right.

The last thing you thought about was the rope-pull ferry.

Who, you wondered, would do your job for you? Mr. Buck maybe.

But the moon had you.

Reeled you into the swamp like you were a big fish.

FOURTEEN

Thankfully, Artie had fallen asleep after calming down somewhat. Getting her out of her wet clothes and into dry ones and then into bed did the trick—yet, for Mushka, many questions lingered. The young woman she called Arietta had been attacked by something. Though her description of it was vague, it jangled in Mushka's thoughts as something familiar. Something her sister, Anna, had talked of once.

The Terror.

Before dozing off, Artie had sipped some hot tea and eaten a soy cracker or two and she had let go of some of her fear—the animal, creature, whatever it was, was unlike anything she had ever encountered in the swamp. Not a gator. Too large for anything like a muskrat or otter. It had sharp bones, pointed like antlers, and yet neither she nor Mushka could imagine a white-tailed deer attacking anyone in the water.

There was, of course, something more.

In a voice slurred somewhat by the partial paralysis of her face, Artie said, "I don't know who saved me. Somebody rescued me or I would have drowned."

"Might could have been the Michaels woman, you think?"

"No. No, she would have stayed around. She would have seen to it that I made it back here."

They talked a few minutes longer before Mushka insisted that she close her eyes and get some rest. The attack had been a shock, not the least factor of which was the partial paralysis of Artie's face. One corner of her mouth had no feeling. She had asked to see herself in a hand mirror, and the sight of herself, even though the contour of her face had changed little, frightened her, plunging her toward despair.

"What did this, Mushka? What's out there?"

And the older woman could only mutter an admission that she did not know.

But with her niece asleep, Mushka went to her sister's Book of Shadows and read its final pages and afterward found that she could not sleep, could not, indeed, keep from trembling. She decided that she would wait for dawn, and then she would share what she had read with Tina.

Together, they would try to determine precisely what Anna Fossor had done.

And whether she had inadvertently invited a dark spirit to emerge from the swamp.

And visit horrors upon them.

Dark magic.

By shortly after dawn, Billie Ruth Private had directed her husband, Simeon, better known as Buck, in a search of every place Joe Boy typically spent time. But there was no sign of him.

"Like as not," said Buck, "he's gone off into the swamp to fish for bass."

"His pole's still here," Billie Ruth countered. "He was out late and wouldn't say much about it. I think he was upset. You suppose he's taken somewheres to find Willow?"

"That could be it, darlin'. Let's not worry none too much. We both know nothin' bad's gone happen to him in the swamp—he's knows it better'n anybody I know. He knows how to keep away from harm. Let's just us be patient."

But Billie Ruth had a bad feeling about Joe Boy's disappearance.

She had called Tina and Mushka, and neither one had seen him. Mushka's account of what had happened to Artie, though, generated new thorns of apprehension. She wondered out loud whether Joe Boy had been the one who had pulled Artie from the water. The two women speculated that he was, knowing as they did the boy's attraction to her.

But where was he?

First Willow.

Now Joe Boy.

And Mushka's voice had the suspicious texture of knowing more than she might want to share.

She had dreamed of being in the fiery furnace with her sisters.

Like Shadrach, Meschach, and Abednego from the Bible. It was her mother's favorite story from the Bible and thus it had become, while she was quite young, her favorite, too. But unlike the three men who faced the great sheet of flame unafraid, Tina and her sisters were deeply afraid, and their furnace was the swamp.

And no protective spirit was there to allay their fears.

Midmorning, Tina was awash in confusion. She hated that state of mind. For she had grounded herself, her life within a life, on being in control of her reality, of understanding things with the clarity that following the Old Ways promised.

Of trusting her dreams.

Of trusting some inner "knower" to tell her things about her life that she needed to know. And yet the fire dream had left her grasping for meaning because she had not been allowed to see how the narrative ended. What happened to her and her sisters in that inferno?

What did it all mean?

Sitting on her deck, her eyes drawn to the high blue of the firmament, to the gathering warmth of what would be another beautiful day on the edge of the swamp, she set aside the dream and thought about her conversation with Aunt Mushka and her sharing the final pages of Anna Fossor's Book of Shadows.

It wasn't that Tina chose not to believe that the curious words were those of her mother—no, in fact, it seemed clear that they were in her mother's hand and were tinged everywhere with her mother's voice. What Tina could not accept was simply that her mother would have chosen to conjure up a dark spirit—the Terror—and cast a spell upon it so that it might serve as a protective or guardian entity for her daughters.

"She must have known about her coming transition," Aunt Mushka had offered. "Her bad heart—she must have figured she didn't have long and so she wanted to have someone watch over you girls. She could see that I couldn't—and she was right. What I'm saying is—she did it out of love. But it's like any spell—it can take on a life of its own. Magic can always turn dark. You know that better than anyone else."

Still, to Tina, it seemed unlikely.

Aunt Mushka had persisted, however, claiming that whatever attacked Artie could have been that protective spirit, the one, ironically, that Anna Fossor had conjured to keep her daughters and her sister from harm.

"So why would this entity attack Artie?" Tina had asked.

"Because it can. What I mean is, spirits like that have a will of their own, especially with Anna not being around to keep it in check."

"I'm sorry," Tina had followed. "I don't accept the direction you're taking this. I have no idea what frightened Artie, but, mostly, I'm not ready to believe that something my mother brought into this realm might be something Willow encountered. That this might explain why she's missing. This thing that Mother called 'the Terror'—yes, all of us recall her talking about it when we were girls. It was just her way of cautioning us about the dangers of the swamp. We never took her words literally."

Aunt Mushka had gone home saddened, afraid, and though Tina tried to hug away her apprehension, she knew that the older woman had convinced herself that the mystery surrounding Willow was inextricably linked to something mysterious in the swamp.

But what Tina couldn't explain away was both the reality of Willow's disappearance and the breakdown and total diminishment of magical powers of herself and Gretta and Artie and Aunt Mushka. Could the Terror be responsible? Had it cast a dark spell upon them?

Could that spell be broken?

And there was something else on her mind.

The phone call from her ex-husband.

"I just wanted to let you know that I'm going into the swamp for a few days. Pa-Po's going with me. We're calling it a fishing trip, but . . . I'm willing to look where the search teams never reached. Not that I agree with you that Willow could have gone into the swamp. I still think that most likely she ran away. She'll come home one of these days. In the meantime, if it'll ease your mind some, I'll cover as much territory as I can."

And he waited for her to respond. To thank him for his magnanimous gesture.

Bastard.

But as she watched a pair of egrets fly across the backdrop of Pan Island, she was glad that she hadn't been too cold to him and glad, as well, that he had called her.

FIFTEEN

The swamp is never what it seems.

John Scarpia poled hard in the late afternoon dappling of sun and shadow. He was negotiating his small fishing boat down the South Fork, and he had the top two buttons of his shirt unbuttoned and he was sweating, and the sweat felt good, though the fiercely atavistic pleasure of penetrating an alien world cooled it the moment it beaded up, forcing a chill.

Night Horse Swamp.

Here was a world in flux.

God, it was a fascinating place.

And it occurred to him that if a landscape could ever be said to wear a mask, this one could play the role. By day it appeared remote, yet you could see into it and you could follow—if you knew what you were doing—the labyrinth of its unmarked waterways.

The night, however, transformed it.

For that's what masks were for—not to *hide* something but rather to *transform* it.

"Pa-Po, how you doing?"

Scarpia's father, a baseball cap pulled down low over his eyes, said nothing, of course. He raised a limp hand almost as if bored or indifferent. Scarpia knew that wasn't the case. He knew that while his father seemed detached, he was actually plugged in rather intensely to the sights and sounds of this mysterious realm as much as his aging senses would allow.

"I thought we'd drop a line in up here where a couple of feeder creeks come in. If I'm remembering this right, it's a good spot for bass. You ready to catch some fish?"

It brought a smile to Scarpia's face when his father touched the bill of his cap to signal an affirmative.

"It's a go, then," said Scarpia.

He shook off a tug of guilt. No, the real reason for the trip was not to fish.

The real reason was Willow.

To get her mother off my ass.

But he knew that wasn't quite true either. Maybe a tiny part of him did suspect that Willow, in her reverence for the swamp, might have set off on some kind of spiritual adventure, spurred by her affinity for the Old Ways.

Yet, would she do it without telling her mother?

Would she have been gone this long?

Scarpia slowed his poling. Sun glinted off the large hunting knife tied to the top end of the pole, the deadly blade a hedge against a surprise attack from a bull gator or even from the uninvited visit of a moccasin dropping down into the boat from a tree limb. Of course, there was also a twelve-gauge shotgun resting next to the rods and reels. He glanced back again at his father and saw the amulet around his neck.

And recalled the moment this trip materialized.

It was after supper the night before, sitting out with his father, drinking a beer and watching the moon rise over the water behind the cabins. Earlier in the day he had explained to his father why Willow had still not come around. "We're looking for her," he had said. "We'll get her back home. You'll see."

Then at supper, he had noticed that his father was wearing the amulet.

The one Willow had given him to ward off evil spirits. Artie had made it.

Something about the gesture of his father putting that amulet around his neck had served as a catalyst, linking his guilt with his need to find his daughter. And thus he had generated a plan to go into the swamp. Call it a fishing trip. Take Pa-Po.

For companionship.

For good luck.

They had drifted another hundred yards, slipping past areas of thickly compacted peat and vegetation that gave the appearance of solid ground, but if one were to step upon them the earth would tremble as if one were walking upon a water bed.

It had been warm and humid. Gnats buzzed in small clouds. A discordant orchestra of frog sounds had embraced them along the way. Occasionally, in the distance, they would hear the swelling thunder of a bull gator. Bird cries volleyed between slash pines and cypresses.

"Pa-Po, it hot enough for a cold one?"

His father, resting his elbows on his knees, had lowered his head. Scarpia knew the old man was on the edge of taking a nap.

"Hey, how would a beer taste to ya?"

Scarpia had raised his voice enough to nudge a response from his father, who had looked up and nodded. Laying the pole in the boat, Scarpia had hunkered down and fumbled with the lid to an ice chest and then plunged his arm into the crunch of ice. He brought up two cans of beer, popped their tops, and handed one to his father who took it and smiled.

"Here's to hooking into something big," Scarpia had said, lifting his can in a mock salute. His father had returned the gesture, smiling even broader.

After a long swallow, Scarpia had pressed the cold can against his forehead. In a companionable silence, son and father had drunk their beer and drifted in the run, relaxed and mellowed by the heat and the alcohol and a setting that few other men had ever seen.

Minutes later, Scarpia had stood up and crushed his can.

"Guess I better give a holler in case there's some lost soul back in here we need to let know we're coming."

It wasn't a spectacular holler—not like the ones Pa-Po could deliver before cancer of the throat took his voice rendering him mute, but it was serviceable. Scarpia had listened for a return response. Heard none.

"Pa-Po, looks like we got this ole swamp to ourselves."

Where two feeder creeks bled coffee-colored water into the run, they dropped anchor and got out their rods and reels and lures. From either end of the boat they cast their lines, both using top-water lures.

Scarpia caught one small bluegill. His father caught nothing and, in fact, snagged his lure on a trio of cypress knees necessitating that Scarpia wade in and extricate it. On the way back to the boat he heard an oak toad warming up for twilight, and the sound brought a smile to his face. To an ear unfamiliar with the swamp, the utterance of an oak toad bordered on being a scream.

"Hear that, Pa-Po?"

The old man nodded.

"You remember what you told me when I's a boy?"

His father shook his head several times and then

doffed his cap and rubbed at his scalp. Scarpia got both of them another beer.

"Well, you know that's an oak toad. But when I's a boy, you told me that sound was made by a black snake. You told me that's how black snakes sing."

He chuckled, and his father followed with a noiseless chuckle of his own.

"You did. That's what you told me. You were always telling me crazy shit like that. Now it's kinda funny. Now I'm glad I remember it."

They drank a third beer, and Pa-Po stood unsteadily and relieved himself.

"The bass outta love that," Scarpia joked.

But he was sinking deeper into himself as twilight fell. He knew that they needed to find a campsite, and he wondered what was causing him to feel a sudden uneasiness. He was thinking about Willow. Thinking about how she and his father had such a good relationship. He longed to see them together again.

At bottom, what John Scarpia couldn't shake was the belief that his ex-wife's delving into the Old Ways had led not only to the breakup of their marriage, but also, somehow, to the disappearance of Willow.

"Pa-Po, keep your eyes open for a good spot to pitch camp."

As the mask of night slipped onto the face of the swamp and the various sounds of its myriad creatures gathered in a cacophony almost palpable, they found a pine-clad hummock where a rusting boiler from a steam engine dominated a clearing.

"This musta been leftover from one of the old cypress logging operations. That what it looks like to you, Pa-Po?"

The old man drank in every inch of the area, his jaw set hard. Scarpia had no idea what he might be thinking.

After tying up the boat, Scarpia and his father set their gear ashore and began picking up any pieces of dry wood they could find. Scarpia came upon the tracks of a black bear.

"A young one is what I'd guess. Pa-Po, you think black bear are gettin' more numerous in the swamp these days?"

His father was standing with his back to him, locked in a silent reverie as he stared into the pine thicket beyond them. Scarpia said, "Something out there? I think I smell something. Skunk maybe."

With a small fire blazing, they settled in, and with the help of a couple of take-out barbeque plates from the Homewinds Barbeque House and a couple more beers, Scarpia let his uneasiness dissolve. The only smell that invaded his nostrils was charred, barbequed pork.

"Does it get any better than this?" he said to his father.

And the old man smiled and chewed away at the meat.

Scarpia considered telling his father the truth about the trip. Then decided against it. Why stir up anything for him to worry about?

Within an hour, the fire dying down, the cache of beer virtually depleted, the two men crawled into their sleeping bags and fell asleep quickly.

Two hours later it was the silence that woke Scarpia.

And the smell.

And then a movement in the thicket.

The campfire had died down completely.

But between his flashlight and the full moon, there was enough illumination to stoke his courage to go exploring. He checked on his father before he left the camp.

Out like a light. Sweet ole fart.

The movement deep in the thicket was that of

something rather large foraging for food, or at least that was Scarpia's guess. The smell was animal, pungent and unmistakably wild. Deciding against taking the flashlight, he instead loaded two shells in the shotgun and braced it across his heart.

The animal sounded like a bear.

Scarpia circled around close to where he thought it was. But he couldn't see a distinct shape. Nothing more than a block of darkness. He recalled the tracks of a young black bear they had seen when they struck camp. He guessed it had smelled their barbeque. Something about the moment made him think of a story he had read once—a kind of ghost story. It was entitled "The Wendigo," and it told of a mythic entity the Indians of Canada believe roams the deepest and most remote woods.

He had edged several yards closer when something instinctual whispered up from his groin that this was no bear.

"Jesus Christ," he murmured.

His mouth went dry.

The shotgun grew heavy.

Whatever kind of creature it was, it had stopped its foraging.

And was looking at Scarpia.

He knew it was, even though he couldn't see it.

Jesus, what is it?

He couldn't remember ever feeling so frightened. Frightened to the bone.

And yet . . .

He wanted to draw nearer to whatever it was.

He *had* to.

Holding the shotgun to one side, he stepped to where he thought he could reach out through a stand of tall saw grass and touch the beast. He wanted to touch it. His fingers wiggled in anticipation of making contact with skin or fur.

The slash came too suddenly to avoid.

He cried out and jerked back his arm and could see that the palm of his right hand and several inches of his wrist had been sliced open. Blood flowed freely. He dropped the shotgun and he ran.

"Pa-Po!"

He roused his father and pulled him out of his sleeping bag. "Pa-Po, oh, Jesus! Get in the boat!"

He shoved him into it, then turned and grabbed the only available weapon: the knife-tipped pole.

Something lumbered from the thicket, moving at him, cold creature eyes boring in upon him as if intent upon seeing what absolute fear could do to a man's face. Bracing himself, Scarpia lifted the pole, then jabbed it at the creature. He felt and heard the pole snap, and out of the corner of his eye he saw his father approaching.

And again the movement of the creature was lightning quick. His father's head ritched back as he was struck in the forehead. Scarpia screamed as he rushed into the creature as if to tackle it. He never saw that the pole danced in the air as if held by invisible hands.

The blade of the hunting knife entered just to the right of his heart.

Knife and pole were thrust through his body.

John Scarpia stared down at the pole as if it were an optical illusion. He reached down and touched it as if wanting to see whether it was real.

Then he staggered and fell to one side.

The man called Shep had watched every moment.

He had been afraid to intervene—no, he had not *wanted* to intervene.

Following the creature at a distance as it lumbered back into the woods, he wondered why this was happening again. Why he couldn't overcome the seductive fascination he had with this creature.

The Terror.

I have been sent here to confront it. Destroy it. This monster of dark magic.

"Why can't I?" he whispered to himself.

Returning to the scene of the attack, he rolled John Scarpia's body over, but there was nothing he could do for him—no magic in the world could have helped. The older man in the boat was moaning softly.

"I'll take you both home," said the man called Shep.

He heaved Scarpia's body into the boat. The older man, apparently only on the edge of consciousness, did not move. And the man called Shep found a hefty limb to use as a push pole and began to negotiate the night swamp and return father and son to civilization.

But the man called Shep knew that civilization was just a mask that Nature wore.

SIXTEEN

A week had passed.

The great, dark absence of the world held sway.

The full moon had come and then had begun to wane. And so, perhaps, had Tina Fossor's hopes of finding her daughter.

Alive.

The death of John Scarpia had been, of course, a tremendous shock to her. The mysterious circumstances, the impact upon the Homewinds community—many things coalesced to sharpen her awareness that something darkly transcendent was afoot.

Dark magic.

Aunt Mushka had no doubts about the matter: to her everything could be explained by the presence of the Terror. Tina was not certain. Was not certain, indeed, of anything except that her daughter was still missing and her ex-husband had been buried in the tiny Catholic cemetery behind St. Stephen's Church.

Though her ex-husband's relatives and many of the citizens of Homewinds did not welcome her attendance, she had gone to the burial mass and the graveside services. So had Aunt Mushka and Gretta and Artie, clad in black and somber, and yet the rift among the sisters remained. Not even sympathy for John Scarpia could heal it.

To keep herself sane, Tina had given much of her

attention to the fate of her ex-father-in-law, whom she cared for dearly. Hospitalized for several days after the death of his son, the man known as Pa-Po suffered from a gash to his forehead. Authorities puzzled over it, for it appeared that he had been struck by a hoof. It seemed, indeed, that he had been kicked.

Though the larger Scarpia family held no warmth for Tina, what she discovered was that no member wanted to take Pa-Po in. John Scarpia's fish camp had been closed. The property would, eventually, be put up for sale. Tina wanted no financial gain from it; she was, however, more than willing to give Pa-Po a place to stay.

After his release from the hospital, she made him as comfortable as possible—in Willow's old room. And she found that he clung to her like a child, especially following several grillings by law enforcement officials who wanted to glean every possible detail of what had happened to him and his son.

Pa-Po wasn't able to offer much help. Nods and shakes of the head.

Mostly he was very confused.

One afternoon while the old man slept, Tina talked with Glen Favors about the ongoing investigation.

"What makes no sense," he confessed, "is how the two of them got back to the fish camp. I mean, John was dead, and his dad, from all indications, would not have been capable of guiding that boat out of the swamp. Who brought them in?"

Tina naturally speculated on the drifter named Shep, but Favors believed that he had moved out of the area before the murder had occurred.

"No one has seen that guy for weeks," he said.

"The swamp is a rough place," Tina said. "Maybe John and his father came upon a bootlegger—I've heard there are a few who continue to have an operation fired up back in the Night Horse."

Favors, uncomfortable with his next suggestion, apologized for even thinking it. "I've learned from Simeon Private that his son—the one he and Billie Ruth took in—well, he's been missing and I—"

"Joe Boy? You're not serious, are you? Are you saying that Joe Boy might be a suspect?"

"I . . . I don't know. Do you recall that he and John ever had bad blood between them?"

"No. They barely knew each other—no, this is ridiculous. Joe Boy is a sweet, innocent young man. He left home—I think he's just been very upset since Willow disappeared, and I know that Buck and Billie Ruth are sick to death about his being gone. Whoever's responsible for what happened to John is probably responsible for—"

She stopped short of saying it. Didn't even want to entertain the possibility.

That Willow and Joe Boy could have met a fate similar to that of John Scarpia.

"I just don't know what to think," said Favors.

After he had left, Tina went to Pa-Po's bedroom and sat beside him as he slept. She still couldn't tell whether the death of his son had sunk in—was he truly aware of anything that had occurred? The only thing that she could ascertain was that he would not—under any circumstances—allow anyone to remove the amulet that Willow had given him.

That evening, when Tina returned to the fish camp for the rest of Pa-Po's belongings, she was drawn to the edge of a gathering near the picnic pavilion. Torches were burning. A crowd of perhaps three dozen semicircled close to a speaker. A young man.

He was clean-cut with reddish blond hair worn

short. He had on a white shirt and tie and his voice
was clear and forceful. He was waving a white book,
and when Tina drew nearer she began to catch
snatches of his speech. He was articulate, and, by
the body language of his hearers, he was convincing,
perhaps even mesmerizing.

And his topic was witches.

Tina felt as if a cold rod were being jammed down
her spine.

It wasn't that she had never heard witches con-
demned, it was more that she had never seen anyone in the flesh who so forced her to think instantly
of what seventeenth-century witch-hunters might
have sounded like.

She listened further, piecing together the young
man's rhetorical position: the good people of
Homewinds, Alabama, should not suffer witches.
John Scarpia was dead because the community allowed these sisters of Satan to reside in the area.

They should be driven out.

Or better yet: *burned at the stake.*

Dizzied by the almost unimaginable hatred and
misogyny of the young man's message, she turned
to grope her way back to the fish camp. But someone was standing in her path.

"He's quite a talker, isn't he?"

Startled, Tina looked into the face of a young
man she recognized instantly.

Emil Sinclair.

"Who is he?" she managed to say.

"He's my brother, David."

Sinclair accompanied her to the rear of the main
office.

"You don't," she said, "you don't . . . agree with
what he's saying, do you?"

The young man shook his head.

"No, of course not. And not that many folks in

Homewinds do. Enough, though, that you and your aunt and your sisters are in danger."

"Your brother—is he insane?"

Sinclair smiled softly. "You could say that. And you could say that he's afraid. That book he was holding. It's called *The White Man's Bible*. He preaches from it. Blacks, Jews . . . witches—anyone pretty much who isn't white Anglo-Saxon Protestant is the enemy."

"I hope you're right that he doesn't have many on his side. That gathering is terrifying."

"For the most part I think David just likes to have an audience. He loves power. He refers to himself as the 'pontifex maximus' of 'the Torch of Dawn.' Troubled white guys are attracted to him like moths to a yard light. But it's not just talk. I think down deep my brother would like to die a martyr to the cause. I'd watch out for him if I were you."

"Thanks for the warning," she said.

With horrible images of David Sinclair stalking her thoughts, Tina went home to fix a late-night snack for Pa-Po and to ponder whether the dark fabric of her reality was about to be torn by forces she no longer possessed the magic to combat.

SEVENTEEN

You know that somehow Willow is sending the music.

You have heard it before.

In her room.

Danzig's "Black Aria."

Willow said it was about fallen angels.

So you listen.

But you have called out for Willow. You have called her name, and she does not return your call. In your head, all you can hear is a voice not quite hers saying a single word.

Coda.

It is another dawn and you are homesick.

You have slept on a piney hummock on the moist ground near the fire you built. You have eaten mostly berries for days and you are hungry for cornbread and for the taste of chocolate milk. And you miss Mr. Buck's chair and the coconut butter smell of Miss Billie Ruth.

You miss the rope-pull ferry.

You miss the breathtaking beauty of Artie.

You are almost ready to go home.

But you have things to think about. You need to lose yourself in thought before you go home again. The swamp is a great and large place to lose yourself

in thought. You have to think about things that are
troubling you. Not sinful things. Not love—not exactly.

Mysterious things.

Mr. Buck always says, "Joe Boy, life is a mystery."
But until these past several days in the swamp you
have not realized the truth of what he says. You have
mysterious things in your mind, and you need to
figure them out some before you go home.

You are sorry that Mr. Buck and Miss Billie Ruth
are worried about you.

You know they are.

But you have seen mysterious things. Things that
scare you.

You have gone back several times to the clearing
where the rusting boiler sits and you stand there
and smell blood and you smell where the creature
was and where the creature killed a man.

Willow's daddy.

And almost killed that man's daddy, too.

That creature walks around in its own world.

The world Willow has gone inside?

You do not know that.

Another mystery is the man who walks on moonlight. The same man who talked with you at the
rope-pull ferry. The one who walked across to the
spit on a path created by the moon. A mysterious
man.

A magic man.

Like Jesus in the Bible.

You watched him put Willow's daddy and Willow's
daddy's daddy back in their boat and pole them to
the fish camp. All the way to the fish camp, not
letting anyone see him. You wonder if the moonlight walker knew *you* were watching.

You think maybe he did.

You get up to face the day. You will think about
all these mysteries as you hunt for food. Yesterday,

you came upon a cabin as you were wading in a feeder creek. You saw smoke coming from the stovepipe chimney of it. You smelled bread and you smelled hot meat. You will return there today maybe and see who lives there.

Maybe someone who has seen Willow.

You are finding things in Night Horse Swamp you did not know were there.

That makes your heart beat fast. Almost like it does when you see Artie.

The sun is just past midpoint.

You are out of sight, but you are watching carefully. Near the cabin you have come upon in your wanderings there is a tall, white-bearded man in overalls. He is wearing an old-time swamper's hat— Mr. Buck has one like it. This man is very gentle. Gentle. You like that word. Watching this man, you think that you would like him.

He is feeding three deer.

It is a sight you have not seen before. A man feeding such skittish animals. Deer do not come close to where people are without running. These deer feed from the man's hand. Corn? Some kind of grain—and they swish their white tails and they are not afraid of this gentle man, tall, with a white beard.

And eyes that do not seem to see the creatures pressing up to him.

Because it is so warm, you swim down one of the main forks. You cannot keep from thinking about the tall, gentle man with the white beard. You want to visit him, but you will swim first. You think about going home tomorrow. Tomorrow is a word that hangs high in the tree of your ability to comprehend. Like mistletoe high in a tall cypress. Only you know how to get the mistletoe. You shinny up the cypress.

Tomorrow is a different thing.

In the distance, as you swim and gambol in the water and keep one eye out for bull gators or for mama gators protecting a nest of eggs, you see the derelict houseboat. You decide to go explore it. You wonder if maybe, just maybe Willow came upon it and claimed it as her own. Set up housekeeping there.

You hold your breath and kick along until you reach one side of it.

Then you surface and push yourself up to where you can climb aboard.

But you don't.

Because you hear voices inside the boat.

A man and a woman.

Warm voices.

You think maybe it is a man and a woman in love.

EIGHTEEN

"What frightens you?"

Gretta admitted to herself that she loved to touch him. Loved to rub her fingertips in the soft, curly, dark hair on his chest. Loved, as well, to hear his breathing after sex—the rhythm of it, rapid, yet ever slowing and, she hoped, contented. She loved the smell of him: sweat and Old Spice and passion.

Toying with her bare shoulder as they nestled in the bed on the houseboat, he paused thoughtfully.

"As a kid that movie *Nightmare on Elm Street* scared the hell outta me. You know, the one with that Freddy guy—knives for fingernails. I'd wake up thinking he was about to come through the ceiling of my room. But what really scared me was the thought that any of my guy friends would find out that a movie scared me. What a wuss I'd have been to them."

"Maybe they were frightened by the same movie."

"Maybe."

She kissed his throat and tasted the tiny beading of sweat there.

He even tasted good.

"It's hard for me to imagine," she said, "that you've ever been frightened of anything."

The afternoon heat bore down on the houseboat, though it was somewhat cooler in the small room they playfully referred to as the "master bedroom."

She listened to his heartbeat and to the downshifting speed of his breathing. She knew he was thinking, reflecting, lowering himself deeper into his emotional past. She waited and was rewarded when he said:

"I'll tell you something I've never told anyone else."

She felt her body tense as she readied herself to listen.

"Being left behind," he began, "*that* was the most frightened I've ever been. That was the worst feeling."

"Left behind? You mean, at a mall or something like that?"

"No. I mean left behind in the sense of . . . being abandoned. You see, my father worked as a roustabout. Mainly off the coast of Louisiana. In fact, I suppose the only reason we didn't move there from Alabama was that my mother had so many relatives here. But anyway, he was gone most of the time. God, I would miss him and look forward more to him coming home than I would to Christmas. My mother used to tell me that his work was dangerous—that one day we might learn that he'd been in an accident."

"Gosh, that's pretty heavy stuff to lay on a kid. How old were you?"

"Oh, maybe eight or nine. I don't know."

"So one day something happened to him, right?"

"Well . . . one day we got this letter in the mail and all it said was, 'I'm not coming home again.' Short and not so sweet. I was devastated. I don't think he ever knew how that tore my heart out."

"I'm sorry," she whispered, and hugged him. "And I hope you know that I won't abandon you."

She liked the warmth of his chuckle.

"Thanks. I know you won't. Not if you really have a choice. It's funny, though, how what my father did has influenced so much of my life. I know it's why—with Robbie—leaving her would be . . . but what I'm doing is selfish. Not fair to either one of you."

Gretta reached up and put her fingers to his lips. "Don't talk about that. Please."

"Sorry." He paused, and she hoped he would drop the issues that had been lifted suddenly into their intimate microcosm. "What about you?"

"Me? What do you mean?"

"Same question. What frightens you?"

She turned over on her back and closed her eyes and gave herself to the pleasure of his hand on her bare stomach. But the world of her childhood came flooding back too quickly. Her throat tightened, and she knew that she would have to calm herself before she could speak. Pleasure and tension. Opposites. Like needing to be with someone and also needing so much of the time to be alone. To have her own private *temenos* on Pan Island.

"It scares me," she began, "to think that something I care deeply about could be taken away from me. It's always been that way. Going back to being a little girl—the times my sister, Tina, took something away from me. A doll or a trinket or whatever. Or when my mother did something like that. Or the Goddess, once I had started believing in the Old Ways, and once I understood that the Goddess could take away something that made you too prideful. Now, its scares me that someone would take you away from me, even though you're not really . . . you know what I mean."

"Another woman? Is that what you mean?"

"It isn't something specific necessarily." She rolled over and held him very tightly. "To cope with the feeling, I have this fantasy of kidnapping you and maybe keeping you on this houseboat as my love slave and . . ."

They both began to laugh.

"I could go for that," he said, when the laughter had subsided and they had kissed.

There was more she wanted, needed to say.

She wanted this man all to herself. If it came down to it, she wouldn't let the world take him away from her. She would not.

"Hey, sweet love," he said. "I hate to say this, but I have to get back to the real world. A little bit of official business."

Minutes later they were dressed and standing on the deck drinking in the quiet beauty of the swamp. Gretta thought again of her fantasy of holding her lover hostage from civilization. She could not believe that anyone else loved or needed this man as much as she did.

But the intrusion of reality was as undeniable as the sun penetrating the canopy of the swamp.

"Has there been any progress on the murder of John Scarpia?" she asked.

She could see how such questions instantly changed his demeanor. How he suddenly became Deputy Favors. The way he stood. The look in his eyes.

"No. Nothing really. I've been on the lookout for that drifter—the one that talked with Tina a few weeks ago. I think he's miles away, though. Otherwise, what we're gone have to do is head out there and see if some bad guys are maybe protecting a whiskey still or some stands of marijuana or a meth lab, maybe. Lots of that going on these days. Tough characters running illegal operations, especially in places impossible to police."

He gestured toward the shadowy reaches of the swamp.

Gretta felt a chill slither across her shoulders.

"Please be careful, my darling," she said.

"You know I will."

And there, at that moment, she resolved suddenly

not to tell him about seeing something on Pan Island. Seeing the creature—maybe the same one—that her mother called the Terror. And not to tell him that she had started linking the creature with the disappearance of Willow.

For she felt he wasn't ready for it.

She felt it was her secret—something she needed to hold on to.

Something that otherwise might be taken from her.

NINETEEN

Seeing Willow took your breath away.

You did not expect to see her. You had swum away from your vantage point where you watched Willow's aunt—the one who lives on Pan Island—say good-bye to the man—the deputy sheriff. They kissed. A long kiss. Watching them kiss made you feel funny down low in your stomach.

You know they are not married.

But you think they are in love.

You saw it in the woman's eyes as she waved at the deputy as he poled away. But he did not pole into a run that would take him out of the swamp. Instead, he went farther into it. You don't know what that means. The woman had her own boat. You watched her go in the opposite direction. She was sad, you believe.

Then you swam away.

You became a water creature again, not thinking about sadness or love.

Not even thinking about Artie or even Willow.

You smelled smoke in the distance.

Twilight falling.

You believed that the smoke was coming from the cabin where you saw the tall, gentle man with the white beard feeding deer. You were curious.

She did not have a face.

Willow.

When you saw her or thought you saw her, she was faceless. Was the swamp playing tricks on you?

She was naked, running across a sand scrub and then into the piney woods not far from the gentle man's cabin. You smelled honeysuckle and kudzu.

Willow's smells.

You called out for her.

Your head barely out of the water, drifting in the current like a gator, you wondered about what you saw: Willow. Her black hair. Her young body. But no face. And the sight of her took your breath clean away. Left you gasping for air.

But you know how to catch your breath, and as you drift along you begin to think that it was not Willow.

It was something like a ghost. Mr. Buck has told you that the swamp has them. A giant "night horse" is one of them. It races through the swamp now and again. You imagine the ghost of Willow with no face riding atop that phantom night horse.

It makes your teeth chatter.

And you are hungry and homesick.

Then you hear the saddest music you have ever heard.

It's coming from the direction of the smoke. From the gentle man's cabin, you guess.

It draws you.

You also keep an eye trained on the piney woods in case Willow reappears.

She does not.

It is saw music.

It hooks you, and you know in that instant what a fish must feel like being hooked by a fisherman. You cannot resist. You are being reeled in.

The gentle man, white beard, is sitting in a cane-backed rocking chair on the porch of his cabin hunkered down over the toothed saw, and with what looks like a fiddle bow he is coaxing sadness out of the saw. Out of the air. Out of the earth. Out of your soul.

It is music that makes you ache.

The death-of-the-day music.

You wade right out of the water and right up not far from where the man is sitting.

You wonder why he doesn't see you.

Is it because he is concentrating on the music?

The music threatens to suck tears from you. You are moved. You are shaken. And, suddenly, you cannot help it. You put your hands over your ears and you say, "Stop!"

And the music ceases.

The old man puts down the saw and bow.

"Who's there?" he says.

The sun is low. He squints out toward you.

You see that he is blind.

The old man stands. He is tall. Taller than Mr. Buck. You have interrupted his music, yet he does not seem angry.

"Who's there? I heard you, friend. Mr. Crowfoot? No, I don't believe so."

You think about turning and running. But this is a gentle man. He is not reaching for a gun of any kind. He is not siccing dogs on you. He seems to have no dogs. And besides all that, you smell food. You smell hot food. And you are so hungry, so tired of eating mostly berries, that you will brave the moment.

"Joe Boy," you say. "Joe Boy Private. I live with Mr. Buck and Miss Billie Ruth."

The blind man smiles. "I know of them. But you—you the fella who runs the ferry?"

It is your turn to smile. To beam. "That's me. Joe Boy. I do."

"Are you lost? You're as far from that neck of things as a body can be."

"No. Not lost. I've been looking for my friend. She smells like honeysuckle and kudzu. She's disappeared. I thought I saw her back there a ways."

You can see how the old man is gazing off into nothingness—thinking, maybe. Remembering a smell? You do not know.

"You're in a world here where things disappear," he said.

There is silence, and you do not know what to do. But the blind man saves you. He says, "Are you hungry, Joe Boy?"

Your stomach growls low. It sounds like pigeons cooing.

The blind man hears it.

He begins to laugh, and then you laugh, and the day darkens just fine, and you begin walking into the laughter.

It is cool and friendly inside his cabin. Just like the mobile home in which you live with Mr. Buck and Miss Billie Ruth, only there is no television, no rocker recliner. No pictures on the wall—of Jesus or nobody. Simple furniture. A fireplace with a low fire and a black-as-night pot simmering something above the licking of the flames.

"Do you like beans, Joe Boy?"

"I do," you say.

You want to tell this man that when Mr. Buck eats beans he waits until Miss Billie Ruth is not in the room and then he "rips big ones." Bull gator farts, he calls them. Beans do that.

"Sit on the stool by the fire. I'll get you a plate. Don't suppose you like biscuits, do you?"

"Oh, yes, sir," you say. "I do like biscuits."

"I have some. Cat head biscuits. They fit right

into a boy's mouth just fine. I have sun tea. Sweet, very sweet."

You think maybe you walked into heaven.

Maybe this old man is God. Maybe.

Then you say, "I saw you feeding deer. From your hand. Never seen that before."

The blind man chuckles warmly.

"My children," he says. "Say, did I tell you who I am?"

"No, sir. I was wondering if you might be God. But mostly, in pictures I've seen, God is reaching down from a cloud. Jesus carries lambs around. I don't know who you are."

"Brother Owen," he says, nodding. "A far piece from God. I do, though, worship his creation. Pleased to meet you," he adds, reaching out for your hand, and you move where you can shake it. It is the most gentle hand you have ever shaken. It is like shaking hands with a big flower petal.

The food just might be the best that you have ever eaten.

You will not, however, tell Miss Billie Ruth that.

Sated, fire-warmed, and comfortable, you watch Brother Owen light his corncob pipe.

"You're not a smoker, are you, Joe Boy?" he says.

"No, sir."

"Good. It's a bad habit. Devil taught it to me. But I get to wondering if everything the devil teaches you is bad. You know what I'm saying?"

You do not know what to say. You think about the devil and finally a question occurs to you.

"Ever see the devil in this here swamp?"

The old man pauses. He looks up at the ceiling even though you assume he cannot see it.

"Lately. Oh, it's like a feeling comes over me, you know. And I've met up with some ferocious things in this ole swamp—gators, wild pigs, snakes—all of it. Lately, something else. Might could be the devil.

Might be something dark and mean that slipped in when God wasn't watching."

Pictures in your head are swimming around, swirling like an eddy. Brother Owen's words make you think about what attacked Artie. It makes you think of the man called Shep who walked on moonlight.

"There's a crowd of bad things these days," you say. "That something dark and mean—I know what you're talking about. And the man who walks on moonlight. Shep. And carries a guitar."

The old man brightens. "Oh, I've heard him. I have. Playing and singing, but I thought I was imagining him. Yes. But he won't come around to my door. Least, he hasn't yet."

You ask again about Willow.

The old man shakes his head.

"What would you do?" he asks. "How far would you go to see her safe home again?"

"Does that mean you've seen her?" And you realize your mistake. "I mean, do you get a feeling she's around? Not a ghost. But a real girl. Willow."

"Things fall into the world sometimes. But you, sir, have not answered my question. How far would you go to save your friend?"

"To the edge of the swamp. To the bottom of it if I had to."

He nods. He pokes his pipe at you. "Good."

"Why?" you ask.

"Because it's the only thing that counts."

You echo his words, and you are confused. But this old man sounds as wise or wiser than Miss Billie Ruth or Mr. Buck or Aunt Mushka or any teacher at school. And you are sleepy and you need to rest, yet you need to know what he is talking about. He knows something. This is what he says.

"My friend, the ultimate human joy is *sacrifice*. No greater joy. No greater gift to offer someone you love."

The fire dies as the two of you surrender to silence. His words blow through your mind like an incessant wind.

He makes you a pallet on the floor in front of that fire. And you curl up and he says to you, "Will you remember that, Joe Boy?"

"All right then," you say. "I will."

His words scare you.

Your thoughts fill with blood.

And you do not know why.

TWENTY

Glen is my life.

The thought came to her, hard, sobering, impossible to challenge.

And what does it mean, she wondered, for a man to assume, to *become* a woman's life? To take it over. To become your sole reason for existing. Could she really not live without him? That sounded absurd.

"I can't let anything take him away from me."

The resolution, spoken out loud, sounded right to her. Sounded real.

But crouching before a small fire in her hearth, she told herself that she—Gretta Fossor—had created a perfectly suitable life on Pan Island. She had embraced Thoreau-like simplicities. Things necessary for living. In this cabin on *her* island she had security, identity, and all the stimulation a woman could need.

Everything except intimacy with a man.

Enter . . . Glen Favors.

She bit her lip.

How could loving a man be such a curse?

No, it wasn't a curse. Of course it wasn't.

It was beauty.

It was a gift.

Like a sunset. Like a refreshing rain shower sweeping in over the swamp. Like blooming flowers. Like the calls of birds.

Like the breathtaking sight of the panther.

She closed her eyes and reexperienced the satis-
fying feeling of his weight upon her. Of their lovemaking aboard the houseboat. Their floating
temple. Their *temenos*. Sacred. Safe. Or was it? She
dismissed the latter thought.

Such a love as they shared was never *safe*. Not as
in "safe sex" but rather as in emotionally safe. It
was, in fact, a dangerous love. She never doubted
that. Most of her, in fact, accepted it. But did she
really accept that this man had become her life?

More important to her than magic?

What would her mother have said?

"Would I care?"

She smiled at the sound of her voice. The empty
rebellion in her tone.

But where in all the sacred tenets of the Old Ways
did it say anything about not loving a man? Where
was it written that a witch was not permitted to love
a human male? She could have both: a life galvanized by all the magical energy of the Old Ways and
a life annealed through intimacy—physical *and* spiritual. With a man.

An incredible man.

As she stirred a pot of lentil soup she wondered
where he was. She wished that he had not gone
farther into the swamp in search of clues surrounding the death of John Scarpia. She wished he had
not promised her that he would find Willow. She
regretted not going with him.

He doesn't know the swamp.

"He hasn't seen what I've seen," she murmured.

With a small bowl of the hot soup, she sat back
on the floor and thought about going after him.
But then feared that if she did, he would read it
the wrong way. He might read it that she thought
he wasn't capable of avoiding the dangers of the

swamp. That male ego thing could rear its ugly head.

She smiled at the glancing pun.

No. She would let him play the role that he must play.

Tired, she finished her soup and let her fire burn down. Then, as she was undressing to retire to her bed, she smelled the smoke. She went back into the front room to see about the dying fire. And the sight of the curious smoke arrested her attention completely.

She sucked in her breath.

And something of dark magic began to shape itself among the shadows.

With her lantern guiding her way, she poled in the direction of the houseboat. The night air was thick and humid. She felt as if she were trespassing. Forbidden territory. But she deflected every other thought except one: *he needs me.*

Glen Favors needed her. He was in trouble.

The smoke told her.

The indistinct shape that emerged from it, and, most of all, the voice—Glen's voice, she believed— telling, *begging* her, not to leave him behind.

"Don't abandon me," it seemed to say.

And the smell of the swamp and the smell of his own fear.

And one other smell: blood.

TWENTY-ONE

"I've seen methamphetamine come outta no-wheres. Like some monster trying to swallow us up alive. Now we gotta do something about it. The man who does is gone be the next sheriff."

The voice Favors played back in his thoughts was that of Willie Roy Slaughter, Catlin County Sheriff and former All-SEC running back. Ten, twelve years ago, Willie Roy was six feet two, two hundred and twenty-five pounds of solid granite possessing break-away speed and hands as soft as talcum powder. An NFL first-round draft choice.

Two serious knee operations later he was back in Homewinds, Alabama.

On the road to being a has-been. Anything but a conquering hero.

And yet, Willie Roy Slaughter had clout, had "voice" among the black folks of the county—and among enough whites who remembered his football ability—to put together solid political support to run for sheriff—first black sheriff ever for the county—and win handily.

Now scandal loomed.

Willie Roy, fifty pounds heavier than his collegiate days, could still run, but he couldn't hide, and so he was grooming Favors to take over the reins while he eluded the grasp of the Alabama Bureau of In-vestigation as surely as he juked linebackers on the gridiron. He liked Favors. Coached him in the game of politics. Willie Roy knew that putting a lid on the county's meth labs would score just enough points for Favors to win the day. And throw a few downfield blocks against the authorities as they probed into Willie Roy's extrapolitical activities.

Quid pro quo.

The problem was that Favors didn't really want Willie Roy's help.

Gotta do it myself.

But Favors admitted that he didn't know everything he needed to know to catch some pretty slick operators. He had a theory—not one he had voiced to anyone else. Not yet. His theory was that John Scarpia and his father had not happened upon a moonshiner. No, more likely they had come upon a meth lab out here in the realm of trembling earth. And its ruthless protectors had dispatched Scarpia and spared his father and sent their boat back to civilization.

What Favors hoped to do was to locate an unprotected lab—hence, this night journey—for he assumed that at night the bad guys would believe no one was crazy enough to venture into the swamp. Daylight hours would be the only necessary time to stand guard.

Power.

Favors hated to embrace it, but lately a vision of himself wielding power had become very attractive. Slaying the dragon of methamphetamine production would be just the ticket for his eventual seizing of power—with or without Willie Roy's assistance. Money was a factor, too. Every local law enforcement official in the South knew that the Drug Enforcement Administration had set aside millions to help catch illegal drugmakers and to help clean up the environmental damage caused by the meth labs, some of which generated refuse such as propane tanks, red phosphorous, hydrochloric acid, anti-freeze, battery acid, and toxic cleaning fluids.

Money in the coffers of the county sheriff at the start of taking office would help establish his stature beyond reproach.

I need to feel like somebody.

Yes, Gretta had made a big difference. Had boosted his self-esteem significantly.

But he needed more.

His promise—the same one made to Gretta as he had made to Tina—seemed safe. At some point, he believed he would get word that Willow had been spotted in New Orleans or Miami. Just another teenage runaway. Maybe he would make a big deal of bringing her home—much to the delight of both Gretta and Tina.

He needed to be a hero.

It sounded shallow, but he didn't care.

As he poled deeper into the swamp and trained his flashlight onto hummocks and sand scrubs, he thought about Gretta's fear of having something taken away from her. He vowed to himself that he would do whatever possible to see that it didn't happen—that her fears would not be realized. And yet, he wasn't ready to belong to her. To be totally committed to her.

Because it would involve abandonment.

Abandoning someone he believed needed him.

And those were his tangled thoughts when he heard the sound of a guitar in the distance.

The only light he dared keep alive was his flashlight.

The guitar strumming drew him inexorably. Man-made sounds in the swamp gave the heart a start. They were almost mesmerizing because one could only equate them with another human being. And

who would be out in the swamp at this hour if not
a drugmaker or a thug hired to guard the lab?

Hunkered down in the boat, Favors grasped his
revolver with two hands and let the swamp run take
the boat where it would. Forty yards later, it seemed
as if the implacable darkness of this nether world
had turned upside down.

"Jesus Christ," he whispered.

The guitar music ceased.

Revolver in one hand, flashlight in the other, Favors watched as the boat meandered slightly to the
right. A hummock swung out of the night, pine trees
and scattered cypress and peat solid enough for a
man to stand upon.

Cheeks and forehead sweating, Favors sprayed the
area with his flashlight, ready to shoot and, even
more so, to be shot at.

"Here we go," he whispered, swallowing back fear
as big as a basketball.

But, at first, he saw no one.

And yet, his thought was not primarily relief.

A gold mine. A fucking gold mine.

It was a meth lab. The music had, ironically,
guided him there. But now it appeared that the lab
had been . . . *abandoned.* Stepping from the boat
onto the hummock, he kept his eyes peeled for a
sentry. Saw none. Relaxed a notch.

"So, what do we have here?"

As he investigated, disappointment washed over
him. It hadn't been an active lab for some time.
More so, it appeared to be a meth dump site, the
vegetation scarred with dead patches where anti-
freeze and battery acid had been disposed of.

What had Willie Roy called the operators of such
sites?

"Beavis and Butt-head"—a reference to the sim-
pleminded teenage characters of a popular cartoon.
In east Alabama, such operations typically enlisted

a small circle of folk, often family members or friends, to create an enterprise that could net up to $2,000 for each ounce of powder or chunks that they produced. All you had to do, Favors had been told, was to break down ephedrine using anhydrous ammonia, ether, sulfuric acid, and other toxics. Not quite Chemistry 101, but not far from it.

And what you conjured up was highly addictive.

Some folks just *had* to have it.

Favors took a deep breath.

The night was breathing a peculiar perfume. He wanted to make love to it.

He couldn't wait to show Willie Roy what he had found.

"Things are finally gone turn my way," he whispered.

And then the man holding a guitar high, very high—maybe eighty feet up—in the closest pine said hello. Favors caught him in the spray of his flashlight just as the man fell headfirst from a jutting limb.

Favors watched in total disbelief as the man, ten yards or less before striking the hummock, tumbled once and then, as if an invisible parachute had opened, glided softly to the ground.

"God bless it!" Favors exclaimed. "What the—"

The man, calming holding his guitar as if about to break into song, said, "You don't belong here. You've come too far. Turn around and go back. Before it's too late."

"Hey, just who the hell are you?"

But Favors was trembling so badly he feared he would drop either his revolver or his flashlight or both. He blinked several times hard and stepped forward. The beam of his light was trained on the man's chest.

"The name is Shepherd. But that's no matter. I'm telling you, friend, you need to leave this area."

"I'll decide that. Just stay right where you are. Shepherd—Okay, I've heard of you. You in on this meth lab?"

"No, sir. Forget about this. You're in danger. I'm telling you."

"Seems to me you're the one in danger. And maybe, in fact, you're the one who killed John Scarpia. Seems to me you have a whole helluva lot of questions to answer. Let's just have you climb on into my boat and we'll go back to Homewinds and have us talk with Sheriff Slaughter."

"No, sir," said the man. "I can't do that. Won't do that."

The smell wafted up from behind Favors. It was strong. Made his eyes burn. Made him swallow hard. Distracted him from bringing in this suspect.

"I'm Glen Favors, Catlin County Deputy Sheriff— and I say you can and will get in this boat, or I'll blow your fucking head off. That clear?"

The man shook his head, a gesture of pity it seemed.

"There's dark magic at work here," he said.

And then he turned and right in plain sight he walked up into the air a good ten feet. Then he turned again and drifted down and stared back at Favors, who whispered, "Jesus Christ—what is this?"

He sensed that it was coming, but whatever it was moved so quickly that he had no time to swing around and protect himself. Gun and flashlight were worthless.

All the air in his lungs was pressed out as something slammed into his back.

He screamed at the excruciating pain.

And before he dropped his flashlight, he angled it so that he could see the points of antlers protruding from his stomach—a dozen of them, it seemed. And blood. A river of blood. And that's what he saw before the pain took him into a blindingly white light.

He felt the antler points slip from his body.

He slumped down and began to crawl toward his boat. He tried to speak Gretta's name, but could not. He tried to focus on the shadowy creature that had attacked him, but the night world was gauzy and darkly indistinct.

He made it to the boat. Rolled into it.

Heard a death rattle scurry up from his throat like a small animal.

Then blackness closed all the doors of his awareness.

TWENTY-TWO

"The right kind of sharing is a lovely thing for a woman."

Gretta did not know why her mother's words should occur to her at such a moment, a moment in which she was desperately searching for the man she loved. Had she heard a scream a minute earlier?

Right kind of sharing . . .

Her small lantern was ineffectual against the darkness of the swamp. But she poled intuitively, slipping past the houseboat and down the run where she had last seen Favors. And by degrees she eased her frantic pace; a curious calm fell over her shoulders like a blanket. And she heard the laughter of children from long ago.

The snake and the hunter.

How often had she and her sisters, as little girls, played that game—a teaching game? It was the only kind Anna Fossor allowed, of course, and she would play it with her daughters and sometimes they would coax Aunt Mushka into joining them as well. All it required was a circle of people, a rattle, and a blindfold. Someone was chosen to be the hunter, someone else to be the snake. The remaining others would encircle hunter and snake—the hunter would be blindfolded and be charged with the task of catching the snake. In turn, the snake was required to shake the rattle every few seconds and to elude the hunter while staying within the circle. A hollowed-out gourd containing a handful of dried watermelon seeds served as the rattle. It was great fun. Much laughter. The game ended when the hunter caught the snake. Anna Fossor wisely maintained that the game was an excellent way to practice using senses other than one's eyes.

Locked in the echoes of girlish laughter from the past, Gretta poled onward, pushing aside her fears about Favors, releasing herself to still another memory, this one of a warm spring day out in the swamp with her mother creating "Markers of Memory." It was a morning during which Gretta had innocently asked her mother, "Is there a game that teaches about falling in love?"

Her mother had laughed softly. "How old are you, Allegretta?"

"I'm ten," she had replied.

"A little young perhaps for thoughts of falling in love."

"But one day I will, and I want to know how to."

"Well," said her mother, her gaze drifting out into the embrace of the swamp, "did anyone teach you how to breathe?"

"Breathe? No, you don't have to be taught how to breathe . . . you just . . . do it. Or you won't live. You'll die if you don't breathe."

"I think falling in love is rather like breathing, and I hope it's never a game for you. And maybe instead of *falling* in love, you'll think of it as *growing* in love."

"Like the way plants grow?"

"Rather like plants grow, yes."

And they had wended their way deeper into the swamp, her mother having challenged her to locate a landscape "marker," some area of the wet, sun-splashed realm that Gretta would be inclined to return to again and again. A place, perhaps, of pleasant associations or memories. In the language of the Old Ways, a Memory Marker.

Gretta had one.

Her Remembrance Pool. She called it that because she would use it as the starting point for remembering other trail markings or "run" markings in the swamp, such markings necessary to keep one from losing her way. The pool itself was semicircled by three large cypresses, but instead of the water being shallow at the spot, it fell away into a hole five or six feet deep where duckweed swirled lazily. Gretta loved the spot. Her Remembrance Pool. And she told her mother that one day something very important in her life was going to happen there.

"I'm sure you're right," her mother had responded. "But now, how do you plan to sanctify your Memory Marker?"

"With fire and smoke."

Three piles of dry rye grass and a flint striker and a simple prayer to the Goddess.

And Gretta had lowered her face into the smoke of the first pile and had been startled to see a mummy—no, not a real one, just the image of a body wrapped all in white. When her mother asked her why she had given such a start, Gretta had responded, "Some day I'll tell you, but not today."

I never got to tell her.

A sigh of regret held her like the embrace of another person.

She imagined being in the arms of Glen Favors.

Glen, my darling.

When her mother's words evaporated from her thoughts, she began to pray to the Goddess—an almost wordless prayer—a passionate desire that she not be *too late.*

But the Old Ways stirred in her blood. Intuition, a dark sense of things.

She knew.

Long before she reached his boat.

She shouted his name over and over until the night sounds of the swamp ceased as if in sympathy with her anguish. Yards before she came upon him, she smelled another presence: the Terror. She knew that tragedy waited. Her body jerked with sobs as she plunged from her boat into the shallows where Favors's boat spun slowly, without purpose.

Her lantern spotlighted a man lying on his side in the boat, his back to her. There was a peaceful look to the position of the body, the natural-looking curl of the upper body, the rucking up of the knees. He appeared merely to be asleep. Gretta was stung by hope. She surrendered to it, her imagination projecting how, in years to come, she and this man would take care of each other, growing old on Pan Island after he had left Robbie for the beloved he had doubted he would ever find. Yet, he had found her, and she him. Would there be children? If he desired them, yes. Would there be room for the Old Ways in their days of deeper intimacy? Perhaps.

But no belief could be as powerful as the love shared by a man and a woman.

That's what her time with Favors had taught her.

Now he was resting. Here in the heart of the swamp. She would wake and greet him with her love, and he would rise to welcome that love and they would be each to each sufficient, needing no one else.

And that's what Gretta forced herself to embrace until she saw the blood. Much too much blood.

She would keep him.

No one was going to take him away from her.

Not his wife. Or the good folks of Homewinds.

As she lay with him in bed in the houseboat, she

was pleased with herself for putting a plan into action. She had calmly, resignedly lifted Favors into her boat. Then had sunk his. She had taken his body and his gun to the houseboat. She had undressed him. Cleaned his death wounds, staying the flow of blood with the pillowcase from the pillow on their bed, though not before she had collected several drops of that precious blood in a vial that she would hold sacred. She had wrestled his dead weight into bed. Undressed herself. Then had gotten in with him and pulled the sheet up over them. And had held him to get him warm.

Because his body had lost its heat.

She wasn't going to cry, but the only way she could keep from crying was to talk.

And pretend that he was listening.

"I know what did this to you, my darling. I can tell by the wounds—I know there's something out there. A creature of dark magic. But it can't hurt you any longer. Now you're with me. You're safe."

His body grew colder and seemingly heavier.

She pulled away from him and reached for his revolver. "Would my spirit join yours if I used this?"

The words filled the partially lighted room, words directed as much to herself as to her lover's lifeless body.

"If I could be certain . . . if I knew that we could be together . . ."

But she did not.

In her thoughts, suicide began to dissolve quickly as an option. Emotionally, she was spent. Revolver in hand, she walked out onto the deck of the houseboat and listened to the night sounds of the swamp and felt the touch of its heat and wetness. She did what needed to be done.

The plop of the gun when it struck the water belonged there—like the sound of a frog jumping in. Now the weapon would no longer tempt her. Back at the bedside, she stroked her lover's brow. She would leave him to rest; she would return to her cabin and hope that his spirit followed. Carefully she stuffed the bloodied pillowcase and the vial of blood into a drawstring purse. She dressed. Then she kissed his cold lips one last time.

"My darling," she whispered, "I vow to you that I'll find the creature that did this. For you, for *us*, I'll get revenge. I promise you."

She sighed and fought back a rising of tears.

Then her body began to tremble with anger.

She thought of her mother and of the way in which the belief system of the Old Ways had been passed along to her daughters, and Gretta could not deflect the dark possibility that somehow witchcraft had played a role in the death of her beloved. But the thought spun inchoately, full of blood and pain, forming nothing of substance for her.

Exhausted, she climbed down into her boat and returned to Pan Island.

Dawn had approached when she glimpsed his diaphanous ghost.

It was not whole; it had not retained "his" shape. His form. It was torn and ragged and confused. Seeing it saddened Gretta. Seeing it also jogged her to action. She could not leave her beloved's body on the houseboat.

Someone would find it.

Sheriff Slaughter. Or someone else. And her beloved would be returned to the woman he did not love.

And he would no longer be mine.

Gretta knew what had to be done. She loaded her boat with rope and heavy rocks. In the dark hour before dawn, she poled back to the houseboat. Lovingly she wrapped the body of Favors in the sheet that covered him. She wrapped his entire body, including his head and face, until he became the vision she had glimpsed as a girl.

Though tired to the bone, she once again wrestled with his body, lowering it into her boat for the journey to her Remembrance Pool. It took the better part of an hour to secure the shrouded body to the cypress roots and to anchor it so that it would not float to the surface. Wet and achy from the rigors of the task, she collapsed into her boat as the sun glanced into the swamp.

First light was both frightening and glorious.

The Terror is out there.

And was the spirit of her mother there, too?

She felt alone. But there was something of a life to move forward with, albeit empty now without Favors. She sat up in her boat and imagined that her beloved was listening as she recounted how she had created this special place long ago. The vision she had witnessed. She imagined that her beloved was pleased to be there rather than in a cemetery.

"Good-bye, my darling," she whispered into the water. "I'll visit you each day. And I won't rest easy until I've gotten revenge. I promise you again—I'll destroy what took you from me."

Several days later.

A bright, warm, early afternoon.

Gretta was planting a dozen tomato starts behind her cabin when she saw her sister, Tina, approach with a woman at her shoulder. Gretta felt herself stiffen in response. She and her sister had remained cold to each other since the night of the slap.

"Gretta, there's someone here who wants to talk to you. I brought her over, and I'm going to wait around until she's finished talking with you."

Gretta nodded. She thought Tina looked haggard

and worn—worry and lack of sleep were taking their
toll. When Tina finished speaking, she turned and
walked aside, and the other woman stepped forward.

"I'm Roberta Favors," she said. "I'm—"

"I know who you are," Gretta interrupted.

She glanced at Tina, who fielded the signal that
the two women needed to be alone.

Gretta gestured for the small, red-haired woman
to follow her to the far end of the island.

"This is a beautiful place," said the woman. "You
really have a pleasant place here."

Arms folded against her breasts, Gretta gazed into
the woman's face and wondered how a man such
as Glen Favors had ever loved or wanted or needed
such an inconsiderable woman.

"So, why do you want to see me?"

"I think you know."

Their eyes met. The rough, bruising exchange of
other woman and wronged woman.

Gretta sighed. Her body was warming as anger
and defiance gripped her muscles.

"Say what you have to say," said Gretta.

Suddenly the other woman was trying to choke
back tears and pressing a hand over her mouth and
turning aside, her body diminishing with every passing second. Gretta found herself almost wanting to
console the woman, but she could not. It was as if
such a gesture would have betrayed the man she
loved.

The man she was keeping in the swamp.

In her Remembrance Pool.

Nearly a minute ticked by before the wife of Glen
Favors—now his widow—composed herself.

"I'm not here to accuse you," she said, her voice
uneven and lined with the aftermath of tears. "I
know . . . I mean, it doesn't matter what people
have been saying about you and Glen. It doesn't

matter. Nothing matters except knowing where he is."

Tears threatened her again.

"He's not here," said Gretta. "If you think he's here, you're wrong."

The other woman was shaking her head. "I told Sheriff Slaughter everything I knew to say. I suppose he's been to see you—the sheriff, I mean."

Gretta nodded. "Yes, and I told him the same thing I'm going to tell you: you're wasting your time."

"Isn't there anything you can share? Any clue? It's just not like Glen—unless something happened to him. Like what happened to John Scarpia. Has something happened to my Glen?"

Through clenched teeth, Gretta said, "I'm not a detective, you know. You're wasting your time talking to me. I don't have anything to say." She hesitated. "I'm sorry your husband's missing. But I'm also sorry John Scarpia's dead and Willow Fossor is missing. Maybe all of those things are connected—I don't know."

The other woman brushed at tears in the corner of one eye.

She was nodding again, and Gretta detested her for doing so.

"Gretta, I just have one more question, and then I'll leave you alone." The hesitation stretched out until Gretta finally spoke.

"Go ahead. What is it?"

She could hear the woman's throat click before as she gathered herself to speak.

"I just want to know—was . . . did . . . did you see Glen the night he disappeared? Were you with him?"

TWENTY-THREE

You wonder what this means.

Willow's Aunt Gretta is waist deep in a pool, and she has her eyes closed and you guess she might be praying but you don't know. You have decided to go home. You hope that Miss Billie Ruth and Mr. Buck will welcome you. You think they will.

You said good-bye to Brother Owen.

When you think of him, you think of the word "sacrifice."

It is a big word. Almost too big for your head. A word so big it might could squirt brain stuff out of your ears like toothpaste when you squeeze the tube too hard.

"Sacrifice."

You will have to find a way to make that word smaller.

But you watch.

This woman, Willow's Aunt Gretta, lives in a cabin on Pan Island.

"She has simple needs"—that's what Miss Billie Ruth says about her. You heard her say that once. You also heard Mr. Buck talk about her. "Doesn't hardly seem natural," he said, "for a young woman like that to be alone. Can't she find her a man?"

Miss Billie Ruth told Mr. Buck, "Maybe she don't want a man."

And Mr. Buck said, "Maybe no man would have her. You ever think of it that way?"

You watch. This woman standing in the pool looks sad. The tall cypresses there make her look sad and small. You see her reach down into the water like there is something there, but you can't see what it is. Her face changes as quickly as the swamp—one moment she's sad, the next filled with joy.

You wonder what this means.

And you wait for her to leave the pool so you can go see what it is that does such things to her face. You watch her as she gets back into her boat. She mumbles something. Maybe she's praying. Maybe she's talking to the water. Or to what is below the water.

You wade into the pool after Willow's Aunt Gretta has gone.

You see something.

You see half-inch ropes tied to the cypress roots.

You suddenly remember something Miss Billie Ruth said to you once: "Curiosity killed the cat."

That's what she said. She explained to you about that word "curiosity." Not an easy word. Curiosity is when you just have to know about something. You just *have* to. Because you are *curious*. But this could be dangerous, you tell yourself.

Curiosity killed the cat.

A small cat? A big cat?

Could curiosity kill the panther?

You wanted to ask Miss Billie Ruth *which* cat, but you did not.

If curiosity could kill a cat, might could be it would kill a boy, too.

You stand in the pool staring at the ropes. Duckweed gathers around you. You think maybe you *have* to take a chance. So you take a deep breath and go under. You feel around and you find something.

Something wrapped in a sheet.

And when you have felt all around this something you jet to the surface.

You cry out in fear and surprise. You cough and spit water and splash away as if this something is after you. But it is not. You get a hold of yourself and try to understand what is going on.

Willow's Aunt Gretta has been visiting a dead body wrapped in a sheet.

You touched that dead body.

Curiosity almost stopped your heart.

Maybe that's what happened to the cat Miss Billie Ruth told you about.

You know for certain now that it is time to go home.

On the way home you run into another surprise.

The swamp is filled with them, it seems.

You were swimming along, enjoying how you always begin to feel like some other creature. Not a boy no more. Not Joe Boy. But something else. A good feeling. And the sun was cooking up the day like Miss Billie Ruth boils up spaghetti sometimes or macaroni. And birds were calling and no gators were around.

You always watch for gators.

You were swimming along trying not to think about the body tied to the cypress roots, trying not to wonder too much about Willow's Aunt Gretta and what she was up to. You were swimming and suddenly you heard the word *Coda* in your head. You thought you knew that word. You kept on swimming and you happened to glance over at the point off quite a ways at where a feeder creek entered the run and your eyes almost popped out.

There was Willow.

Your heart was so glad you just couldn't even say anything. You started swimming toward her as fast as you could, but this time she wasn't a ghost at all. This time she was real. Willow. You swam closer, and as you did you got a funny feeling in your stomach. Not a real bad feeling. But not a real good one either.

Willow was naked.

And had no face.

Just like before.

But you kept swimming toward her and hoping she wouldn't run away. She didn't. She had her same black hair, and you tried not to stare at her nakedness—not the same nakedness as Artie's. And you could not understand what had happened to her face. No eyes or nose or mouth. Just flesh-colored face. Like skin pulled over a tanning board.

"Willow!" you called out. "It's Joe Boy!"

You waved from the water. She did not wave back.

But she spoke right into your head.

Stay away!

Those were the words that bounced from one side of your head to the other. They were loud in your head. As loud as your rope-pull ferry signal. Loud like a hammer against a plowshare.

You stopped swimming. You were close enough to Willow to chuck a rock at her.

"Come on home, Willow!" you called out. "Come right on home!"

Then it seemed like she looked around as if someone else might be there. You thought maybe she was afraid of something. You sensed it, too. Someone or something close to her. But you couldn't see. Then she started to run away. Then she stopped and spoke into your head again.

I can't!

Those were the words you heard.

Then she was gone.

And you felt all empty inside wanting to understand.

* * *

Miss Billie Ruth just about hugged the snot out of you because she was so glad to see you. She smiled and chortled and hugged and kissed you. Then she got mad at you for going away and "worryin' me to death." Which wasn't true because there she was—alive as always.

Mr. Buck rubbed your head with his knuckles—it's the same as a hug and a kiss. He knew Miss Billie Ruth wouldn't stay mad at you for long. He let you sit in his chair while Miss Billie Ruth made you cornbread. She held on to her anger the way the day holds on to light. She gave all the way up on being mad when you said, "I love you."

Mr. Buck laughed and told you, "You're a smart little prick, Joe Boy."

And you tucked that word "prick" in with all the other good-sounding names Mr. Buck has called you. You had no idea why Miss Billie Ruth told Mr. Buck not to call you that, especially after he said, "Oh, go on, woman—it's just a term of endearment."

Whatever that is, you know it takes the chill off your heart.

You lie awake that night and think of how a few days in the swamp can turn you upside down. You think about Brother Owen and Willow's Aunt Gretta and the body wrapped in a sheet. You think about Willow with no face. You think about what could be making Willow so scared. You think maybe you know. You think maybe it is the same something that attacked Artie.

That's what you think.

You decide something big.

You decide that tomorrow you will tell Willow's mother what you know about Willow.

You want to rescue Willow.

But you will have to be as strong as the world to do it.

TWENTY-FOUR

She did not believe him.

Yet, as May became June and her daughter had been missing for exactly a month, Tina Fossor did not really know what or whom to believe. She had reached the end of her rope. Dark-night-of-the-soul time.

She needed an answer from the outside.

Joe Boy had come to her the day before with his awkward revelation, with news that during his days spent in the swamp he had seen Willow—twice. But when Tina had pressed him for details, when she had virtually demanded that he take her to the spot where he had seen Willow, he had refused. No, not exactly refused. Simply and matter-of-factly, he had explained that it would do no good.

"We can't help her. Willow said to me, 'Stay away,' and I told her, 'Come home, Willow, come home,' and Willow said to me, 'I can't.' Willow didn't have a face."

It was no use badgering the boy.

He was flustered and confused and, most of all, scared. It was apparent that he had experienced something rather dramatic. But what? Tina found it very difficult to believe that he had actually seen Willow—Willow with no face. Had the boy's vivid imagination been working overtime?

And now Willie Roy Slaughter had come to visit

her again. He was out on her deck on a gloriously sunny and warm late morning. She and Sheriff Slaughter had gotten to know each other pretty well through his several "official" investigative sessions. Questions. Questions and more questions about the death of her former husband and about her daughter and the possible connection between the death (murder?) of John Scarpia and Willow's disappearance.

"Now my deputy is missing," he said, shaking his head, then thanking her as she handed him a glass of iced tea.

"I know," she said. "But I can assure you that I don't have any information to help you on that."

She could tell that he was more uncomfortable than usual. He was a large man, muscular, though a beer belly was stealing some of the impressiveness from his physique. Holding the glass against his sweaty forehead, he said, "I spoze this question ain't gone surprise you none. Spoze you know what I'm gone ask."

"Sheriff, contrary to popular opinion, not many witches are mind readers. No, I don't know what you're going to ask."

He chuckled. Then drew himself up until he was apparently the size he needed to be.

"Your sister—the one who lives out on that island there—she and Glen . . . well, folks say, well, you know how this goes . . . I been told your sister and my deputy, maybe they was havin', you know, an affair."

"Seems like Gretta's the one you need to be asking that."

"Yes, ma'am. Well, I did, in a roundabout way, that is. I questioned her, of course. Glen's wife demanded it. But your sister didn't say much. I suspect she didn't tell me a whole heap of what she knows. I got no proof—and I'm not sayin' she had anything to do with whatever happened to Glen. He jus' plain fell off the planet is the way it looks."

"So is that what this is about? The disappearance of Glen Favors?"

The sheriff sighed heavily. Gulped once at his tea and looked as out of place as darkness at noon.

"No, ma'am, it's not. Folks get crazy notions—if you could have my job for a week you'd see how crazy some of their notions are—and so, what I'm trying to say is . . . well, about what happened to your husband—ex-husband, I mean—some folks wondered if you and your sisters somehow did something. Like voodoo or a spell or curse or something—hell, I don't know—to bring on the violence he ran into. You wouldn't believe the things I've heard."

He had to stifle some derisive laughter.

Tina picked up the line and gave it her own spin of sarcasm.

"They think maybe we *conjured* up something, right? With help from Satan, of course."

He looked at her. She assumed he could hear the barely repressed anger in her voice.

"Yes, ma'am—something like that," he said quietly.

"So, are we going to be burned at the stake in the Piggly Wiggly parking lot?"

Sheriff Slaughter shifted uncomfortably, then regained himself.

"Not if I can help it," he said.

"Would this have anything to do with Mr. David Sinclair?"

"Yes, ma'am, it would."

"May I assume that my sisters and my aunt and I will be fully protected from that man and his followers?"

"Mrs. Fossor, what I'm tryin' to say is that no law

enforcement official in this whole land can protect a citizen from all the crazies out there."

"So this visit is a warning?"

He paused. She could see the heaviness of the moment on his shoulders.

"Yes, ma'am. I spoze you could say it is."

"And I suppose, in turn, I should thank you. Is that all the questions for today?"

She could see that at least one more had occurred to him.

"The drifter, ma'am."

"Drifter?"

She knew, of course, that he was referring to Willis Shepherd, but she hadn't seen or heard from him for quite some time. She opted to be coy with the sheriff.

"Yes, ma'am. Apparently he's still in the area. Blond hair, long, you know . . . jus' looks like a bum. A hippie. A drifter. Can't say he's a suspect or nothin' like that. Jus' be a good idea for the local sheriff to know what he's up to. You know what I mean?"

"I do. Should I handcuff him if I see him? Citizen's arrest?"

More uncomfortable than ever, he glanced at her as if to gauge the degree of her seriousness.

"No, ma'am. Nothin' like that. Jus' tell 'im the sheriff would like to have a talk with 'im."

That evening late she had fixed Pa-Po a snack of chocolate pudding and settled him, as usual, into Willow's bed in Willow's room where he seemed perfectly at home. He was a dear man—sweet and gentle and no trouble at all. He could keep himself contented for hours listening to the radio, watching TV, or sitting out on the deck peering into the landscape of the swamp. Tina often wondered what he saw there. Had he witnessed his son's death? If so, he wasn't sharing the experience with anyone.

Restless, Tina decided to go down to the rope-pull ferry and sit on the wooden dock and let an approaching thunderstorm bathe her with its sights and sounds. It hadn't rained hard since the day Willow disappeared—the swamp was turning bone dry again.

From her vantage point at the end of the derelict wooden structure, her feet dangling over the edge, she could see across to where Joe Boy was sitting on a stool waiting just in case an evening traveler needed to be escorted over to the spit. She thought again about his odd report to her on seeing Willow. While Tina certainly continued to believe that her daughter was alive and would return home one day, she was beginning to believe the running-away-from-Homewinds theory might be dead-on.

But she was losing hope.

It was fading the way a rainbow eventually does after a storm.

"Don't let it."

Nearly falling in, Tina yelped in surprise at the sound of the voice. She wheeled around to see the man known as Shep, who seemed to have casually walked up out of the earth. She had not heard him make a sound until he spoke.

"Oh, good heavens, you startled me," she said.

"Sorry. But when I sensed that you were losing hope, I had to step in to tell you not to."

"You must have read my mind."

He hesitated. Hunkered down next to her, the only light being the meager one on her back porch, his face was a rage of shadows, and yet his eyes glimmered softly, warmly. "Yes, I did."

She tried not to act surprised; and, in fact, some psychic ability seemed perfectly in keeping with this curious man. "You must not be your ordinary garden-variety drifter or troubadour or whatever it is you call yourself. And I suppose you know that Sheriff Slaughter is looking for you. Twenty questions time."

Shep nodded. "For what it's worth, I didn't kill your husband, and I had nothing to do with the disappearance of Glen Favors . . . or your daughter, Willow, either."

"I have a bad feeling about Favors," she said.

The man grew quiet, then seemed to be drawn to a flash of lightning back over the swamp. "You probably won't be shocked to hear that he met the same fate as your husband."

"Does Gretta know?"

"Yes. But let's not talk about what's out there. Not right now. Not tonight. There'll be time later to talk about dark magic and what we're going to have to do about it."

"*We?*"

"Yes. You, me, your sisters, your aunt . . . maybe even that boy across the way."

"Why should I talk with you at all? Why should I trust you?"

"Because I can help you."

"How can I be sure of that? And, besides, what makes you think that I need help? I've taken pretty good care of myself and those around me over the years."

"I don't doubt that—but then do you know where your daughter is right this moment?"

She felt herself flinch. Her chest burned with a stab of anger. "Do you?"

He looked down at his comically worn boots, then cut to the swamp. "I have a good idea—yes."

"Out there?" She gestured with her eyes in the same direction of his gaze.

"Yes."

The rush of feeling came before she could prepare herself, steel herself for the weight of so many days of anguish and worry crashing down. She began to cry, softly at first, then more intensely as the man took her by the shoulders and pulled her close and began to sing to her.

His song. A song the dark powers sing.

With words she could not later remember.

TWENTY-FIVE

"Help me! Help me! Oh, please, help me!"

The screams yanked Mushka from her sleep. Rosebud, who had been dozing at her feet, squalled once and leaped to the floor for safety. Dodging the cat, Mushka scrambled from her bedroom desperately trying to focus on the terrifying cries.

They were coming from Artie's room—of that she was immediately certain.

But so much else was a blur. Especially the strange dream she had been locked in.

"Help me! Somebody help me!"

The pathetic calls quavered and ricocheted crazily along the hallway.

Dashing into Artie's room, Mushka reached the young woman's bed and could make out, there in the shadows, the young woman flailing her arms, her voice tearing along a line separating reason and fear-induced insanity.

"I'm here, baby, I'm here," Mushka exclaimed.

When she switched on the small lamp near Artie's bed, she lunged to embrace her niece's hysteria. But she was pushed away, shoved back as a new round of cries began.

"See them? Horrible! Horrible! Oh, look, Mushka, look!"

Artie's eyes were inflamed, her face pale and sweaty. Her naked body was not covered by the sheet

or the thin comforter. Her breasts swung free as she
pointed at her arms, and when Mushka followed the
direction of Artie's finger, she gasped at what she
saw.

She could only stare, momentarily paralyzed, as
the young woman shrieked and then began slapping
at her wrist and arm with her left hand.

Slapping at the spiders.

Seemingly dozens of them.

Some small. Some large. All of them dark and
creepy.

And under the young woman's skin.

And moving.

It was all an illusion, of course.

A nasty turn of dark magic.

Generated by what?

Mushka had no definite answer there. Only a very
good suspect. "You feeling better now, sweetie?"

It had taken more than half an hour to quiet Artie. And ten minutes or more before the spiders—
Artie's tattoos—stopped their weird scurrying all
over the young woman's body.

"You saw them, didn't you, Aunt Mushka?"

The older woman was pressing a cold rag to her
niece's forehead. "Yes," she said. "Yes, I saw something."

"They looked so real. Didn't they look *real* to you?
Oh, Mushka, I can't stand this. We have to make
this stop."

This.

As was often the case, Mushka found herself trying to get at what *this* was. She nodded at her niece,
whose face, especially the right side, continued to
show signs of an odd palsy. Her right hand continued not to function fully. Mushka had helped her
dress and had made some strong, honeyed, herbal

tea and had propped her up in bed with pillows behind her head.

"Yes," said Mushka. "I'm resolved that we got to do something. The fabric of our lives is being ripped apart."

"What's doing it, Aunt Mushka? Is it the Terror?"

After pausing briefly, Mushka nodded again. "Yes, I believe it is. The dark force preying upon us. Driving us into fear. Driving us over the edge. Or trying to."

"Did it take Willow? Do you think the Terror took Willow?"

"I think so. But I've dreamed that she's maybe alive. I dreamed that I was swallowed by the swamp and down there in the stomach of the swamp I saw Willow." She hesitated, smiled at Artie, then patted nervously at her throat. "We have to be at our strongest to fight it. You and your sisters—the bond between you has to be reforged. We can't defeat something like the Terror as long as the three of you have bad feelings toward each other."

Artie agreed. She sighed helplessly before glancing again at her arms to see whether the dark illusion had returned. The two of them suddenly grew quiet. Pensive. Rosebud jumped up onto Artie's bed, and the young woman began stroking her, and when the cat had lapsed into contented purring, the young woman said:

"Why? Why now? What has caused the Terror to come into our lives? And isn't there something we can do to recover our magic? Isn't there something in the power of the Old Ways to help us?"

"I think I've come to know what might could be going on. Oh, if only your mother was here. None of this would have happened. Not a bit of it."

"I don't understand," said Artie.

Mushka smiled. "Here's my two cents on it, if you feel like listening."

"I do."

Artie pressed Rosebud to her breasts, and Mushka gathered herself and began her speculation, qualifying nearly every statement, but slogging on as if her words, metaphorically, had to press through swamp mud. She offered that the entity known as the Terror had been conjured by Anna Fossor initially as a protective force and that for years it had remained so, its mission to protect the Fossor family from evil forces attracted to the dark recesses of the swamp. Everything changed when Anna Fossor died, when only her spiritual presence remained behind to keep the Terror in check.

"And like all entities of dark magic," Mushka explained, "this one possessed a heart of deceit, a soul envious of what our family had—the love, the togetherness. And maybe it chose Willow because it knew how much we all loved her. It knew that taking her would hurt us more than we could bear."

Artie's face registered puzzlement, and yet Mushka could tell that her narrative carried some persuasiveness.

"But what can we do?" Artie asked.

Mushka shook her head. "Might could be the only thing that would appease the Terror is sacrifice."

"Sacrifice? What do you mean by that?"

"Not sure I know, really," said Mushka. She tried to keep her expression from showing signs of confusion and pain. "But, now, let's stop our talk of this. You need some rest. What can I get you before I leave you be?"

"Would you give Gladys Michaels a call? She'll be at her restaurant today. I'd like to see her, okay?"

"You got it, sweetie."

"Folks are scared. That's what gets all this stirred up. The talk of witch-hunts—big talk about violence.

Vigilante talk. David Sinclair knows what buttons to press. It's all about fear. Homewinds is just a pissant little town that's scared."

It was a warm afternoon. Mushka and Gladys Michaels were sitting at the kitchen table with cold drinks waiting for Artie to awaken. Mushka had let Michaels's words settle in before responding.

"We know how some folks can never accept us—it's always been like that for followers of the Old Ways. Nothing new under the sun. We know a lot of folks would dearly love to see us all pack up and head for parts elsewhere. But Night Horse Creek and that ole swamp out there is our home. And we don't do nobody no harm."

"But the death of John Scarpia and the disappearance of Glen Favors—you can see how folks might conclude that y'all had something to do with things turning the way they have. And what with Willow being missing, too, and—"

"Oh, course, I see," said Mushka. "I'm gettin' old, not blind. But let me ask you this: do *you* believe the Fossor witches are evil?"

Out of nervousness perhaps, Michaels laughed softly. "No. No, not at all. Anything but that. Artie—she's everything that's beautiful in my life. She's suffering, I know that. Something has caused her to lose her magic. And I don't believe her aunt—who she loves very much—put a spell on her. But I do believe this: your family is in danger, and no one in Homewinds can protect you."

Mushka was, by subtle degrees, beginning to like Gladys Michaels. Saw honesty in her. "You in love with Artie?"

Michaels blushed. "Shows, doesn't it?"

"It does. And, you know, I'm glad to hear it. The Fossor sisters need all the love they can get these days. They need to be free of all the darkness surrounding them—love can do that, can't it? I mean, love has a way of settin' people free, doesn't it?"

Michaels's smile gathered warmth. "Yes, you're right about love. Sometimes it's the only response to evil."

TWENTY-SIX

"I told her how we're friends. But she doesn't need to know about the rest, does she? Oh, Glen, I can't share you—not with her. Robbie doesn't deserve you. She never has."

Gretta Fossor was waist deep in her Remembrance Pool talking, late morning as had become her habit, to the decaying body of Glen Favors. The warm weather and the swamp water and the rotting flesh combined to sting her nostrils, but she didn't mind. She was near him. Near the man whom she loved more than anything else she had ever loved.

But the ongoing alchemy of the swamp was changing her.

She could feel it.

The transformation into something savage—someone committed to revenge.

"I'm going now, my darling. You know I can't stay long. You know I have to be careful not to come too often. They're watching me. Watching what I do and where I go. The sheriff is suspicious and so is Robbie and others."

Wading free of the water, she sat down next to a cypress knee and brushed at her hair. She knew it was a mess. She knew that she looked like a wild woman—dabs of her lover's blood on her cheeks and forehead. Her war paint.

It gave her courage. Courage to face her enemy.

She glanced around.

"I know you're out there, goddamn you!" she suddenly cried.

The Terror.

The hateful creature that had taken the man she loved. Just for spite.

But she had vowed over and over again that she would get revenge. She would find a way to destroy the creature—with or without magic.

There has to be a way.

She bowed her head and sobbed softly into her hands. When she was cried out, she rose and climbed into her boat.

"Come again tonight, my darling. Come and walk around inside my soul."

Nearly every night he had.

His ghost, that is.

It would appear during the night and behave as if it were working on the cabin, building new rooms. Imaginary rooms. Building it for the two of them? And it made Gretta long to be a ghost, and yet she continued to reject the idea of suicide—what if such an act damned her to a realm where she and her lover could not be together?

It was too great a risk.

"Good-bye, my darling. May the Goddess watch over you."

As she began to pole away, she saw the panther drinking from a feeder creek. She met the eyes of that magnificent creature and knew that she could never enter into her thoughts—could never again be wild and free like her.

The weight of her situation pressed down upon Gretta on the return to Pan Island.

Guilt.

Suffering.

Her reasoning was this: had she not become the lover of Glen Favors, he would not have gone into

the swamp after being with her at the houseboat.
He would be alive. He would be his vital self.

I can't bear up under this, she told herself.

And as her boat drifted down the run, she
glanced around at the serene beauty of the swamp
and saw only death there. Where once the loveliness
of yellow butterwort and the silken, green tubes of
the pitcher plant would have captured her eye, now
she saw only ugliness.

The Terror had stolen life and beauty.

And, most of all, magic.

Back in her cabin, she sprawled on her cot as if
exhausted. She did not want to think. She did not
want to feel. She wanted only to be totally numb—
emotionally paralyzed. In that condition, she could
survive, or so she told herself.

The warm afternoon ticked on.

She slept fitfully.

Then was awakened by a knock at her cabin door.
Believing suddenly that it was Glen and that she had
only dreamed his death, she clambered from the
cot and ran to embrace him. But her visitor wasn't
Glen. It was her Aunt Mushka, greeting her with a
smile and a trio of gardenia blossoms so white and
perfect that they appeared to be made of porcelain.

"I picked 'em from the bush by my back door."

Gretta stood as if transfixed. She could feel herself trembling.

"Oh, Mushka," she whispered.

And fell into her aunt's arms.

"What on earth has come on you, dearie?" said
Mushka as she held Gretta's face, and studied her.
"What have you done to yourself?"

Before they went outside to sit together by the
edge of Night Horse Creek, Mushka took a washcloth and cleaned Gretta's face, then tried to run a
brush through her hair before abandoning the project. It mattered little. Gretta felt better simply being

in the presence of her aunt. They found a bit of shade under a willow, and she listened as Mushka narrated Artie's spider nightmare.

"But now what about you?" said her aunt. "What dark secret is in your heart? What's turned you into this strange, sad woman?"

"I'm not keeping a secret," said Gretta.

Her aunt knew better and said so. "It's leaking out of you like resin from a cedar tree. I'm guessin' it's about that deputy fella."

"Oh, Mushka, I don't want to talk about it. All I want is revenge." Gretta could feel anger rising in her, anger from visions of the Terror and flashes of scenes in which she imagined the creature taking the life of the man she loved.

"You know what's out there, don't ya?"

"Yes. And I need to know how it can be destroyed—because that's all that I'm living for."

Her aunt gestured that she understood. "That's what your sister, Arietta, wants, too. And Cavatina probably. The Terror is responsible for Willow being gone. I'm sure of it. We all want that creature to be out of our lives, but before we can get on with things, we have to get our magic back. We can't do that if all you girls are hating one another."

Gretta nodded. "You're right, of course. But magic is what we've always shared. If we don't have it, how can we be blood sisters again?"

"Maybe I have a plan," said Mushka. "Maybe I have a way to bring down the Terror as well. My old eyes are startin' to see some things. I could be wrong. I might be foolish. And I wish your mother could be here—I pray to her spirit for wisdom, just like I pray to the Goddess for wisdom. But the Terror won't let those prayers be answered. So, what I'm sayin' is this: all we have is each other. You and me and Arietta and Cavatina—we have to have the strength of all four of us or we won't have a chance against dark magic."

There, under the willow, as the Night Horse Swamp gathered heat, they embraced each other and felt a new alchemy—one of love and blood devotion—begin to transform them.

TWENTY-SEVEN

Nunc ex tenebris te educo.

Tina laughed at the upsurge of good memories. Sharing her deck with her at twilight was Aunt Mushka, and the two women were holding on to the day—and the beauty of sunset gilding the swamp—as long as they could before they surrendered to the amassing army of mosquitoes and sought shelter inside.

"How many times did you use that line to cheer me up? Whenever as a little girl I got into one of my funks, you would come over—I bet mother sent you, didn't she?—and you would say that you had some magic words to chase away my gloom."

Mushka chuckled as she listened to Tina recall her association with the Latin words.

"You fell for them every time," said the older woman.

"You were so convincing," Tina followed. "I mean, you would do this thing with your hands, and you would shut your eyes tightly and sort of grimace, and then when you said the words you would give them a whispery spin, and I just knew that they were *real* magic words."

Nunc ex tenebris te educo.

"Now I bring thee out of darkness," Mushka whispered, yo-yoing her eyebrows melodramatically as she translated the Latin. "And do you remember when those words helped you get your turtle back?"

A new round of laughter ensued.

"Oh, I remember. Aunt Mushka, I tried for years to figure out how you got my turtle—what had I named it? Yes, I remember: 'Ringo,' after the drummer on The Beatles—yes, that was it, and that turtle had crawled under the house and I bawled my eyes out because I thought I had lost it."

"It was just plain luck," said Mushka, "that that turtle came lumbering out after I said the magic words. I was on a roll, doncha know?"

A pleasant calm followed their exchange.

It was good to be together.

It was good to have the memories to share.

"Thanks," said Tina. "Thanks for coming over. I needed to laugh because all I feel like doing these days is crying."

She embraced her aunt, and then after swatting a mosquito or two they abandoned the deck.

"I brought something for you," said Mushka, once they were inside.

From a large paper sack she lifted free a tarnished silver case.

"Oh, Aunt Mushka is that—"

"Your mother would have eventually wanted you—as the oldest of the girls—to have it. For the magic it holds. And maybe for protection, too."

Tina reached into the case and pulled out the athame. Its black handle glimmered and the double-edged blade looked as wicked as sin. Holding it made her feel momentarily powerful. "You know what this makes me think of?"

"I believe so," said Mushka. "I hope, at least, that it reminds you of the last time you handled it—it was the night you girls had your falling-out. And I've been thinking that maybe now is the time to get the three of you back together."

Tina smiled. "You're right. It's just that it's not easy. Sometimes I feel that the three of us are so different and that we're becoming strangers."

They talked into the evening, keeping the focus mostly on Gretta and Artie and what Mushka had seen recently in their lives. And they talked, as well, of the Terror and of how it might be destroyed. But never far from their words or their thoughts was Willow.

"If she's out there, Mushka, what is she going through? How is she surviving?"

The older woman paused a moment, then said, "You forget that we all taught her how to survive in the swamp. It can't be easy, but it can be done. Physically she will survive fine. But I have to wonder what is happening to her soul—if the Terror has control of her, I . . ."

Tina pressed the back of the woman's hand to reassure her. "I don't know quite what to think. You and Shep have pretty much convinced me that she's out there, and I feel that I have to go find her, but I seem to lack the courage."

"This man you call 'Shep'—you and he becoming close friends?"

"I think so. I don't know. I really don't know him. In fact, I feel as if I'm aiding and abetting a would-be criminal at times. Sheriff Slaughter seems to have questions about him."

"But you don't?"

"Not those kinds of questions—I mean, he didn't have anything to do with the death of John or the disappearance of Favors and Willow—I'm sure of that. My questions have more to do with, well . . . with issues of fate."

"Fate? How so?"

Tina hesitated thoughtfully. "I want to understand why he's suddenly come into my world, into *our* world—the world of Night Horse Swamp."

"That sounds easy enough."

"It does?"

"Yes." Mushka's eyes twinkled as she reached out and cupped Tina's chin with her fingers. "Just ask him."

Tina was waiting for him around midnight, dead certain in her heart that he would come, for the simple reason that she sensed he was attracted to her. A woman knows—she doesn't have to be a witch to see attraction written in a man's eyes or to hear it in his voice.

But something was preoccupying Tina's thoughts as a nearly full moon rose over the swamp and pulsed its beams into her living room. It was Aunt Mushka's final question: *Are you falling in love with this man?*

"Am I?" she whispered to herself.

One simple answer was *no* . . . not love. Or not love in the sense of heart-pounding, passionate, sexual love. Willis Shepherd was no fallen angel. No handsome John Scarpia. And yet. And yet he had something about him. A quiet strength. A gentle touch. A presence.

And more.

Mystery.

Magic.

No, I'm getting ahead of myself.

She had questions about this man who called himself Shep and who seemed to live nowhere in particular and be aware of so much even as he was seen so little. He claimed to know about the fate of Glen Favors.

And he believes Willow is in the swamp.

In the shadows of her living room Tina closed her eyes and mused, "Who are you?"

A man's voice jolted her out of her reverie.

"The man who cannot return."

Tina swung around to find Willis Shepherd standing not five yards away, half hidden, one of his misshapen hands pressing his guitar against his side at a jaunty angle. He smiled the awkward smile of a man who had been withholding the truth about himself.

From a woman who was bringing light to his darkness.

For Tina the minutes of conversation, gathering intimacy in a moment-to-moment futurity, had a galvanizing effect upon her—just as she anticipated they would. At dawn, after he had left despite her invitation for him to stay, she replayed pieces of their dialogue in order to deconstruct it in hopes that fresh meanings would emerge.

"A man who cannot return to what?" she had asked.

That's where it started. Where the lines between two lives began to blur and, by invisible degrees, nearly disappear.

He had paused, not for rhetorical effect, she believed, but rather because he had not thought through the direction of his statement. "To being what I have loved being. To being what I need to be."

"I'm sorry. I'm afraid I don't follow you. You're a musician, a troubadour—a lonely, warm-questing spirit. A storyteller. What has changed that?"

Even in the meager light his blue eyes held her, eyes bluer than any sky she had ever seen. An almost preternatural blue.

"I haven't been exactly honest with you," he said.

"If you tell me you're in reality a serial killer or an FBI agent, I'm going to be very disappointed."

She liked his laughter. She also liked how hard he was trying to connect with her.

"I'm not really a musician or a troubadour, though I do love to sing and play the guitar. But, no, I'm definitely not a serial killer or an FBI agent—or even a Republican for that matter." Their laughter mingled warmly before he continued. "And I didn't just *happen* to be here, to show up on your deck the day your daughter disappeared."

"I had a feeling," said Tina, "that something transpersonal might be at work."

"Well, it is. But before I say anything more, I want to know if you forgive me for misleading you—for being so mysterious."

She drew herself deeper into the cautious intimacy of their exchange, then smiled. "Sounds like perhaps you didn't have a choice, so, yes, of course. There's really nothing to forgive. Not as long as you're willing to explain who and what you are."

"Okay, fair enough." He leaned toward her with his hands clasped and resting on his knees. For the first time since she'd met him, he didn't try to conceal those hands. They were badly scarred, and it was difficult for her not to stare at them. "Do you know what a 'Cunning Man' is?" he said.

Tina reflected.

She thought of her mother lecturing her and her sisters on the many traditions of witchcraft and the Old Ways. "Yes, I think so. A white witch. One who may possess psychic and healing powers, one who in former times was called to a small town or village to perform some supernatural service. Some task. For a fee or a gift of some kind. 'Cunning' from the Old English term *kenning*—meaning 'wise.' "

"Very good. Your mother taught you well."

"Is she responsible for your being here?"

"Yes, indirectly at least. I've been aware of the situation here for a number of months beginning just before your mother had her passing. I've known that the Terror is here—drawn here, ironically by your mother, who rightly believed that dark magic can often be benignly protective."

"But when Mother's presence no longer controlled the Terror, it was free to . . . what?"

"To do the bidding of its dark heart. To take your daughter. To weaken or completely stop the flow of your magical powers."

Suddenly confused, Tina shook her head. "A few moments ago you described yourself as a man who could not return to being what you loved being, to being what you needed to be. Are you saying you can no longer be a Cunning Man?"

He shrugged, and there was regret in the gesture. "I came into the craft—I *became* a Cunning Man through heredity. Through my father and his father and his father before him. The Shepherds are said to be distantly related, in fact, to the great English Cunning Man, James Murrell. And I've always been very proud of my heritage. Proud of my role. Proud of my special ability to come wherever I might be called to deal with forces of dark magic. But something has happened to me here at Night Horse Creek—several things have happened—and now I find that it's hard to continue . . . I believe I'm losing what it takes to be a skillful Cunning Man."

He hesitated, bringing his hands, palms up, close to his face. "I'm weak. Too weak, I'm afraid, to help you and your family—too weak to fulfill what I came here to do."

"I sense that you have much more to share," said Tina. "If I make a fresh pot of tea, will you go on with your narrative?"

As she brewed the tea, Tina released herself into a fantasy of sharing her life with this man on the edge of the swamp. And of Willow joining them.

Pa-Po, too. And of all the Fossor women being close again.

And the Terror gone forever.

When Shep took the cup of tea from her, she said, "I want to know about your hands. Was there some sort of horrible accident?"

Setting down his cup, Shep raised the gnarled and scarred hands. "They're not so bad off that they prevent me from strumming my guitar. But, no, it wasn't an accident that did this. It was the Terror."

Tina grimaced. "You've fought with the Terror?"

"Yes, long ago and far from here. The Terror is ancient, you see. One of the denizens of the Otherworld—one that will live on until there is no dark magic in this or any other universe. Yes, I did battle with the Terror when I was bold and brash and thought I could defeat anything. Those antler blades slashed my hands. I could have healed them—I possessed that kind of power—but I needed to remind myself, constantly, that my opponent was extremely dangerous. And so I left my hands like this."

"You must have great respect for the creature."

"I do. In fact . . . perhaps too much. In my brief time here, my feelings about the Terror have taken on a different dimension. Something has happened that scares me—shakes me to the core of my being."

"What is it?"

His eyes pulled hard on her sympathy and understanding. "My fascination for the dark beauty and power of the creature has deepened. Deepened to the point, I fear, that it may prevent me from completing my task."

"But you must still feel that you can drive the Terror away . . . or you wouldn't stay, would you?"

He could suddenly read her thoughts. She knew that he could.

He could hear the questions she was silently asking.

Can you defeat the Terror?

Can you restore our magic?

Can you bring Willow home?

"I don't know," he whispered softly, sadly.

She held his hands and tried with her touch to erase his self-doubts.

"What do you need to be strong again?" she asked.

The shadows ticked on, and the room seemed to dissolve around her.

"You."

It was the answer she was hoping for. She raised his hands to her lips and kissed them several times. And then he continued, this time with a flood of words she knew he must say.

"I saw you," he said, "and this beautiful place a long time ago in my introcosm. I started falling in love with you beyond space and time. I would have come even if the moment hadn't demanded that I come."

"But doesn't your love give you strength and courage?"

He freed his hands from her grasp and shook his head. "I'm afraid that's not how it works. If anything, human love siphons off the magical powers I have. It's as if love and magic have, for me, a similar energy source and cannot coexist easily. It's something beyond my understanding. All I know is that I have grown to care very deeply for you, and as that love has grown, so has a certain regret."

She caressed his face and searched his expression as if hoping to find there some clue as to what she could say to reassure him, but what she found there needed something beyond words.

"Stay tonight," she said. "Stay with me."

But he would not.

And dawn found her adrift on a sea of memory, alone, lost.

And needing to be rescued.

He was waiting for her that next evening just where he had asked her to meet him. He had built a small fire there under Night Horse Oak, and as she approached him, his face bathed in firelight, she realized that she was, indeed, falling in love with him.

But she wondered who was rescuing whom.

He had been reading a book as she neared, and when he saw her he stashed it in a large backpack by his guitar and stood up. They fell into each other's arms and a wordless embrace held time at bay. And Tina was surprised at how good it felt to have someone to hold on to—the warmth of a man's body and the comfort of knowing that that man cared for her.

"Was everything all right when you left your house?" he asked.

"Yes, I . . . Should I be concerned? Is the Terror near?"

"No. But I sense that something potentially destructive is, though I'll have to admit that my powers of discernment are not at their peak. As I've said, I doubt that I'm going to be as much help to you and your family as I should be—as I need to be."

They held each other a few moments longer before sitting near the fire.

"It's so odd that you mentioned my house. I felt a tiny chill when I closed the door. Like a portent, only I couldn't determine whether it was good or bad. I mean, I had the feeling that Willow might be close. That when I returned she might be there, sitting at the kitchen table talking with Pa-Po, her grandfather. Yet, the feeling seemed to have an equal measure of alarm to it—I don't know. Ever since the day Willow disappeared, all of the energy I used to receive from my beliefs hasn't been there for me."

She could tell that he understood.

"It will come back," he said. "Your magic. I know it will. Somehow it will."

She smiled at him and leaned toward his face and kissed his cheek, and she felt that she was riding a spiral of love upward into the starry night. "I hope you're right. Not just for me. But for Gretta and Artie and Mushka. And for Willow, too."

Their exchange turned to reflections upon the beauty of the night: the sounds of the swamp, including the distant bellows of bull gators and all manner of birds, and, finally, to an even more reverent tone in which Tina found herself musing upon her mother.

"She was a remarkable woman," she said.

"Does it make you uncomfortable to be here so near to her grave?"

"No. Actually just the opposite. I sense her presence whenever I'm here."

"Do you sense it at this instant?"

"Only somewhat, and that surprises me. Is it possible that the Terror has the power to keep her presence from being evident to us?"

"It's possible. The truth is that despite my many experiences with the Terror, there is much I don't know about the creature—the rules of its dark fantasy, I mean. Unfortunately, the creature enchants me: it is elegant and subtle and all that it must be."

"You really are in awe of the creature, aren't you?"

"Yes. I hate to admit it, but I am."

"Mother used to say that the Otherworld has both beauty and horror and that beauty is not always doomed. Horror, she said, has the power to diminish us, make us smaller. Only beauty—and I think she might have added love—has the power to expand our souls."

"Magic has that power, too," he said. "One of the difficulties, however, is that dark magic can, under certain circumstances, equal the power of white magic. The Terror holds a tremendous reserve of dark magic at its disposal. And it is a seductive power. It frightens me."

"Don't let it frighten you tonight," she said.

"No, I'll try not to."

She suddenly remembered the book he had been reading when she arrived. She asked him about it, and from the backpack he retrieved a book with a green cover.

"Have you read the Harry Potter books?" he said.

The laughter they shared was muted and warm and laced with the pleasant irony of being witches—*real* witches—and finding much of interest in the popular books.

"Yes, of course," she said. "Willow and I have read them. But which one is this?"

He held it up for her as if he were about to lecture on it. "*Quidditch Through the Ages* by Kennilworthy Whisp. All you would ever need to know about the wizard sport."

Again they laughed in a teasing tone, emotions on the edge of embarrassment.

"Do you think this J.K. Rowling could be a 'Cunning Woman'?" she asked.

"Ah, most certainly," he said. "She appears to have what it takes. At least, she knows her magic inside and out."

"I wish I did."

"Don't forget that the real stuff is just a bit more complex than what parades across the pages of these marvelous books." He held the book lovingly and then added, "This is not all I have in my backpack. Check this out."

"Oh, marshmallows! How wonderful! I haven't roasted marshmallows for . . . well, since Willow was a wee child."

Mentioning her daughter's name almost instantly stole some of the warmth from the moment. But Shep was there to squeeze her hand and whisper her back to the intimacy of the evening. They cut roasting sticks and gorged themselves on the hot, sticky marshmallows and laughed at how messy they got and snuggled closer as the temperature dropped and a fine mist crowded in over Night Horse Creek.

"Thank you," she whispered. "Thank you for bringing a kind of magic back into my life. I've missed being with a man—and I've *never* been with a Cunning Man."

He chuckled. "I'm nothing to write home about. You, on the other hand, are everything a man—any kind of man—could possibly want. Your intelligence, your beauty, your warmth—you touch my soul, and you tempt me to want to change my life completely. To abandon the one I was born into."

She gazed into his eyes and saw how much he meant the words he had spoken, and yet she had no desire for him to become someone different because of her.

"Be who you need to be," she said. "If being that person permits you to include me in your world, then I'm happy."

"What do you feel for me, Tina?"

She flinched at the curious sensation of warmth and chill at the same time.

"You must be able to tell," she said. "What you need to know, though, is that I wouldn't be free to be the woman you deserve until the dark magic that has my family in its grip, that has taken my Willow away, no longer has power over us. We have to free ourselves from the Terror."

"I know," he said. "I understand."

"But will you help? Will you help us destroy the Terror?"

He turned away. The darkness of the swamp drew his attention. He seemed to lose himself momentarily, seemed incapable of responding. "In time, I will. Yes, Tina, I will."

Then he reached once again into the backpack. "Now I want to show you what I found during one of my many treks into the swamp."

Something in his manner caused Tina's nervousness to press to the surface. She giggled rather like a girl, then held her breath. When she saw the items, tears instantly welled in her eyes. She pressed her hands to her face.

Willow's textbooks, her satchel, her sandals, and her long, red dress.

"Do you recognize them?" he asked.

Speechless, tears streaming down her cheeks, Tina nodded.

And after they had held each other and shared a passing of time deeper than words, he looked down into her face and said, "I'll take you home now."

"But won't you stay with me?"

He shook his head. "I need to go into the swamp again. This time I need to go with my soul and not just my body. I have to recover all the things I've lost—courage and more. Because if I don't recover them, I won't be able to help you . . . and you won't be able to love me."

"No, please," she said. "Don't say it like that."

But he held her by her shoulders, and she knew that she could not make him change either his mind or his words.

"You'll come back when you're ready, won't you?" she said.

"Yes, and then we'll go after Willow and perhaps then a new family will take shape. If the Goddess allows it—and it harms no one. Time is of the essence because Midsummer will be here in two weeks. Magic of all forms will be at their strongest. That includes the dark magic of the Terror. The creature has to be defeated before Midsummer breaks upon us . . . or it might become far too powerful to ever be controlled."

Tina could see that he had more to say, but she didn't press him.

They kissed and said good night, and then he was gone, blending with the shadows and mist as if he were a gust of wind.

Standing at the door to her modest home, Tina felt very alone, and in her thoughts one word—one mysterious, magical word—blazed.

Coda.

Pa-Po was blessedly asleep.

After she checked on him, Tina returned to the kitchen and spread out the items Shepherd had given her: *Willow's.*

She touched each one lovingly, and though she tried to hold back the rush of emotions, tears came. She missed her daughter tremendously and wondered whether she would be able to wait for Shepherd to recover his powers before she would join him to go after Willow and bring her home. Midsummer was approaching. Nature would be alive. The swamp would be darker and more mysterious and threatening than at any other time of the year.

Was she being foolish to depend upon someone else?

A man? Hadn't she tried to depend upon John

Scarpia only to find that her trust was betrayed? Was Shepherd any different?

I love him.

And never had she fallen so quickly in love with a man.

The reality of it all frightened her.

"Mother?" she whispered.

But though she had momentarily sensed a presence, when she glanced around at the shadows nothing materialized. She looked down again at Willow's things, choked back another round of tears, and decided that it was time to turn in.

Patience.

That's what she told herself she needed. And a new beginning on the road to trusting a man.

Willis Shepherd. Cunning Man.

She needed him to be her hero. Her savior.

But she knew that even as she was forming a bond with the curious stranger, she remained perfectly capable of fighting her own fights. She was a single mother; she had built a business on her own—she was strong and resourceful and could protect herself if necessary. Yes, her magic had been diminished—her ability to cast spells had virtually evaporated—and yet she did not feel defenseless.

And with that thought she went to her dining room sideboard where she had placed the silver box containing the athame. She gripped the weapon, and as she did so she felt an upsurge of savagery. Yes, it was there if she needed it. She would place the knife under her pillow and maybe she would dream of blood. Or dream of protecting those she loved from the Terror.

Yes, she would be fearless.

She would be a woman filled with wilderness, but she would also be a woman capable of loving and seeking intimacy and trusting . . . once again.

Minutes later, as she was about to undress, and

as she was entertaining a fantasy of lying naked in the arms of her new love, a sudden pounding on the front door caused her to suck in her breath and reach for the athame. The insistent pounding continued. She had no idea who it could be at that hour, well past midnight.

When she opened the door, the young man almost fell into the room.

"Mrs. Fossor, I'm sorry, ma'am. But you're in danger. A whole lot of danger."

"Emil Sinclair? What is it? What is this about?"

Out of breath, sweat beading on his forehead, the young man stood nervously, his hands rigid and trembling. Even as he blurted out his words he looked over his shoulder in the direction of the ferry dock. "It's my brother. It's David. Oh, God, he's coming, Mrs. Fossor."

"What does he want?"

"Don't you see? There's no time to talk. He and about three or four others from the Torch of Dawn—his goons—they're coming, and I think they plan to burn you out, to burn your home and your aunt's, too, I'd bet. You can't stay here. You have to—"

Joe Boy's plowshare signal suddenly rang out into the night, and Tina could see, through the rectangular panes of glass in her door, several dark figures approaching from the dock. Like a scene from an old horror movie, they were carrying torches, and she could hear one of them shouting something about not suffering a witch a live. Ugly voices filled with violence and hatred.

Emil Sinclair was insistent. "You have to go—now! He's serious! He's crazy, Mrs. Fossor. You can't stay here."

"I'll call the sheriff," said Tina.

"No, there isn't time. You have to get out now."

As they dashed through the house to the back

door, Tina heard glass breaking and smelled smoke.
The torching had begun. David Sinclair and his
witch-hunters were setting the night on fire.

To their minds—cleansing it of evil.

First light.

Tina was sitting on the ferry dock cupping a mug
of coffee with hands still shaking in the aftermath
of the terror-filled night. There was blood on those
hands. Her Aunt Mushka had gone for water and a
washcloth to clean them. Artie was there, too, her
face a mesh of worry wrinkles. Gretta was up near
the house talking with Sheriff Slaughter and Emil
Sinclair. Joe Boy was sticking his head in and out of
one of the broken windows. Pa-Po had gone back
to bed.

Shepherd, though, had fled the scene.

Tina understood. It would not have been wise for
him to stick around.

David Sinclair, a severe wound to his shoulder,
had been taken away in an ambulance on the other
side of the spit. His three companions had been
arrested and transported to the sheriff's office by
two of his deputies.

Tina could not escape the feeling that it had all
been a bad dream.

A nightmare. But not real.

"Here, darlin,' let me clean you up. You doin'
better?"

Aunt Mushka, bearing an almost comical degree
of concern in her face, hunkered down near where
Tina was sitting and began to scrub at the blood
that gloved Tina's hands.

"I don't know how I am," said Tina.

But a replay of events had started to reel through
her thoughts. Not a clear or accessible linear narrative—just pieces, images, and raw moments—

flames and cries of dark retribution and an act or
two of magic.

One scene dominated.

Having escaped the house with Emil Sinclair, she
had realized that Pa-Po was still inside. Tearing away
from the young man's grasp, she had raced back in,
her only intent being to rescue her father-in-law.
The old man, clad only in a T-shirt and underpants,
had clawed himself awake as Tina shook him. Seeing
her with the athame in hand had frightened him.
On top of that, he had wanted to take the time to
put on his overalls.

"No, Pa-Po! We have to get out. The house is on
fire."

The smoke alarm had been beeping its nasally
warning.

And then, in the swirl of confusion, Pa-Po had
not followed her out, turning inexplicably instead
toward the kitchen. Tina had gone after him and
that is where she had met David Sinclair, torch in
one hand, a white-covered Bible in the other.

"Die, witch!" he had shouted. "Burn in your own
den of hell!"

The moment lost all clarity. In reflecting, she
could recall only the sickening thud of the knife
blade ripping into David Sinclair's shoulder and his
scream of pain. And the next thing she knew she
was outside, scrambling to the side of the house that
was on fire.

And seeing Shepherd.

And watching, as if through opaque glass, as he
exercised his magical powers to put out the flames
with a flick of his scarred hands. Then running to
his arms and being held by him as she lost consciousness.

The reel of memory flickered to an end.

Aunt Mushka was saying something.

". . . Cavatina, honey, are you hearin' me? The

sheriff, he needs to speak to you some more. You feelin' strong enough to do that?"

Tina gestured that she was.

Yes, she was going to be strong. She was going to face what had happened. But when she felt Artie's embrace and, a moment later, Gretta's as well, she knew that the torch attack had siphoned off her strength, and had her sisters not been there, she would have fallen to the ground.

TWENTY-EIGHT

Gretta envied her sister for spilling blood.

She wondered how gloriously redemptive it must have felt to drive the blade of the sacred athame into an enemy such as David Sinclair. Although she knew she shouldn't have, Gretta had taken the knife from the scene. She had plans for it. With it in hand, she believed she would have the courage to draw the blood of *her* enemy—not a witch-hating, crazed young man—but rather the Terror.

It was midmorning of a day that promised to be hot and dry.

Gretta had left Tina in the supportive company of Aunt Mushka and Artie. Sheriff Slaughter was continuing to investigate the episode. Yet, it was likely no criminal charges would be lodged against Tina. She had stabbed David Sinclair in self-defense. He and his no good companions had tried to burn down her house. Fortunately, the damage was moderate and limited to only one side of the structure.

But the attack seemed symptomatic of the world of the Fossor women.

Their peaceable kingdom had been visited by violence.

They would have to meet that violence with their own violence.

Gretta welcomed it.

As she swept the small rooms of her house, she

thought about how she would journey into the swamp armed with the athame and hunt down the Terror and exact a bloody revenge for the death of the man she loved.

The man who waited for her at the Remembrance Pool.

She was adrift in those dark musings when she heard the panther scream.

It was a call. She knew it. It had to be.

Coda.

Yes, the panther, in the strange symbiosis that she and the creature had formed, was calling her into the swamp, insisting that she follow.

What is she trying to tell me?

Dropping what she was doing, Gretta gathered up the athame, then clambered into her small boat and started poling. She watched as the panther padded along nearly out of sight, moving steadily ahead, then slowing when she got too far ahead, slowing to let Gretta catch up.

"Dear creature, where are you going? Where are you leading me?"

Speaking the words softly to herself eased Gretta's anxiety somewhat. It was a spellbinding situation—following the wild, beautiful creature as she coaxed her along familiar runs toward *something*.

Gretta knew not what.

But the first glimmerings of what it might be emerged as she approached the Remembrance Pool and saw three gators gliding silently to the same destination.

Oh, please, no!

And she knew what the panther was warning her about.

"No! No! No!"

Gretta screamed at the top of her voice as she plunged from the boat, athame in one hand and the pole in the other. But the gators had sniffed out

the decomposing body of Glen Favors and were intent upon devouring it.

"No-o-o!"

Wading into the trio of gators, she began to stab
at the rough, dark green bodies, heedless of the
danger she was putting herself in. She could see
that while two of the gators had retreated slightly,
one had a grip on the sheeted body of Favors.

She stabbed at its back and then was knocked
down by the swish of its strong tail. Thrashing about
in the water, she righted herself and began again to
attack the gator. Blood billowed up mixing with the
dark water. She smelled it. She stabbed as hard and
as furiously as she could, but it was no use. She
could not dispel the most vicious of the gators, and
she could see that the other two, confident now that
they, too, could share in the spoils of the morning,
were advancing.

Gretta screamed.

But she was too weak to stop the beasts.

She began to sob as she turned her back on the
scene and waded to safety.

When she looked over her shoulder one more
time, she saw something extraordinary.

In the midst of the frenzied gators, the figure of
the Terror rose from the pool as if it had been lying
in wait at the center of the earth. Its antlers glis-
tened in the late morning dappling of sun and shadows and droplets of water; its eyes were dark and
brooding, and its presence spoke of something
primitive and otherworldly.

Gretta found that she could not hold her gaze
upon it.

For it was too frightening to behold.

But the horrors did not cease.

And Gretta could do nothing to prevent the Terror from stealing the corpse of the man she loved.
Once the gators had been chased away, the magnifi-

cent creature had lowered itself into the pool and
disappeared.

The swamp lapsed into a preternatural silence.

The sheeted corpse of Glen Favors floated to the
surface.

And then became animated.

Gretta gasped in disbelief at what she saw next,
for the corpse of Glen Favors began to move. It
stood, and the sheet in which she had so tenderly
wrapped it fell away. Favors was fish-belly white, but
to Gretta he was handsome even in death. The
strength of his facial features ghosted out from the
puffy, bloated skin and flesh. The gator had torn
away part of one arm and some of the flesh along
his ribs; she stared at what stood before her and
could recall how perfect that body had been—how
it had felt to caress that body and to be touched by
those hands.

Suddenly his eyes opened.

But he seemed not to see her.

Then something came over him, and at first
Gretta assumed that she was only imagining it: imagining that his face disappeared and became merely
a featureless mask of flesh. It was hideous to see.
Gretta screamed.

And the faceless corpse began to walk zombielike
as if under the command of some zombie master.
With eerie, mechanical steps, the corpse strode deep
into the swamp as Gretta, powerless to prevent it,
could only watch as what had once been Glenn Favors slipped out of sight.

TWENTY-NINE

She knew he was watching.

And it delighted her. She could imagine that his boyish lust was generating saliva that would escape from the corners of his mouth in thick strands. She could imagine his eyes going glassy, yet focused on her every move. She giggled at the thought of his penis growing erect.

It wasn't kind of her, of course.

Her mother would not have approved. Neither would have Aunt Mushka. Perhaps Gladys Michaels would have understood. But Artie did not care. As the late morning warmed, she stood where she knew Joe Boy could see her, and she began, with her left hand, to unbutton her white blouse. She could imagine that with each button the boy would swallow back his desire and stare harder. Button by button. Then the blouse opening to reveal the gleaming whiteness of her push-up bra, the cups barely containing the swell of her breasts.

She slipped out of the blouse and stood in clear view of her back window, pretending that she did not know she was being watched. Then she began to unzip her pink shorts, pausing as the zipper reached bottom and the whiteness of her panties could be seen. Because the shorts fit tightly, she had to tug at them and grind and bump her bottom back and forth to work her body free of them.

She smiled to herself at the effect she knew she was having on the boy.

I need this, she told herself, as if reminding herself that despite what the Terror had done to her right arm and hand and to the right side of her face, she was still a sexually desirable young woman and that to be desired in that way gave her a certain kind of strength she could obtain from no other source.

The sight of her spider tattoos caused her to shiver, but at least they weren't moving.

In only her bra and panties she stood and began to trail her left hand up from her left knee, up along her thigh, then to the inside of her thigh, hesitating at the line of her panties, then moving up to her stomach and gently rubbing there. Just above the ring in her navel. Just above one of the spiders.

She closed her eyes and smiled again and held the smile.

Imagining . . . imagining . . . almost envying what a man (or a boy) must feel when he is captive to sexual desire.

The hand then snaking behind her to unclasp the bra.

Hesitating as her breasts heaved slightly before gently resting against her flesh.

Then removing the bra and laying it aside before her hand returns again to her stomach and then slides up between her breasts. Then flattening her palm against one nipple and pressing hard as her tongue slips between her lips and she lets her head fall back slightly. And she sways from side to side and reaches down to remove the panties all in one continuous motion, leaving her invitingly naked.

She walks to the window and raises it and calls to him.

"Joe Boy, please come in."

She is delighted by how openmouthed nervous he is. But he cannot resist.

He is sweaty. More from his arousal than from the heating of the day. Or so she assumes. He balks at first. But her eyes convince him to stay. She says nothing as she helps him take off his clothes. His throat clicks in nervous anticipation, and she laughs softly and pulls him to the edge of her bed and they sit and she strokes his warm, moist cheek and says, "I need you to be with me, Joe Boy. Will you lie with me, please? I need to be held, and I need someone to listen."

He is speechless. His body is stiff.

She is pleased to see that his penis is erect, though he tries somewhat to hide it with his hands. He is embarrassed. Uncomfortable. He suddenly starts to dash away, and she has to grab his arm and hold him and coax him back.

"Please, Joe Boy. I need you. Please."

His eyes swim in a swirl of confusion. She sees how deep his anxiety is. She leans over and kisses his forehead and takes his hand and gently presses it to her breast, and he is trembling like a very frightened dog. She smiles and then laughs warmly when she hears him hiccup. She looks into his eyes and fears that he might be on the edge of tears.

"It's okay, Joe Boy. You're my friend. I like you. When two people like each other, they give each other affection. They like each other's body." She pauses to put her hand over his hand, a hand that is tentatively fingering her nipple. "I like your touch," she says. "Won't you lie here with me under the sheet?"

He is breathing hard with his mouth open. Like a fish.

His body is very warm as she lies on her back and holds him against her, his head nestled at her throat.

"Joe Boy, I know that all of this is hard to understand. But I'm a woman, and I need to be desired.

The Terror has stolen my magic. I can't exercise my magic as before, and I need to feel wanted. The Terror has taken so much from me and from my sisters and from Aunt Mushka, too. And I think the Terror has taken Willow."

With the mention of Willow's name, she feels his head jerk. He clears his throat as if to speak, but no words are spoken. She believes that she could hear his heart beating.

"It's all right for us to touch, Joe Boy. Nothing will happen to you. Nothing bad. I won't put a spell on you or anything like that. You're not afraid of me, are you?"

He shakes his head.

She loves the feeling of power she has over the boy. It feels good because she has become, otherwise, so powerless—so dependent upon others. And she has the power to give pleasure, just as she once gave pleasure through the artworks she created. Through the magic that once coursed through her hand.

She would give Joe Boy pleasure.

And she would feel his desire for her, and it would help erase how dead she had felt lately.

"Joe Boy," she said, "I want you to enjoy this. Don't be afraid. Just let me touch you and make you feel very good."

Her fingertips tap at the head of his penis, and she hears him suck in his breath and then moan, and as her fingers slide down the shaft and danced along the glowing warmth of his skin he begins to thrust at her with his hips and to moan louder.

Until she grips his penis tightly and begins to pump it.

And she can feel his entire body throbbing, and she wants his penis inside her, and she spreads her legs and shifts to let him get on top of her. But then he cries out, and in the next instant she feels sticky

wetness on her stomach, and he is scrambling out
of bed and he is yanking on his clothes as if terrified.

"Oh, Joe Boy, it's all right. Don't go, please."

He escapes with the fury of someone who had
stolen something.

Artie lies naked in her bed and laughs.

And feels stronger than she has felt in weeks.

It was twilight, and the portrait was not going
well.

Artie could not create the effect she was after—
not with her left hand. The charcoal was too difficult to control. The beauty of Gladys Michaels was
beyond her ability to capture. But she continued
because she had to see it through. Frustration was
building. Fear, as well. She had begun to think
about her sister, Tina, and the attack of the witch
hater and of Gretta and Aunt Mushka and Willow
and how their family—followers of the Old Ways—
did not deserve what had happened to them.

She tried to think about Joe Boy.

She did not regret her moments with him. He
would not forget—of that she was certain, and yet
as her eye marked the curve of Gladys Michaels's
jaw as she sat nearby on a stool, posing, believing
that she was being a good friend and lover, Artie
could not keep a dark image of the Terror from
seizing her thoughts.

"How is it coming?" said Michaels suddenly.

Artie's hand paused inches above the drawing paper.

She knew she would not show her dear friend
what she had produced. She would crumble it up
and start again—and this time pray that something
other than the head of the Terror would materialize
on the paper.

THIRTY

And so now you will go to hell.

Your head is filled with sin. It is leaking out of your ears like blood and out of your nose like snot. You remember how it got there. Every moment.

You have been sinful with Artie, beautiful Arietta, and when anyone looks at you they will be able to tell that you have been sinful. Maybe without even looking at what is dribbling from your ears and nose. You will be marked with sin—like a stain. Like the stain of blackberry juice. Like one of Artie's tattoos that you felt moving beneath her skin when you were in her arms and sinning with her. You are glad that school is out for the summer. Your classmates and teacher won't have to be around a sinner like yourself.

You wish that sinning didn't feel so good. But it does.

You can't eat your lunch.

"Joseph, are you feelin' poorly?" says Miss Billie Ruth.

You are at the kitchen table, and you can smell yourself. Smell your sin. And you hope that none of Arietta's spider tattoos crawled from her skin under yours.

"I'm not very hungry," you say. You sip at a glass of iced tea and wonder why beautiful Arietta invited you to her bed. It's a puzzle like so many others.

It's a puzzle you won't be able to solve. No use wasting your time on it. She said she needed you. You won't ever understand what that means.

You are waiting for Miss Billie Ruth to announce to you that she knows that you have been in bed naked with Arietta and a stiff, hard dinkle doo and that you will go to hell before sunset. You watch her as she goes about cutting up vegetables—carrots and celery and radishes and a head of lettuce for a salad, though Mr. Buck does not like salads and neither much do you. Not like you like cornbread. And sinning with Arietta.

You are suffering.

Miss Billie Ruth is making you wait and think about your many sins—just *how many* you are not sure—before she delivers the bad news. You wait. You are very surprised when Miss Billie Ruth says, "Joseph, why on earth are you sitting around this kitchen when you could be out enjoying the day? Go on away from here and soak up some sunshine. Might could be somebody needs the ferry—have you forgotten about your job? Go on now."

She shoos you out like you were a bantam chicken pecking away in her garden.

So. You don't know what to think. You take your sinful self outside.

Mr. Buck is cleaning some kind of automobile part. You smell gasoline. He has yanked some part from his old pulpwooder's truck and he is scrubbing at it the way Miss Billie Ruth washes dishes at night.

And you think that maybe Miss Billie Ruth has assigned Mr. Buck the task of telling you that you're going to hell. So. So you go stand by Mr. Buck and wait for the dark sentence. But you are puzzled to find that he says nothing about your sinful ways. Instead, he talks about the weather.

"Never seen it so dadgum dry, Joe Boy. That ole swamp's gone go up in a frightful roar of flames one of these days. All's it gone take is somebody's cigarette butt or a stroke of lightning—just one, then, blooey—up she'll go."

"It is real dry," you admit.

Mr. Buck stops cleaning the thingamajig and stares at you a moment before he returns to his chore. "A good day for a boy to be fishin' or swimmin', ain't it?"

"Yes, sir, it is."

You wait. Seems like he would have said something about hell by now.

You are very, very puzzled.

You decide to go into the swamp to think.

And maybe wash away some of your sins. You've heard that sins can be washed away, so maybe you'll try it. You'll also try to wash Arietta out of your thoughts.

That won't be easy.

You're also thinking about Willow and wondering if she ever thinks about you and if she somehow knows about your sinning with Arietta and whether Willow ever plans to come home again.

You wonder what God is up to today.

Maybe planning to punish a sinful boy.

You just don't know.

Things get worse when you meet up with the tookbird.

You had been swimming in a deep run and thinking about Arietta's nipples—just couldn't help it—and you don't feel that many of your sins have been washed away and so you are kind of blue and you decide to crawl up among some cypress knees and let the ole mother swamp talk to you.

Well, not really in words you could make out. But, all the same, the swamp has been stirring. You can feel it. Gives you an itchy sensation—which you don't like much. These days the swamp is getting meaner. Better watch out, you tell yourself. And so

you are sitting and trying very hard *not* to think of
Arietta and this took-bird flies up and lands on a
cypress knee a few feet away. It is a little yellow bird
that some folks call a water thrush, and while it's
not unusual to see them in the swamp, you particularly notice this one because . . .

Because it looks you directly in the eye.

Stares. Hooks you with its stare and won't let you
wiggle free.

You turn stone cold.

Because it's an omen.

When birds look inside your face like that, it's an
omen.

Of death, most likely.

Then it flies away. And you shiver.

You figure that God sent the took-bird.

And you know why.

It's deeper in the day now. Late afternoon. Hot.
Humid. Slow heat cooking the swamp and all kinds
of creatures out sunning themselves: turtles, gators,
snakes, frogs—sunning themselves and watching
you, a sinner among them.

You notice how creatures these days aren't much
afraid of you.

Something has turned them—that is, colored
their blood mean and fearless. You notice three or
four gators that have their eye on you. A snapping
turtle looks at you with hunger in its jaws. The more
you glance around, the more you get the feeling
that everything in the swamp with a heartbeat would
like to suck you dry of blood.

There is death in the air.

Yours maybe.

Up among some reeds you see a cottonmouth
moccasin, black and thick in the middle, hunting
for frogs most likely, and it occurs to you that maybe

rather than waiting for the swamp to get you dead, maybe you ought to do it yourself.

Just wade on over and ask that cottonmouth gentleman to do the deed.

Or better yet, catch his tail and swing him around and cuddle him to your neck just the way the beautiful Arietta cuddled you to her neck and just let that poisonous gentleman sink his fangs into your big ole throbbing vein and pump a shit load of venom into you. "Shit load" you borrowed from Mr. Buck—you hope he won't mind if you use some of the words he can't use around Miss Billie Ruth.

You imagine yourself smiling after that moccasin has delivered his dose of death.

You will smile because you helped out God.

One less sinner for Him and the rest of creation to tend to.

You wade closer to the snake. Now you can see that what you thought was a gentleman is actually a lady reptile because you see that she has a brood of young ones. A mama cottonmouth. She sees you and you are not welcome.

Some folks insist that a cottonmouth does not hiss.

They are wrong.

Suddenly mama cottonmouth opens her mouth and shows her cotton and that hiss you hear means you better move your ass, boy, because she's coming your way and it isn't to give you a kiss.

You swim away like you're on fire.

You keep on swimming until you make it all the way back to the ferry.

You crawl up on the dock and though it's pushing ninety degrees you are shivering like it's twenty.

You wonder if maybe that mama cottonmouth did you a favor.

Maybe she scared the sin out of you.

THIRTY-ONE

Keep your faith in the Old Ways strong.

Tina could hear the words of her mother and knew that she must heed them. Especially now. Especially with the world turning its sharp points toward the Fossor women. Especially with dark magic holding sway.

It was late, and she was thinking about her mother's wisdom and about visiting with Aunt Mushka, who had just left, having shared some plans and having made an unusual request. A disturbing request. But Tina loved Aunt Mushka, and she knew that Gretta and Artie did, too.

And Willow.

Yes, Willow loved Aunt Mushka very much.

Lonely and melancholy, Tina had gotten out the photo albums of Willow as a small child and found herself smiling at her dark-eyed daughter's growing-up process and feeling pride in her intelligence and the sensible way in which she had embraced the Old Ways.

And Willow's symbiosis with the swamp.

She'll be okay.

Yes, Tina had reached the point at which not only had she become convinced that Willow was somewhere in the swamp, but also she had assured herself that Willow would be safe there, that she could take care of herself.

But will she ever return?

It seemed an odd question, and yet, it seemed to fit the moment. What Tina feared was not that the Terror would physically harm Willow but rather that the creature would *change* her, work its dark alchemy and transform Willow into someone who could no longer live in the real world.

And what about that real world?

Tina had told authorities that she did not expect them to continue an official search for her daughter—she told them, a lie of sorts, that she had accepted the obvious possibility that her daughter was gone. Forever.

As to the incident of David Sinclair's attack—there would be a hearing and, quite likely, a trial, depending upon the nature of the charges Tina wished to file. Assault at the very least. Attempted murder another possible avenue. But Tina's thoughts were not on that frightening scene. The damage to her home would soon be repaired. The Torch of Dawn would probably not continue to be a threat to her or the other Fossor women. True, she wondered about the disappearance of the athame, but she assumed that one day it would turn up. Sadly, however, the Sinclair attack had led to John Scarpia's relatives coming for Pa-Po, maintaining that it wasn't safe for him "to live with witches." She couldn't blame them, though she sensed that the old man did not want to leave. She had no legal right to keep him—it was out of her hands, she reasoned. And there were other, more pressing worries.

Her preoccupation was with Shepherd and, relatedly of course, Willow.

She had told her Aunt Mushka about him and about her feelings for him, and it was upon that lead that her aunt had confided in her: "I'm goin' into the swamp, doncha know, to bring back Willow."

And it did no good for Tina to protest, to encourage her to wait until Shep returned. Aunt Mushka was resigned. She would not go alone. "I'll get Joe Boy to go along for company. He knows the swamp, and, like you said, he's seen Willow. Maybe he can find her. Maybe I know a way to take her from the Terror."

There was one thing more.

"Cavatina, you promise me this, darlin.' If I don't come back, burn the book. You hear me?"

Though Tina protested, she issued a promise.

And she knew that the book was a reference to Anna Fossor's Book of Shadows.

Destroying it seemed a gesture of desperation, but Tina agreed if the move became necessary.

"You'll come back," she said. "I know you will. And so will Shep, and when he does we'll all find a way through this darkness. We'll find strength in the Old Ways—strength and hope."

THIRTY-TWO

"I don't plan on comin' back. You need to know that up front."

The moon was full and bright, but the witches of Night Horse Swamp were not engaged in occult practices or rituals of any kind, in fact. Aunt Mushka was sitting with Joe Boy on the ferry dock, their legs dangling over the end as if they hadn't a care in the world.

And yet, the conversation was very serious.

Aunt Mushka was going into the swamp.

After Willow.

When Joe Boy continued his silence, Mushka kept her tone even and matter-of-fact. "If sacrifice is what it takes, then that's what I'll do. If I have to sacrifice this ole self to release Willow, then the Terror can have me whole—it doesn't matter. Not if we get our Willow back."

Silence ticked on between them as if they were not even within hollering distance instead of just a foot or so apart. Mushka could feel Joe Boy's nervous tension. She had asked him to go with her, and she had assured him that Miss Billie Ruth and Mr. Buck knew that she needed him. She was preparing herself to go an extra mile or two to make sure the boy said yes.

"The swamp's turned shadow," he said, finally, and in a small voice.

She nodded. "I know. I've seen it, too."
Turned shadow.
It was the way folks talked about the swamp when
they saw evidence that dry weather or some other
phenomenon was working on the mysterious place,
affecting the animals and giving off the general impression that people were less welcome there than
ever.

"We might could get killed out there," he added.

"It's a chance I gotta take, Joe Boy. And if you
care about Willow as much as I think you do, you'll
take that same chance."

"The gators are all fussed up and mean."

"I know that."

"And Willow, she told me she don't want nobody
comin' after her. She told me that. She spoke right
in my head."

Mushka said she understood, but she pressed on.
"Seems to me there's somethin' else botherin' you.
Care to lay it out where we can see it?"

She heard him take an almost comically deep
breath. Then he issued a low whistle of regret and
said, "I'm sinful."

"You're what?"

"Sinful," he said. "Filled up with sin. Like an ole
tick fills hisself up with blood suckin' on a dog's
ear."

Mushka couldn't help herself.

She threw her head back and cackled. Like an
old witch. "Oh, lands—you are a case, Joe Boy. Sin?
Oh, my, that's a powerful notion for somebody to
have. But tell me this: how'd you happen to get
filled up with sin?"

She was barely regressing a giggle at the boy's
seriousness, but he was squirming uncomfortably.

"I don't think I want to tell 'bout that."

"You steal somethin'?"

"No'am."

"Well, I can't hardly believe you'd go out and kill somebody—so it's probably not that."

"No'am. Not killin.' "

"What is it then?"

"It's bad."

"How bad?"

"Miss Billie Ruth would say it's 'dirty thoughts' and more."

"Hmm . . . dirty thoughts, is it? More than dirty thoughts?"

"Yes, ma'am."

"About what? Oh . . . now was it about women?"

"Just one."

She put her hand on his shoulder. "But I'm guessin' it was not Willow."

"No'am."

Then she pretended not to know. "Well, it's a blessed mystery to me."

"It's somebody you know."

"Hmm . . . well, there's Cavatina and Allegretta—"

"It's Arietta."

"Oh, I see. . . . Well, she's a beautiful young woman, I know that's right. Lots of young men probably have certain kinds of thoughts about her—some women, too."

Joe Boy looked at her and frowned. "I just can't go. I can't tell you 'bout what I did. And I can't go because I'm full up with sin so far I'd sink the boat."

Aunt Mushka cackled even louder than before.

"Oh, you are a piece of fresh cornbread," she said. "But listen here: if you think you're all weighted down with sin, the best thing you can do is a good deed."

"Like what?"

"Well, like helping me bring back Willow. Can't get much more good than that, can you?"

For the first moment in their conversation Joe

Boy's frown eased. A shy smile climbed onto the corners of his mouth. "No, ma'am. I think maybe you're right. Doin' good might could do the trick."

"It will—just like turnip juice can make warts disappear. You and me are goin' back deep in the swamp and do the biggest good deed—we goin' to bring home our Willow. We goin' to shine a bright light on all the dark magic hangin' over this swamp."

And so it was that a few hours later—just a spell before dawn—they gathered in Mushka's kitchen with backpacks of supplies for camping out several nights in the swamp. Mushka said a prayer to the Goddess and then, for good luck, she poked her thumb and Joe Boy's thumb and shook the tiny drops of blood into Rosebud's milk dish and swirled the blood into the fresh milk and called the cat.

"This a swamp folk guarantee of good luck," Mushka told the boy. "That is, long as your cat drinks it. If not, you'll have bad luck."

Holding their breath, they watched the cat circle the dish, ignore it in that irritating way that cats have, and then, just as the old woman and boy had given up on the possibility of anything like good fortune for their trip, Rosebud began lapping as if famished.

Mushka and Joe Boy cheered.

"One more thing," she said. "We goin' to carry with us a fresh bouquet of swamp flowers. This'll do the trick."

The boy smiled at the sight of the gathering of fresh flowers: orange milkwort, pink gerardia, meadow beauty, dwarf laurel, swamp milkweed, and yellow star grass.

"It's beautiful—like Arietta," he murmured.

Mushka gave him an understanding hug and said, "Well, sir, enough of this. Daylight's burnin'—let's go get our Willow and see if we can empty all that nasty sin out of you. I got a good feeling—right down into my fingertips. Feels like maybe my healing touch is comin' back. I sure hope so. Way things are goin', I'll probably need it."

Gretta woke at the sound of the panther growling. She could tell it was very close.

Is it on the island?

Excitement as well as fear inching up her throat, she scrambled out of bed and listened. She found her flashlight and went to the front door and hesitated before opening it. She could hear the panther, hear her breathing low, raspy, fierce breaths. Part of her cried out within to try to scare the animal away—shout it out of her life. But another part wanted the animal close. Needed it close.

Steeling herself and lowering the flashlight beam, she pressed open the door.

The panther sat on her haunches and stared at Gretta.

Not a threatening look or a threatening move.

Then the animal did something that surprised Gretta deeply—brushed past her into the cabin and lay down in the shadows. Heart racing, Gretta went about building a small fire in her hearth, though the night was mild and dry. Together, panther and woman gave themselves to the reverie of the flames, and in doing so, something passed between them— Gretta, however, could not be certain what it was. All she knew was that it somehow involved going into the swamp and facing the Terror. And in that exchange with the magnificent panther, in the curious bond that formed between them, Gretta experienced an epiphany: she now saw Nature as a transpersonal force, unknowable even through the sacred processes of the Old Ways, a realm of mystery and beauty and darkness—and except for moments

in which man and animal formed a haunting symbiosis, Nature wore a mask of indifference to humankind.

And Nature could harbor dark magic.

"I'm coming," Gretta whispered to the panther.

And with that, the animal turned and padded
away, slipped out the door and across the island and
into the water and swam toward a sandbar where
Gretta's flashlight beam surrendered to the night.

Coda.

The word danced along the dark hallways of
Gretta's thoughts, seducing her to enter the Otherworld both praised and warned of in the tenets of
the Old Ways. She doused the fire and lost herself
in the smoke, hoping that her magical abilities to
see might have been galvanized by the panther. But
only one vision emerged.

The Terror, its pig eyes tiny and brutish, ghosted
through the smoke.

It held sway. And it defied Gretta's need to respond to the panther's visit.

Grasping for courage, she readied herself to go,
and when she had finished putting supplies into her
small boat she watched as, in the distance, another
boat moved silently down a watery road of moonlight.

Aunt Mushka and Joe Boy.

The swamp, she reasoned, was calling them, too.

To rescue Willow.

I'm going for revenge.

She had the magical athame, her weapon of
vengeance.

Glen, my darling, I'm going to do this for you.

But when she pushed off from Pan Island, she
could feel the dead, cold eyes of the Terror watching from its dimension within the swamp, from a
place never brightened by the rays of dawn, a place
of deadrise and silence.

*   *   *

The cold mist wakes you.

You gather a few sticks to keep the meager fire going, and you fight through the webs of the dream—not a dream *you* were having, but one that your friend and journey companion, Mushka, was having.

You have been a spectator in her dream. You have been privy to her thoughts, though you can remember neither the dream nor her more recent thoughts, the ones she had just before she fell asleep, and now she continues to sleep, curled up on the other side of the dying fire in her sleeping bag.

You stoke up the fire and huddle closer to it. The mist is cold and wet and you are almost miserable. Scared, too. Some. You know something: another boat has been following you and Mushka. Someone else is camping in the swamp.

You look across the flames and study the face of the old woman, her eyes closed, her mouth open slightly. You don't want to enter her dream again or her thoughts for that matter. It's scary slipping into someone else's dream, someone else's thoughts. But you and the old woman are close that way.

You like her. She is a strange friend. You like it that she admires how much you know about the swamp and how much she enjoys having you be her companion. You especially like how certain words course through her thoughts like brightly colored lights: words such as "love" and "sacrifice" and "hope."

You take those words from her thoughts and you juggle them in your own mind like colored balls. You try hard not to drop them. Love is everywhere in Mushka's thoughts—you've noticed that. She

loves life. She loves Nature. She loves people: her
nieces at the top of that list. Willow most of all.

You think maybe she loves you, too.

Love is close to sacrifice in Mushka's thoughts.

Sacrifice.

You remember Brother Owen talking about sacrifice as the main thing—the only thing that counts.
You have strolled around in Mushka's thoughts, and
you're pretty sure that her love for Willow would
lead her to sacrifice herself—to save Willow.

Hope is among Mushka's thoughts, too.

Hope in the face of evil.

The evil is the creature out there somewhere—
maybe watching you as you stoke the fire and watch
your old friend sleep.

It occurs to you that maybe the creature is just a
bad dream, but you reason that it's probably real.
You're certain it has control of Willow—somehow.
It's one of those things about dark magic you did
not understand.

You would like to have as much hope as Mushka
does. Something, however, keeps you from it. Your
sinfulness is what you suspect to be the problem.
That is part of why you have come along on this
journey. It's like Mushka said—doing good is a way
to get rid of your sinfulness. You hope that is true.

You have hope. Just not a lot of it.

You have fear, too.

A slug of it.

So you sit and the mist thickens around you and
the swamp is much too silent and you wonder who
else has journeyed into the swamp—and why they
have—and then you let your thoughts go where they
want to go and, sure enough, at first you think of
Willow. Willow with no face somewhere out in the
swamp. Waiting to be rescued? You don't know.

When Willow slips from your thoughts, you just
can't hold back what you think about next: Arietta.

You wonder if just *thinking* about her is sinful. You guess it probably is because you can't just think about her out picking berries and shaping clay figurines or eating a slice of watermelon. No, you think other thoughts. And soon enough you're thinking what Miss Billie Ruth would say are "dirty thoughts."

Of Arietta's nakedness.

And what it does to you.

You begin to think that sin is like those hungry gators that followed you and Mushka all the way to this hummock. Sin just doesn't let go of you until it's got you. Bitten into you and chewed on you and then swallowed you whole.

So you sit there by the fire imagining that you are in the belly of sin.

Eaten up and being digested.

It makes you shiver.

So you get closer to the fire.

Which doesn't help because the fire makes you think of hell.

Which is where you're going if you don't stop sinning.

Breakfast was fried apples and potato cakes browned just right.

"You sleep good 'n fine, Joe Boy?"

"No'am."

"Why on earth not?"

"I got to thinking too much."

Mushka laughed. "What's a boy thinking about so much that it keeps him up all night? You worried about finding Willow and takin' her away from the Terror? I bet that's it."

"No'am."

"What is it, then?"

"Just words—and thinking about bein' ate up by sin."

"Who-o-o, goodness—Joe Boy. You're somethin' else, fella. You got some kind of imagination."

"I wish I didn't," he said. "I wish I didn't have no more thoughts than a catfish."

"How you know an ole catfish don't think about things? Bet he thinks about supper. Bet he thinks about lady catfish."

The boy smiled shyly. "Lady catfish? Oh, you're bein' silly."

" 'Spect I am. Just needed to see you wipe that frown off your face. Can't start out again on a journey with a boy frowning."

Joe Boy smiled as large as he could and batted his eyes playfully and Mushka laughed and swatted at him with her new hat. It was a Tilley hat—all white with a shoestring lace you could use to tie it under your chin so a breeze wouldn't blow it off your head, but Mushka didn't want to use it, so she didn't. She asked Joe Boy what he thought of her hat and he said, "You're awful stuck on it, seems to me."

"Cost me an arm 'n a leg—it's a good 'n fine hat, doncha know."

Joe Boy nodded.

And then they broke camp, dousing their fire before loading their boat. Minutes later, they were deeper into the swamp as the day burned forward like a fuse on a bomb. It was hot before noon. They drank lots of water and sweated—"sweated like hogs" is what Mushka said—and they identified flowers as they journeyed and they noticed how all the creatures were more quiet than was usual. Bone quiet.

"Those gators are still followin' us," Joe Boy pointed out as they got into the current of a deeper run.

"I've seen 'em, and I just don't like the feel of things," said Mushka. "Do you?"

"No'am."

And they were both pretty sure that another boat was on their tail, though whoever was navigating was doing a good job of keeping out of sight. The old woman and the boy speculated on who it could be—somebody fishing was their top choice. The sheriff was a close second.

They stopped twice for Joe Boy to shinny up tall cypresses for mistletoe. Each time he did Mushka thought about the dream she'd had and thanked the Goddess that nothing strange occurred while the boy was up the trees.

By early afternoon they were looking for a resting place.

"Don't want to have a sinkin' spell," said Mushka, mopping the sweat from her face.

It was on the heels of her remark that Joe Boy started sniffing the air.

"You smell what I smell?" he said.

Mushka lifted her head and held on to her Tilley as a breeze kicked up. "Why, it seems I'm smellin'—"

She glanced, wide eyed, at the boy, and she could tell that he was growing excited.

"Yes'am," he said, "it's honeysuckle and kudzu— Willow's close by."

Mushka's hand raked nervously at her lips. "Oh, Joe Boy, I believe you're right."

Both began calling Willow's name and waiting as the boat drifted and the heat and humidity pressed down upon them. They got no response, but Joe Boy noticed a cutback feeder creek off to their right and they maneuvered into it. Quickly, however, the creek narrowed and grew shallow, causing them to have to get out of the boat and drag it along until the water deepened slightly, just enough for them to get back aboard and follow a slow meander.

"Seems like we's goin' in a circle," said Mushka.

"I'm smelling Willow again," said Joe Boy.

Then both of them looked ahead. Mushka couldn't believe her eyes. "Have you ever seen this before, Joe Boy?"

He was momentarily speechless. "No'am. I ain't *never* seen *this here* before."

In the next half hour they settled in on a small sandbar, all the while marveling at the scene.

"You reckon it's a sinkhole?" said Mushka.

"I'm gonna see how deep it is," said Joe Boy.

Mushka watched as the boy waded into the water a few feet, then made like an otter and darted under, his bare feet foaming up the surface as he dived out of sight.

"It's a curious place," Mushka whispered to herself as she glanced around.

Here's what she saw: an almost circular pool, maybe sixty feet across, the water blue green as opposed to the tea-colored water of the main swamp runs. Edging down to the water on three sides was the thickest vegetation she had seen anywhere in the swamp, replete with vines and tall woody stalks of something that looked like sugarcane or sorghum. The knobby hides of three or four gators could be seen in the floating hyacinth directly opposite her. All the growth on the bank was as green as green could be. Jungle green, she mused to herself, while on the side where she and Joe Boy had camped, there was a sandbar and then, a few yards away, another feeder creek carrying any overflow from the pool back out into the swamp.

It gave Mushka a slight chill to stare at the scene. While Joe Boy was under the water, searching for bottom, she took a chance and called Willow's name, but as before, she got no response. Seconds later, Joe Boy burst through the surface, shaking water droplets like a hunting dog.

"Deeper'n anywhere I've ever been," he said, gasping.

"Golly Moses," said Mushka. "You mean you never touched bottom?"

"No'am. Got down where it felt like hands was tryin' to crush my head, so I came back up then."

They stood on the sandbar and released themselves into the bewitching effect of the scene, one that invited thought to enter realms of chimera and incantatory netherworlds. Finally, it was Joe Boy who broke their reverie.

"I think Willow would love this place."

"Me, too," said Mushka. "You're right as rain."

And then they began to pretend she was there. Joe Boy snickered as Mushka talked to the imaginary girl they had conjured up, telling her how worried everybody had been about her and how search parties had combed the swamp for her and how her mother had put up posters all over town and had even been on WSFA television in Montgomery talking about the disappearance of her daughter. Mushka also mentioned the death of John Scarpia and some other bad things such as the fact that Glen Favors was missing and that a witch hater named David Sinclair had tried to set her mother's house on fire.

They didn't talk about the Terror.

"Oh, my heart aches for the real Willow to be here," said Mushka when the fantasy had faded. But not the hope.

"Mine, too," said Joe Boy. "Not really my heart—but, you know, I miss her."

Mushka smiled. She needed to change the subject. "Doncha sometime just feel like you want to

be far, far away from the dark things in your life? I
know I do."

She tapped at her chin pensively. She and the boy
sat down on the sand and she said, "Joe Boy, if you
could go anywhere in the world, where would you
go?"

He shrugged. "The swamp's as good a place as
any."

"Oh, there must be another place—you know, a
place you wonder about or dream about. New York
City maybe. Or someplace with mountains."

Drying in the afternoon rays of sun, he stretched
back on his elbows.

"I don't want to go to hell," he murmured.
"That's one place I'd rather not ever see. Maybe I
wouldn't mind visiting heaven—if there really is
one." He hesitated. "How 'bout you? Where you
want to go?"

Mushka sighed heavily. She was feeling good despite the heat and despite the fact that they hadn't
found Willow—not yet. The mysterious pool had
somehow transported her into pleasant projections
of time and place.

"Oh, I'd like to see the mountains and an ocean
or two. But I don't care about big cities or about
ever seeing China—too many dadgum people over
there. India's the same way. I don't know—maybe
what I'd really like is to visit a place I made up in
my mind. Sort of my own country."

Joe Boy scrunched up his face. "You made up
your own country?"

"I did."

"What's it called?"

"I call it . . . 'Vasaria.' Isn't that a good name? I
heard it somewhere, but I can't never remember
where."

"Yes'am. I like that name. I think maybe I'd like
to visit it with you. Could I?"

"Sure. You and Willow both—when we find her. I'll make you official citizens of Vasaria. I can do that because it's *my* country. I'm the king of it."

"You mean queen, don't you?"

They laughed, and then the wind picked up and before Mushka could grab it, her Tilley hat flew off and tumbled several times in the air landing atop the water but out of her reach.

"I'll get it for you," said Joe Boy.

But it was skating away from him as he swam toward it.

Mushka had just said, "Oh, please don't let it sink. It's the best hat I've ever had," when a little gust of panic hit her. And then she saw something that filled her old veins with horror.

She trembled on the sandbar in the aftermath of foamy water and blood and of screams from deep in her bowels, and she could recall nothing more than plunging in to save her friend when the gators closed in on him. She knew she had swung and swung and beat and beat at them, and she had tugged at Joe Boy and his cries of shock and pain could be heard from one end of the swamp to the other.

Truth to tell, Mushka did not know how she managed to get the boy to shore.

In one piece, that is.

She tore away his wet clothes even as he writhed and moaned and grabbed at his bleeding legs.

"Hush down now," she said. But all the blood scared her. The wounds seemed much worse than they were—when she realized the truth of that, by slow degrees, she calmed herself. "You goin' to be all right, Joe Boy."

He yelled and started to cry like a baby; then he

suddenly pushed himself up on his elbows and said,
"Is my leg gone? Is it?"

"No. My lands, no. Hush now, and lay back down
and let me see what them gators have done."

She glanced out at where the creatures had slithered away to the far side of the pool. Then, with
fear choking at her throat like strong fingers, she
blinked her eyes rapidly and smeared away the
blood from two sets of bite marks on the boy's left
leg. She breathed out in small, accelerating puffs of
air.

"Okay," she said, more to herself than to the boy,
"let me see what we've got here."

I need my magic.

The words branded across her thoughts.

One bite line dotted from the back of his knee
to the middle of his calf; the other on the front of
his thigh in a four- or five-inch gash.

"Not so terrible bad," she said to the boy, reaching down to pat at his face; it was waxy with sweat
and borderline shock.

He was losing blood fast.

Streams of it.

Prickly panic rising in her fingers and spreading
up her arms, she tore at the hem of her long dress
for a couple of bandages. The tearing of the cloth
sounded horrible to her. As if the fabric of every
ounce of her sanity were being ripped apart.

But they did little good. Too much blood. Cloth
soaking through too quickly.

Please, Goddess.

Then aloud: "Please, Goddess, give me back my
healing magic now or this here boy's a goner."

Joe Boy's eyes were blinking half blinks. The
whites were showing.

"Goddess!" Mushka cried out at the top of her
voice.

Her upper body heaved, and for a matter of seconds (minutes?) she went away. She disappeared. Into a white mist. She returned only when she felt it in her hands. The prickly panic had drained away, leaving her fingers and hands feeling different.

Feeling strong.

"Thank you," she whispered. "Thank you. Thank you."

She took another breath and pulled away the bandages and concentrated.

She pressed one hand over one wound, the second hand over the other, and she closed her eyes and maybe she offered a prayer or maybe she just imagined—imagined as hard as she could, as hard as her body and soul could allow—the flow of blood stopping.

And it did.

"What happened to your hat? Did we save it or did the gators get it?"

Those were Joe Boy's first words after he had rested and recovered some. Mushka had built a fire. Twilight was coming on.

She shook her head. "It doesn't matter, really. You tried, and doncha know it's my fault those gators tried to have you for lunch? I'm sorry, Joe Boy. I seriously am."

He looked down at his legs. Mushka had applied a few more feet of the hem of her dress as bandages, but the real story was the almost miraculous way in which the bleeding had stopped.

"You got your magic back, didn't you?" said the boy. "Lucky thing for me, huh?"

"I think it came around again 'cause I got so scared I was goin' to lose you. I prayed, and it sure felt good when my healing powers filled up hands— like rain after a dry spell. It felt more than good."

"Thanks," he said. "I owe you one."

"Don't go sayin' that. I did it 'cause we're pals. 'Sides that, what would I uh told Miss Billie Ruth and Mr. Buck?"

They talked some more and had a light supper and decided that tomorrow—yes, they could feel it—tomorrow they would find Willow. It was something to look forward to. And they were bathing in those good thoughts when an intruder came stumbling into the campsite.

Gretta looked half crazed.

But minutes after Mushka settled her down at the camp she and Joe Boy had created at the blue sinkhole, Gretta became more of herself again and ate some food and relaxed and listened to Mushka talk about the gator attack. Joe Boy wasn't all that strong yet; however, his recovery verged on being miraculous.

"I came to find the Terror," Gretta explained after she had heard what Mushka had to say and had expressed her concern about Joe Boy's wounds.

"I thought that was it. Joe Boy and I, we knew someone was behind us. Didn't realize it was you."

"You're out here after the Terror, too, aren't you?" said Gretta.

Mushka shook her head. "More interested in finding Willow and bringing her on home. But, we know that wherever Willow is, that's probably where the Terror's goin' to be. All three of us are likely foolish as we can be. We got no weapons to speak of—and we don't really know how to fight the Terror if it comes to that."

"I brought this along," said Gretta.

She held out the athame. Her hand trembled. And then she began to cry softly, and when Mushka had calmed her, Gretta talked about Glen Favors. She told the whole story. Everything.

"I couldn't help it," she said when she had finished her narrative. "I couldn't bear to have him taken away from me, but I see now that it was stupid, and I feel like the Terror is playing with me. Playing with all of us."

Mushka held her niece and told her that she understood.

"You did what your heart told you to," she said.

You got yourself saved. From the gators, at least.

Mushka got her magic back and a lucky thing for you or you would've bled to death and you suppose that would have been fair payment for the sinning you've done. And now it's the middle of the night and you don't like the feel of things—*too quiet*—and even though you've been saved, you don't feel like you're out of the woods yet. Not in terms of your sinning.

So you're determined to do some good: help Mushka find Willow and maybe even help Gretta fight the Terror. Your leg feels much better. You wonder, though, if you're strong enough to do whatever it will take to deal with all the wicked things rolling around in the night.

Mushka calls it all "dark magic."

The words swim through your thoughts like the biggest, meanest gator in the swamp.

You've had enough of gators.

More than enough.

Mostly, you'd like to be home. You'd like to be in Mr. Buck's chair.

Or, if you dig right down to the truth, you know where you'd really like to be: in Arietta's bed, and part of you doesn't give a shit if it is sinning.

That's just how you feel.

The night crawls on.

Gretta is asleep and so is Mushka. Or maybe not.

The old woman jerks and mumbles, and when she does you can hear her inside your head. It's like a shadow (or a ghost?) of her real self has stepped out of her body and wormed right into your skull and is talking to you.

Talking about a dream she once had of finding Willow and . . .

Some of what she's saying is drowned in static or something like static.

It scares you to have Mushka inside your head.

It's happened before. But not in the middle of the swamp.

Not somewhere on the other side of the night.

Dawn is glorious.

Mushka is up building a new fire and getting water ready for hot tea. She glances around at the puffs of gray-white mist rising from the sinkhole and she feels pleasure—the pleasure of submitting to a mysterious place. Of surrendering one's need to understand the length and width and depth of a place. Just be here, be here, be here.

If she could erase the gator attack on Joe Boy, this would be an absolutely delightful spot.

This would be the kind of area Anna Fossor would love.

And venerate.

Yes, there is something holy about this scene.

With the fire crackling and water boiling and strips of bacon frying, Mushka's companions rouse and shake off the night.

"I'll check your wounds after breakfast," she says to Joe Boy.

"Yes'am."

"I slept like the dead," says Gretta. "I don't believe I dreamed at all."

Morning unfolds.

Mushka shares with her companions the joy she feels in having much of her healing power back.

"Makes a body feel like singing," she says.

"You think my seeing powers have returned?" says Gretta.

"Have you tried them?" says Mushka.

"No. No, but I really don't want to. Not just yet."

Joe Boy winces as Mushka peels one of the bandages back to survey his injury.

"It's pretty sore," he says.

"Good. That means it's healing."

She looks at the second bite area as well, and with both wounds she touches her fingertips to the ragged cuts, closes her eyes, and works her lips silently.

"I think that helps some," says Joe Boy.

"It's supposed to. It sure is." Then she smiles broadly. "I don't believe you're goin' to die, Joe Boy. But you got to promise to leave gators alone."

"I thought I was. I never saw him coming."

"He was trying to rescue my hat," says Mushka, filling in the narrative for Gretta.

"Must be one heck of a hat," says Gretta.

"Down at the bottom of that sinkhole now," says Mushka. "But that's all right. I'm just glad Joe Boy's not in the bottom of the belly of one of those gators."

There is a warm, near laughter that spreads among them, and then they close into their separate worlds after breakfast and let the beauty of the swamp fall upon them like a gentle rain. They stay that way for a half hour or more. Time becomes pointless to measure. The sun is wheeling up in the sky and birds are calling and frogs croaking and insects buzzing. The swamp is very much alive.

No one says anything more until Gretta, sitting Indian style, lolls her head back and suddenly sniffs the air.

"I smell Old Spice," she says.

Her body tenses and she looks around.

"Honeysuckle and kudzu," says Joe Boy, and he, too, is looking around.

Mushka feels something catch in her throat.

Her eyes are drawn to the blue water of the sinkhole—and she hopes she is not seeing things.

Glen?

Gretta stands up. She doesn't see what Mushka sees. Neither does Joe Boy.

Not at first.

Gretta releases herself into the impossible, into a projection, a fantasy that the man she loves is still alive. He's out there somewhere, out there in the soul-arresting greenness of the swamp, somewhere just out of sight.

I have the right eyes.

That's what Gretta tells herself. She has the right eyes to see in the swamp, to see what others might not see. But she cannot see the man she loves.

Because he is not there.

"Mushka?" she suddenly exclaims.

Joe Boy comes to attention. He stands, and Gretta assumes that he sees what she is seeing: Mushka is wading out into the blue water, her arms extended, her hands gesturing as if in an invitation to embrace someone.

Willow.

Gretta gasps at the sight of the young woman.

She is naked and standing waist deep on the far side of the pool.

It is Willow, but she has no face.

Mushka is speaking, her voice cracked and thin and edged with a combination of fear and elation.

"Willow? Willow, honey? Oh, it's your Aunt Mushka, sweetheart. I've come for you."

Mushka wades deeper, and behind her, still on the sandbar, Joe Boy and Gretta watch, hardening their stares as they try to piece out whether Willow is an illusion or not.

The sun spears brightly into the serene area.

Mushka is choking back tears of gladness. "Oh, Willow, Willow. Your mama's goin' to be he so happy—all of us are."

But the young woman—if she is real—does not move.

Suddenly Joe Boy cries out. "Hey, look it there!"

Mushka, however, does not see what he is pointing at. Her eyes are trained upon the young woman so naked, so adorned in flesh, her face swallowed up in it.

"Hey! Hey! Come back!" Joe Boy cries.

And Gretta, seeing now what the boy is seeing, joins in the cry of alarm.

But Mushka does not, cannot see.

To her left as well as to her right, boiling up within twenty feet of where she has waded, mating balls of moccasins burble the water the way an outboard motor would.

"Aunt Mushka!" Gretta screams.

Then she and the boy are in the water, scrambling, reaching to stop the old woman.

"Willow, honey," she is whispering, "it's goin' to be all right. It's goin' to be good 'n fine. You'll see. We've come to take you home."

The wild animal stench fills the scene in the next instant, and between the old woman and her niece the water shatters like a plate-glass window. Gretta and Joe Boy hold back. The mating balls of snakes dissolve.

And the Terror rises from the depths of the blue hole.

It wears a horned mask, and it lives and breathes and grows strong in the surprise and confusion and

horror it creates. It buries itself deep in the souls
of those in its presence.

Then reality drops away.

You believe she will die.

You think about the words "scared to death" and
you once thought that they were just words, that no
one could really die of fright.

But now as Gretta tries to revive the old woman,
pressing on her chest and giving her mouth-to-
mouth resuscitation, you believe that you have lost
your friend.

"Joe Boy," Gretta exclaims, "we have to get her
to a hospital as quickly as we can. Help get her into
the boat."

And you do.

You don't want her to die of fear.

You, too, were shaken by the sudden appearance
of the Terror, but you remember little of what happened—only the eyes of the creature, eyes filled
with hate—and the nest of antlers and the smell
that burned your nostrils.

Coda.

You remember the word shrieking in your
thoughts.

The mystery word you had heard before.

"I think she's still breathing," says Gretta. She is
gently slapping the old woman's face, and then you
help her put her in the boat. "Oh, we've got to
hurry, Joe Boy."

And you see someone in the deep green of the
nearby foliage.

Someone watching.

But not moving to help.

You almost call out to that someone.

You know who it is.

But there is no moonlight for him to walk upon.

THIRTY-THREE

Tina couldn't believe how much at peace her Aunt Mushka appeared.

It was as if the woman had gone somewhere beyond sleep—into the country beyond sleep. And where exactly was that? Tina did not know. It was just one more thing she didn't know, and in her thoughts she had a spare room filled with things she did not know. She kept them there as if they were things she might one day need. Like clothing. A skirt or a blouse currently out of fashion. Some day it might be "in" again. Who could say?

"We shouldn't have let you go," Tina whispered into the silence of the hospital room where her aunt lay with tubes running to and from her body, dressed in a hospital gown that appeared too large. Or perhaps her aunt was shrinking. A white, sheetlike partition separated her aunt from a roommate who was recovering from an operation—Tina couldn't remember what kind.

She sighed, then got up out of her chair and stood by the side of the bed and looked down at her aunt the way people will look down at someone asleep, confident that they will be able to see something new there. A piece of that person's soul perhaps. Or some sign that they truly understand that person—have an intimacy with them. But Tina wasn't certain of anything like that simply because she knew her aunt wasn't there.

Wasn't just asleep. She was beyond sleep.

Coma.

The word made her shiver.

And she tried to imagine what her mother would say at this moment if she were there standing on the opposite side of the bed also looking down at the beyond-sleep woman, the "coma woman"—and offering her perspective on Mushka's decision to go into the swamp to retrieve Willow.

Tina closed her eyes.

"Mother? Are you here?" she whispered.

But no one answered.

Then a nurse slipped in to tend to the patient, and Tina decided to go back to the waiting room.

Her aunt had been in a coma for two days.

Doctors could not say when or whether she would lapse out of it.

They did not know, Tina assumed, what country beyond sleep Mushka was visiting.

Maybe she won't want to return.

It was an odd thought, and yet it fit her mood as she negotiated the hallway, alive to what an alien place a hospital can be, a place to which no one *wants* to belong.

But Tina was trying to concentrate on something else. On a question.

What next?

She had not heard from Shepherd. She missed him, and maybe, if she were to be honest with herself, she doubted him somewhat. Doubted what? His ability to help bring Willow back? Yes, that was certainly part of it. Beyond that?

Tina shook her head.

What next?

She was face-to-face with the implacable demands of "next."

And, worst of all, she doubted that her sisters could help.

In the waiting room, Tina let herself glide along in the moment, knowing full well that she was delaying considerations of what to do next. Where to go from there. Minutes later, Gretta and Artie and Billie Ruth and Buck Private and Joe Boy arrived to join her, and as a group they commanded two sofas in one corner of the waiting room, though Joe Boy wandered off down the hallway, limping slightly, to stand outside Mushka's room.

After a burst of conversation—mostly questions about Mushka's condition—the group sank into a nervous silence. Billie Ruth and Buck excused themselves to go to the cafeteria, leaving the three sisters to stare mostly at their hands or the cheap paintings on the wall or, fleetingly, to glance at each other's eyes as if to pick up emotional signals of some kind.

"We shouldn't have let her go," said Tina, the words slipping out as if they had come without volition or dropped the way a leaf on a tree suddenly might.

Gretta and Artie looked at her. Tina could feel their eyes as she herself studied her hands.

"She found your daughter," said Gretta. "She found Willow. She had the courage to go in there and find her."

The tone was both defensive and somehow accusatory.

Tina felt her stomach roil. "Do you think I should have gone? Is that what you're saying? Don't you think I want Willow back?"

Gretta shook her head. "I didn't mean—oh, I don't know what I mean."

Artie slid closer to her on the patterned sofa and draped an arm over Gretta's shoulders. Tina felt something rising in her throat, something she would have to swallow back just as she would have to swallow back guilt.

Silence, like invisible grains of sand, filled and filled and filled around them until it seemed to Tina that the three of them could not move. But all of it drained away when she finally spoke, her voice curiously flat and unplugged. Her words were directed at Gretta.

"Tell us everything," she said, "everything you saw."

Tina felt that there was no one else in the world as Gretta began to narrate events. Reality was an exclusive club of three sisters and perhaps a ghostly mother looking on from the Otherworld. And in Gretta's account, Tina heard how desperate her sister had been to hunt down and destroy the Terror, to get revenge for what had happened to Glen Favors.

Evidence of dark magic was everywhere in the narrative. Tina sensed how much the three of them were aware of it, but it was Gretta's closing remark that spun her into confusion and jabbed her with a sharp point of pain.

"Joe Boy said that when we were taking Aunt Mushka away . . . well, he saw your friend, Shepherd. He was watching. He must have seen the whole thing, I think. And he did *nothing* to help us."

The nurse tells you it's all right.

So you stand by the side of the bed, and you hold her hand and it feels funny—not quite warm and not quite cold, not quite dry and not quite moist. Your leg is feeling pretty good, and you want to tell her that and you want to thank her again for her magic. Without it, you might have bled to death—that's what everyone has told you.

You want to say something about the creature called the Terror, but you can't find the words. You saw the creature. You saw how it stood between Willow and those who care about her, and you begin to doubt. "Doubt." It's another funny word. You figure that it's a word that doesn't come from a good place, and you also figure that people who sin—boys like you—are likely to doubt. Maybe doubt is a sin.

You just don't know.

But you are beginning to have doubts.

You doubt that you will ever stop being sinful, because you can't seem to get Arietta—her body, especially—out of your thoughts. You want to be naked with her. A big sin. And you have started to doubt that anyone can ever rescue Willow from the Terror. The Terror is just that—a terror and more.

And now you doubt that your friend, Mushka, can ever be well again.

"I'm sorry," you mutter.

She doesn't hear you, of course. So you say it again. In your head this time, and you squeeze her hand and—in your head again—you say, "I want you to get well so we can be like always. So we can go into the swamp again and pick mistletoe and plants you use to heal with." You hesitate, bite your lip, and add, "I want you to know I'm here."

Something hits you like a spark of static electricity.

You almost let go of her hand, and you might have had you not heard her voice.

In your head.

"I know you're here."

You open your eyes and blink, and you see that a nurse has finished tending to the other lady in the room and when she walks by you she smiles.

After she has left the room, you close your eyes
again and concentrate and speak in your head.

"Are you feeling bad? Does your head or anything
hurt?"

"No, Joe Boy. I'm feeling fine because I'm not in
my body."

You blink and then you stare at her face. With
your other hand you touch her forehead. Her body
is there, no doubt about that. You close your eyes
again.

"If you're not in your body, where are you?"

"In a wonderful place."

"The swamp?"

"No."

"How far away is it?"

"It's clear at the back of my mind."

You have to pause to think about what she has
said. You don't have a place at the back of your
mind—as far as you know, at least.

"What's it like?"

"Wonderful. Oh, Joe Boy, it has mountains and
oceans and jungles. And it has castles and lots and
lots of magic."

"Sounds like a neat place. What's it called?"

"It's called Vasaria."

"I remember," you say. "That's your special place.
The one you made up."

"Yes, and I'm there."

"What you are doing?"

"Sitting by a beautiful stream in a deep, dark
woods. A magical woods. I believe if I sit still enough
and put myself in tune with nature, then I'll see
something very unusual."

"What?"

"A unicorn maybe."

You nod.

You've seen unicorns in books at school. You
know that unicorns are imaginary creatures with a

single, magical horn. Like a horse with a horn. Only different. The first time you saw one in a book at school you started to wonder if maybe the swamp had unicorns. But you looked and looked and never saw one.

"That'd be good. A unicorn."

"You know what I wish, Joe Boy?"

"That you could see a unicorn?"

"Well, that, too. But what I really wish is that you could be here in Vasaria with me. We could have a real good time. Lots of places to explore. Wouldn't you like that?"

"Sure. Yeah, sure."

Then there is silence, a long silence, and you think that maybe your friend is tired of talking in your head. But then you hear her. She sounds farther away.

"I might not come back," she says.

You don't know what to say at first.

"But you can't do that," you say. "You have to come back."

"Why? I like it here."

You have to think hard and fast. Your thoughts are on fire. You have to come up with a good reason for Mushka to come back—or else she might not. Really and truly she might not. You think so hard it makes your head hurt, and then you say the only word left in your thoughts because all the others have scattered—the way marbles scatter if you drop a bunch of them on Miss Billie Ruth's kitchen floor.

You pick up the one that's left, and you say it.

"Willow."

More silence. A scary silence.

"What about Willow?" your friend says.

"You have to come back because . . . if you don't, you won't never get to see her again. And when she comes home, she would want to see you."

THIRTY-FOUR

Willis Shepherd sits on the sandbar by the blue hole and hugs himself in defeat.

His guitar is at his side. It gives him no comfort. No songs can cheer him. No lyrics stir his soul. He cannot even sing of his yearning to have a wife and children and be whole and complete as a person, no longer a Cunning Man.

No longer a witch. No longer a follower of the Old Ways. Just a man.

I've failed.

"Goddess, I'm a coward," he murmurs, though he doubts that the Goddess is much concerned with him.

What he cannot do is erase the memory of seeing the old woman being confronted by all the horror and mystery that is the Terror. The full weight of that horror and mystery bore down upon her here at this curious place where the creature prevented her from rescuing the daughter of the woman Shepherd is deeply in love with.

I didn't help.

I couldn't.

"Oh, Cavatina, I am so sorry. I have failed you. I have failed your daughter and your family. Because . . . because I cannot overcome the pull of the Terror."

It is the pull of mystery. It is both magic and mystery.

A lethal combination.

So he sits and stares at his hands and considers leaving. Not just the swamp. He thinks of leaving who he is. Giving up his life as a Cunning Man to become—what? A drifter. A lonely, warm-questing soul on the road. Homeless. Loveless. For he believes that he does not deserve a woman such as Cavatina Fossor.

Or maybe he will end it all.

The possibility burns momentarily in his thoughts and he finds the flame of it fascinating. Yes, perhaps that is the way to go. Take yourself as far into the swamp as possible and then merge with its waters, embrace its darkness, and disappear.

He is suddenly resigned.

He rises and picks up his guitar and begins wading into the twilight wishing only that he could see the woman he loves one more time, though knowing that he lacks the courage to be the man he needs to be for her.

Moonlight is his companion.

Twilight thickens to night, and the night sounds chorus around him.

The swamp water is warm and reassuring. As he wades into the dark heart of the swamp, he regrets that he will not again look upon the magnificence of the Terror, its stark beauty, its ancient form, and that he will not again find himself in its arresting presence.

Dark magic.

He knows as he journeys further from the possibilities of love that the Terror is watching him, hidden, but there and everywhere that is the heavy darkness of the swamp. And the creature is pleased, he assumes, because the Cunning Man sent to defeat it has given up.

Surrendered.
Time and space begin to lose meaning.
Shepherd slogs on.
Until he hears music.
The death-of-the-day music.
And he is drawn to it.

"I've been waiting for you."

Shepherd is surprised by the old man who has been sitting on the front porch of his isolated cabin playing a saw. He is especially surprised by his words. He does not know this man who, though obviously blind, gestures for him to come into his cabin.

Inside, there is a low fire burning in a fireplace. Shepherd smells coffee.

"How is it that you know me?" he asks the bearded man who seems so at home with the shadows that dance upon the walls of his cabin. "Who are you?"

The man looks somewhat puzzled.

"I don't really understand how I know you," he says. "A kind of intuition, I suppose. I could *feel* you coming. I could feel how despondent you are, and I knew, somehow, that you were seeking me out. What we seek, seeks us. My name is Brother Owen, self-declared saint of the Night Horse Swamp. Blind and maybe more than a little batty."

The man chuckles, and Shepherd can see that neither truly knows what is happening. Both men are caught in a web of enchantment as big as the night sky.

"That coffee smells good," says Shepherd.

"Sit down and have a cup with me," says the bearded man. "And tell me your story. Everybody has one, especially when they plan to shuffle off this mortal coil."

Astounded, Shepherd takes a cup of steaming coffee and sits down in front of the fireplace.

"You knew that, too—are you a witch? A follower of the Old Ways?"

The bearded man's smile is warm and expansive. "No. Just a human being who long ago came back here into the swamp to find myself. To find truth."

"And did you?"

"Well, of a fashion, yes. Pieces of myself. And the truth? What I've learned is that if we find truth in any sense of the word, we find it inside ourselves."

Shepherd nods. "Sounds like wisdom. I'm in short supply of that at the moment."

"I had heard you around," says the bearded man. "Heard you playing and singing, but I didn't think you would ever show up at my door. But something dark and mean brought you—sent you, didn't it?"

"Yes."

"Tell me. Tell me your story, and in return I'll tell you the only thing that counts."

"It's a deal."

So the man called Shepherd talks for a long while about his family, about assuming the sacred task of being a Cunning Man—and of becoming attracted to the Terror and coming to Night Horse Swamp and meeting the Fossor witches. And of falling in love. And of failing.

Brother Owen has lit his corncob pipe, and when Shepherd concludes his narrative he lets silence crowd around them before he speaks.

"That boy you saw at the sinkhole—he's been here. He understands a whole heap about the swamp and is learning about life. I told him something a while back, and I think it's worth repeating. You likely won't agree with it, but all I ask is that you hear it and take it with you. Forget about your selfish plan to end it all. You have something worth living for . . . and dying for if it comes to that."

Shepherd stands up. He is not certain he wants to hear more. "But you just said that it was selfish to consider suicide."

"I did. When I say 'dying for,' I'm not talking about suicide. I'm talking about the greatest of human joys."

"Love?"

"It's related to love—it surely is. What I'm talking about is *sacrifice*. My feeling is that whatever is out there—that creature you call the Terror—the only way to defeat it is through sacrifice. It's something you have within you to give."

"I don't know what I have within me anymore. I feel hollow."

"You have it. I can tell you do. Think about it. If you have to, go out and walk around in yourself and let that ole swamp fill you up with what it means to be alive. Then, when you're ready, go where your love is needed."

"I've seen all of this swamp I want to see. What I'd like now is oblivion."

"A poor choice."

"There's nothing more in this swamp—in Nature—that can bring me around. The Terror has stolen my sense of wonder and awe . . . and almost destroyed my ability to do magic."

"You want transcendence, I take it?"

"Of course. Everyone does."

Brother Owen puts down his pipe. "Are you certain this swamp doesn't have something that can shake you to your soul? Something that's here and has been for who knows how long—maybe forever? Something older and more horrifying than the Terror?"

"I'd have to see it."

"Stay here tonight then and at dawn we'll go to the dark heart of this beast—that's what the swamp is: a living, breathing beast. And no one will ever be able to fathom it."

So they struck off at dawn the next morning in Brother Owen's dory. Shepherd marveled at the old man's sense of direction, his intuitive feel for swamp runs. The day promised to be another scorcher. The water was down and murkier than Shepherd had ever seen it. The air virtually crackled with dryness.

"How far away is this place?" he asked.

"Don't try to measure it in miles," said Brother Owen. "If the Bushyeye—the Indians indigenous to the swamp—were still around, they could tell you, but they've gone. The pull of civilization got to their young folks. But once upon a time they were the keepers of the swamp. I was shown the spot where we're headed by a Bushyeye woman. She and I almost fell in love."

"A nice story."

"It might have been. Yes, it might have been. But in the end there were too many differences between us. I'm too much of a loner to be a good companion—that's the truth I had to find inside."

When Shepherd, following Brother Owen's promptings, had poled for another hour in the steamy, sun- and shadow-drenched swamp, he said, "How will you know when we're close to this place?"

The old man, who was sitting in the front of boat, turned to smile at Shepherd. "The Bushyeye call it 'the Pulse,' and I won't have to tell you when we're coming up on it. You'll feel it. You'll know. I won't have to say a word."

And that was true.

The drop in temperature was the signal.

"What happened?" said Shepherd.

He could see that they had entered a slow run, and he felt as if he had been asleep for several min-

utes despite the fact that he was standing in the
dory and had apparently continued poling. It was
as if he had been hypnotized.

"The swamp is playing magician," said Brother
Owen, and he chuckled. "Putting on a show for you.
And feel the air—notice anything?"

The temperature had fallen considerably.

"What on earth is going on? Yeah, this is very
strange."

"About another twenty or so yards, and you'll see.
We're entering the realm of the Pulse."

Shepherd had trouble believing his eyes when the
dory drifted near a large pool of ghostly gray water
choked with vegetation—an area seemingly generating its own fog, which, in turn, curled among
stunted and dead trees.

A sandbar appeared to float in the center of the
area like an apparition.

"Do you see now what I was talking about?" said
Brother Owen.

Shepherd hesitated.

"I suddenly feel," he said, "that this place is going to become part of my destiny. Maybe, in fact, it
already has."

"It has for both of us," said Brother Owen. "You
see, the Terror will not be pleased that I've brought
you here. No, not pleased at all. But I feel now that
I did the right thing. All the dark magic surrounding the Fossor witches has seeped into the fabric of
the swamp. There needs to be a cleansing—and so,
we'll wait for what wants to come."

THIRTY-FIVE

Evening visiting hours were drawing to a close. Gretta had left the hospital with Artie, but Tina had lingered behind to sit in Aunt Mushka's room and think. And the issue of concern was, of course, mostly the woman in a coma; however, what increasingly stole into Tina's consciousness was what had happened after the attack at the mysterious sinkhole somewhere deep in the swamp.

Tina couldn't understand why Shepherd would not have helped Gretta and Joe Boy.

What is going on?

She loved Shepherd, but the loyalty she possessed toward her family was strong, so strong that Shepherd's choice puzzled and hurt her. She wished that she could see him and ask him. Could, in fact, Joe Boy have been mistaken? Could it have been someone else watching and deciding not to become involved?

"Is it okay if I say good night?"

The voice abruptly pulled Tina from her dark musings.

"Oh, Joe Boy—yes, of course. Yes, come in."

The young man cautiously approached the bed. "Miss Billie Ruth and Mr. Buck are waiting out in the hall, so I'm won't stay very long."

Tina smiled. She got up and joined him at the side of the bed. "If Aunt Mushka knew you were here, she'd be pleased. You and she are really good pals, aren't you?"

Joe Boy nodded.

Tina placed a hand on his shoulder. She was trying to gauge the degree of his sorrow and his pain before she spoke again.

"If she could, I think she'd tell you how much she appreciated your going out into the swamp with her."

The young man turned and met her words.

"She knows I'm here," he said.

Tina blinked back her surprise. "You mean, you . . . you think she senses your presence?"

He shook his head. "No." Then he reached for the old woman's hand. "When I do this, she can talk to me—in my head."

Tina could feel her heart beating high in her chest. "What—what does she say to you?"

"Well, when I was here before she told me where she is."

"I don't understand—where she is?"

"She's in this place she made up."

"You mean, an imaginary place?"

"I guess so. It's pretty real, and she likes it there. She calls it 'Vasaria.' I think it's a neat name."

"Yes. Yes, it is. It sounds . . . romantic and kind of mysterious."

"She doesn't want to come back from it."

"Oh, I see. What do you think she means?"

"Well, I think she'll be in the coma as long as she stays in Vasaria—that's what I think."

Tina found that she was holding her breath as the young man's words filtered into her consciousness, and suddenly she realized that she believed him—believed that he was carrying on some kind of paranormal communication with her aunt.

"Do you think there's any way we can get her to leave Vasaria?"

Joe Boy was momentarily silent. He was looking down at the woman in the bed, and he continued to hold her hand. It was as if he was trying to decide how much of his closeness he wanted to share with Tina. Then he said, "I told her why she should leave."

"You did? And why—what did you say?"

"I told her if she didn't come back from Vasaria she wouldn't get to see Willow."

Tina felt something tear loose around her heart. Something at once warm and cold. She pressed her fingertips to her mouth, and she cleared her throat. "I'm glad you told her that, Joe Boy."

But it appeared he really wasn't listening. The lean of his body toward the bed and the way he seemed to be concentrating suggested that perhaps he was once again hearing the voice of his comatose friend.

"She knows you're here," he said, then glanced at Tina, then back at the old woman. "Aunt Mushka knows you're here."

Tina edged closer. She reached out and pressed her aunt's wrist. "Can she talk into my head?"

"I don't think so." But he hesitated, and Tina assumed that he was asking her. "No," he followed, "only one head at a time." He smiled and Tina matched his smile.

"That's fine—I just—we're all concerned about her," she said.

"She knows."

"I feel at a loss to say . . . Words fail . . ."

Then Joe Boy released the old woman's hand and turned to face Tina. "She said something she wants you to do—you and your sisters."

"She did? There's something—what did she say?"

"She said you have to promise to do it."

"Yes, of course. Oh, yes, I promise. What is it?"

* * *

The half-moon ghosted through the late night mist.

Tina, feeding small sticks to the campfire, wondered what her mother would think of this meeting. Off to one side, in Willow's backpack, was the object of concern, the object that would hopefully bring the three Fossor sisters together.

And perhaps coming together would not just reforge the bonds of sisterhood—perhaps it would also rejuvenate the magical abilities that each possessed, that each would need to battle the Terror and bring Willow home.

"Mother, are you here?"

The mist was cool and wet and heavy as it descended around Night Horse Oak.

"Mother, this is what Aunt Mushka wanted. We should have done this before now—we should have responded to the dark magic, but instead of working together as blood, we disconnected. I know that you're disappointed in us. We haven't behaved the way you taught us to. And maybe we also lost some of our faith in the Old Ways. We hope to change some things tonight."

She wanted to say more. Words, however, dissolved in her thoughts like the droplets of mist as they neared the small flame. Gretta and Artie were approaching. Tina stood up and waved to them and tried on a smile.

It was difficult.

Sisters.

Yes, there was something sacred in the aura they created.

Something that for weeks they had turned their backs on.

The embraces they shared were warm yet guarded. Nervousness was evident as they situated themselves near the fire. Tina had told them again what Aunt Mushka had requested. She also told them that they should share in the task only if they truly believed it was the right thing to do. No coercion. No guilt trips.

"Thanks," said Tina. "Thank you both for coming. I don't really know whether there's a step-by-step ritual for this kind of thing. I thought it might be best if we kept everything simple and more personal." She hesitated and searched the expressions of her sisters, and in those expressions she read a willingness to follow her lead. "And I thought it would be appropriate to bring Mother's Book of Shadows in Willow's backpack." She hesitated again and held the backpack out in front of her momentarily, then placed it on her lap.

"I'm glad you did," said Gretta. "Mother would have approved. There was a lovely closeness between them."

Artie nodded her agreement.

Then Tina started to lift the book from the backpack, but stopped herself. "Does anyone . . . you know, want to say anything before we start? I know that I do." She gathered herself, then said, "Willow's disappearance has been a nightmare, and I'm terribly sorry that I've—well, I feel that I've pushed both of you away and that I've not been a good sister, and I've not been sensitive to all that you have been facing—the loss of your magic and other difficulties in your personal lives. I'm sorry."

And something seemed to fall away at that point: invisible walls of separation seemed to crumble, for Tina could see that her sisters did not hate her. She could see understanding in their eyes.

"I think it's good," said Gretta, "that each of us expresses her thoughts on things. I have to confess that my life has changed in recent weeks—what I loved most has been taken away, and I'm left with a bitterness in my heart I can't dissolve. But I haven't stopped loving you, my sisters, and I'll never stop worshiping our mother. I want Willow to be home again. I want Aunt Mushka to be well. But both of you should know that my life now largely centers on revenge. I will not be able to live with myself until the Terror has been destroyed. If burning Mother's Book of Shadows can help bring back our magic, then I want to participate in this ritual—because in fighting the Terror I sense that we will need all the magic that we can generate."

Tina smiled at Gretta and reached out for her, and the two of them gripped each other's wrists.

"Don't lose faith in the Old Ways," said Tina. "I think your magic will return, but not if you've lost faith."

"I know," said Gretta. "Loving Glen—well, there have been times when I've been tempted to abandon everything that I once held sacred. He's gone. He lives in my heart. But he's gone, and I know that the Old Ways are still with me. Revenge is not a holy act—I understand that, and yet it's something I must pursue. I *must*. And I don't believe that we can live free and good lives if the Terror exists—if dark magic rules Night Horse Swamp."

Attention turned to Artie, who to Tina would always be the beautiful, talented younger sister, though now she appeared older, the blush of loveliness gone from her cheeks and grace nowhere evident in the movements of her withered right hand.

"You two and Aunt Mushka are so much of what is important in my world. I have a lover now, and she's in my heart as well, but you are family—blood, and Willow is blood, too, and I want her home and safe. And I join with Gretta in needing revenge. I've been a victim of the Terror, not in the same way as Gretta has been—I haven't lost a lover, but I've lost the magic that allows me to create and perhaps it's just vanity, but my sense of self, my physical appearance has been affected, too, and I want desperately to recover that creativity and that sense of self. I hope that this ritual will open the possibility for that recovery." She paused and then, tears threatening, she added, "I love you guys. I want you to know that."

"And we love you," said Tina.

The three of them embraced and a few tears came and the warmth shared was not constrained.

"Blessed be," Gretta whispered. And the words were echoed by Tina and Artie.

Then Tina said, "I guess it's my turn." She found that her eyes were drawn to the fire and the soul-numbing reverie of the flames, and she could see herself suddenly as a tiny creature throwing off the difficulties of life and merging with those flames. How glorious it would be, and yet it would not be *her* life, not the life she needed. "What I need," she continued, "is your support, not just for this ritual, but for a very dangerous mission—I want you to be my companions on a journey into the swamp to rescue Willow and to do whatever is necessary with the Terror."

"It has to be destroyed," Gretta interjected.

Tina nodded. "Probably so, but I want you to understand that most of all I need to have my Willow back. She has been my main loss, but I've also lost the man who was my husband. I've been fortunate in one way, though, because the Goddess has seen fit to send someone new into my life, a man to love and to be loved by. The Terror has power over this man despite this man's knowledge of the Old Ways, despite his magical abilities. So, if you're willing to share in this ritual of burning the Book of Shadows and opening yourself to the return of your magic, be aware that magic may not be enough. We're facing an extraordinary force, and we haven't much time to prepare ourselves for our dangerous venture. Midsummer is only a week away. A new moon. The swamp will be at its darkest, and if the Terror continues to hold sway at the end of Midsummer's Eve, then the creature may control Night Horse Swamp the rest of our days. This is it. We have to be stronger than we have ever been."

Tina found in her sisters the recognition, the awareness of the high stakes involved with their choice to help her. She smiled. "Okay, then, let's see what happens."

Moments later Tina held the Book of Shadows out above the licking flames. Across from her, Gretta and Artie held hands; Gretta pressed the athame between her breasts. Both women had their eyes closed tightly.

"Goddess," Tina began, "look upon and bless this ritual that in part we perform to honor you and the holy tenets of the Old Ways. The charge of our mother was ever the same—'know yourself'—and it is in that spirit that we come now to these flames. We offer the sacred magic of numbers as we prepare to deliver this sacred book to the fire. First, the number one for the universe, the source of all. Next, the number nine: a number of the Goddess. Next, the number fifteen: a number of good fortune. And, finally, the number one hundred and one: the number of fertility in memory of the one who gave us birth and symbolically in memory of my child, Willow, who is missing and deeply missed."

And with that the book was given to the fire.

It burned with a hard, crystalline flame, and ashen flecks of its pages sparked blue light, casting an aura of mystery over the scene. The three women stood away from the heat and searing light, joining hands and discovering a oneness that they had not shared for a long time—perhaps since childhood.

Not completely understanding all that was taking place, they were rigid with awe.

And then, as the book was nearly consumed, the flames died down and a black smoke rose eagerly and appeared to be animated with a life of its own. Gretta pulled free of her sisters and leaned her face into the smoke.

"I see someone," she said, her voice gathering excitement. "Someone is coming. I see her. A woman." Then she stepped back.

"Oh, look!" Artie exclaimed.

Then Tina saw it, too, and she knew, beyond doubt, that they had engaged in the proper ritual.

"It's Mother," she said.

And it was.

Her ghost at least. Or the apparition of her shaped from a whitish smoke rising from within the darker clouds.

The shape remained only for a few moments, but long enough for validation.

Long enough for each of them to know that their mother was with them.

"We're not alone, are we?" said Gretta.

"No," said Tina, "but we have to act. And we have to find the courage to go into the swamp and do what we must do."

"Will we go in the morning?" asked Artie.

Tina shook her head. "We need to wait, I think. Shepherd said he would go with us. We'll need his help. When he returns, we'll go."

"But how long can we sit around?" said Gretta. "You said yourself that Midsummer's Eve will be here soon. I think it's risky to wait."

"I do, too," Artie followed.

"No, listen, please. Let's wait. Shepherd promised he would return—he promised he would help bring Willow home. So, I'm asking you to have faith in

him and in me. We'll go when he comes back from
the swamp."

She hesitated, looking for signs of their assent.

Gretta glanced at Artie. "Well, at this point, I feel
we do need to keep our trust in each other strong.
I'll accept your judgment on this. Artie, will you?"

"Yes."

"Good," said Tina. "Coming together again as
sisters—I think we've already won half the battle."

"What about our magic?" said Artie. "Will it return now that Mother's Book of Shadows has been
destroyed?"

"I hope so," said Tina. "We're counting on it."

Gretta took Artie's hand. "Some of it has. Just a
minute ago, I could *see* the visage of Mother, even
though I didn't recognize her at first."

Reassured, they turned then to the tasks of putting out the fire and preparing to leave.

But just as the flames had been extinguished and
the ashes and coals were being stirred and separated, they sensed it. Another presence. This time
not their mother.

And just as suddenly a cool wind kicked up and
they had to brace themselves against it.

It was the Terror.

Each of them knew it.

The creature was there as if to remind them that
dark magic continued to hold sway.

And when the wind lifted and it was calm and
silent again, Tina sensed something more. She
turned, then spun slowly and called out, "Willow?
Willow, are you here?"

The twin scents of honeysuckle and kudzu filled
the air.

Gretta knelt quickly near the diminishing trails of
smoke and breathed deeply.

"I can see her," she said.

"Where?" Tina exclaimed.

"No, wait. I'm sorry," said Gretta. "She's gone. I sense that she's in another realm. I've lost the image."

"Willow!" Tina cried out. "We're going to bring you home!"

But a deadrise of nothingness held the scene.

THIRTY-SIX

Artie could feel it in her hand. She could feel it alive and pulsing in her fingers.

The sketch of the face of the Terror was complete. Yes, her magic was drawing back into her again. Like blood flowing again. Like life itself.

"Why did you want this log of dead pine?"

It was Gladys Michaels. She was there to keep Artie company while Aunt Mushka was in the hospital. The two women had been talking seriously about moving in together, but everything was on hold until matters of dark magic could be dealt with.

"For carving," said Artie.

The breathless excitement of having back her magical control over a sheet of drawing paper made her words sound strained.

"But what is it that you plan to carve?"

Artie turned from the drawing of the Terror and smiled warmly at her lover. "A mask."

"Of . . . oh, I see. A mask of the Terror."

"That's right. It'll be a good test. If my magic is truly back, then I'll be able to capture the same grotesqueness in the pine as I have on this sheet."

"And when you've finished carving the mask—what then? What will you do with it?"

Artie hesitated. She studied the squat log of pine at her feet. "I'll take it into the swamp and try to capture a dark spirit with it. I'm not quite sure how."

Michaels went to her and wrapped her arm around her. "I'm scared. I don't want you to go. Do all three of you have to be in on this?"

"We're sisters. We're the Fossor witches, and the Terror has tried to destroy our lives and has come real close to doing so. Now it's time to end all the darkness—rescue Willow and see that the Terror never returns to Night Horse Swamp."

"But can you do that?"

"I don't know. Having our magic back will make a huge difference, I think. I have it in my hand again—I can feel it."

"And all the beauty of your face is glowing once more. And I'm sorry to be so selfish—I just don't want anything to happen to you."

"Nothing will," said Artie.

Then she pulled away from Michaels and got out her wood-carving set and began to transform a sliver of the log into a likeness of the creature that ruled the swamp—that controlled her family and threatened to plunge it even deeper into darkness.

They were perfect pieces of swamp cedar, small branches with vibrant green foliage, and she had stacked them reverently in her firepot, which she had set in her hearth. She kept thinking about what her mother had once said about cedar: "Cherokee Indians believed that cedar trees warded off ghosts."

Gretta smiled at the notion.

In the canon of beliefs of the Old Ways, cedar was a protective spirit. For Gretta, it was a galvanizing force when burned, and when the smoke was breathed it opened up strange worlds.

But only if I have my magic.

Trembling with anticipation, she lighted the stack

and listened to the initial sizzle and crackle and watched the first sinuous threads of smoke lift and yet remained tethered to the cedar. On her knees, she leaned out close to the smoke and let it caress her face. She tried not to breathe it. What she needed was for her magic to be released—for her inner eye to be opened.

In a few heartbeats, it was.

Yet, at first she had virtually no idea what she was viewing: two men in a dory somewhere in the swamp. The dory was stationary. One of the two men was bearded and rather old. She did not recognize him, but she believed that he was blind. She assumed, through her glimpse at his long, blond hair, that the other man was Shepherd—Tina's friend. Tina's love interest. A Cunning Man.

Something remarkable was arresting their attention.

Gretta blinked. Concentrated.

And saw the Pulse, though she did not know that was what it was called.

She drew in a breath and abruptly pulled away from the smoke. The vision of the haunting landscape frightened her. Where in the swamp was such a place? And why were Shepherd and the bearded man there?

Gathering herself again, Gretta leaned into the smoke, but this time she did not see the men in the dory or the grotesque, dead-looking stretch of landscape; instead, she caught a blurred image of the corpse of Glen Favors, struggling as if trapped *between* two realms—earthly reality and the Otherworld.

"Oh, Glen," she whispered.

Then, pressing in upon the image of the man she loved, another scene.

"Willow," she murmured.

As if in the next frame of a movie reel, Willow

was there, not far from the corpse of Glen Favors, and she was wading in the swamp, and then, over and over again, the scene repeating itself with maddening sameness, Willow would disappear—as if she had reached out and opened a door into the invisible and walked through it.

And was met there by the Terror.

Gretta shook her head and the vision dissolved, replaced immediately by another.

Of a burning cabin.

Hers.

And a giant image of the head of the panther ghosting through the flames.

"No. No, this can't be," Gretta muttered, alarmed by the sight of her home on fire.

She couldn't pry her attention away from the scene. She could only watch helplessly as some future point in time spiraled back to touch the present moment with the promise of the destruction of what was so dear to her.

Summoning as much energy as possible, she ducked her head and turned her face away from the smoke. Tears choked her throat and stung her eyes.

"Oh, Glen, I need you."

She stayed there, on her knees at her hearth, for the better part of an hour. Then, resigned to the mysteries that lay ahead, she got to her feet, more determined than ever to join her sisters on a dangerous journey into the swamp.

To face the Terror.

Rosebud was hungry.

"Be patient, kitty. There's something I have to do first."

Tina didn't mind tending to Rosebud while Aunt Mushka was in the hospital, though it might have made more sense for Artie to since she was in Mushka's house—and yet, Artie could sometimes be undependable. So. So the cat was transferred to Tina's.

Rosebud was meowing insistently and spinning around in that slow, impatiently demanding way cats have.

"I said I'd tend to you in a minute."

Tina watched her computer screen come up.

Spell-casting time.

Had the destruction of her mother's Book of Shadows been enough to release her magical powers from their imprisonment? She did not know. But as she sat before the screen and tossed about mentally trying to imagine what kind of spell could be put on a creature like the Terror, she realized that she did not know what kind of entity the Terror was. Could Shepherd help her? She assumed he could.

Where is he?

Can I count on him?

She might have asked herself whether she had *ever* been able to count on a man. Even her father. But after a few minutes—during which time Rosebud had plopped down on its bottom in the middle of the floor to pout at the lack of response to pleas for food—something else grabbed her attention.

The panther.

It was only the screen saver taking hold, and yet at that instant, for Tina, it was much more.

"Magic word. That's what I need to get it going."

What occurred then was something she would later characterize to herself as preternatural—a visit from the Otherworld. And the visitor was her mother.

Tina could feel her approach from behind her chair.

She could feel her slip into her body—it took her breath away.

And she could feel the ghostly presence slip out of her body.

And into the computer.

She could see and hear the machine waffle and blip and blink.

She imagined that she heard the panther on the screen growl.

"Mother? Mother, please help."

And then Tina's mind went blank except for one word.

Coda.

"That's it," she whispered to herself. "That's what I've needed—a word. A magic word."

She hadn't realized that it had been available to her all along.

Suddenly she glanced away from the screen to Rosebud.

"Kitty," she said, "I know you're hungry, but wouldn't you feel better if you took a little nap first?"

The cat was indifferent, of course.

Tina smiled to herself.

Then she closed her eyes and began to test her ability to once again cast spells.

"Coda," she whispered.

And typed the word across the screen.

Then repeated it again and again all the while imagining the effects of the spell she was casting.

When she had convinced herself that she had waited long enough, she opened her eyes and laughed softly at what she heard.

The contented purring of a sleeping Rosebud.

THIRTY-SEVEN

Your head is filled with voices.

So many you cannot hear any single one of them clearly, and because of that you are sitting on the rope-pull ferry dock after supper hoping the din will die down. You keep hearing one word repeated over and over again.

Coda.

You have heard it before, but no one seems to know what it means.

Now, Miss Billie Ruth and Mr. Buck will soon be calling for you so you can go to the hospital to see your friend, Aunt Mushka.

She will talk into your head.

And you will let her. You need to know, however, what is really going on.

You wish Willow could be there.

You wish she hadn't stepped into another world—sort of like the way you step into the elevator at the hospital and it just takes you up to the next floors.

Like magic.

You wonder what kind of elevator Willow took.

You wonder what it will take to bring her back home.

You don't really want to be part of all that is happening. You'd just like to dive into the water and become someone else. Another Joe Boy. A swamp thing. And swim down deep where the water runs cooler.

And the world becomes silent.

"How's your leg doin'?"

It's the first thing Mushka says to you when you are standing by her hospital bed holding her hand. Everyone else is there, too: Miss Billie Ruth, Mr. Buck, Tina, Gretta, and Arietta—you try not to let your eyes meet Arietta's because it will make your face warm like a heat lamp.

"It's good 'n fine," you say. "A little sore. Not much."

And you know it must be strange for the others in the room to hear you talking like that, talking, it would seem, to yourself. So you turn to them and say, "She just asked about my leg. You know, the gator bites."

They all have bright-eyed wonderment in their expressions.

You try to pretend they're not there so you can concentrate on your friend.

"Did they burn the book?" she asks.

While you were still out in the hallway, Willow's mother told you they had burned Anna Fossor's Book of Shadows—more than that, each of the sisters was experiencing signs of magic returning.

"Yes'am."

"They got some magic back?"

"Yes'am."

"Is Rosebud doin' okay?"

"Yes'am, I think so."

There is a long silence then and you begin to fear you've lost contact with her, so you squeeze her hand and say, "You still there?"

"Oh, yes, I'm sorry," she says. "I was thinking about what's goin' on in the swamp and about how

when you get beyond the world we've all lived in
you begin to understand the way things work. But
not everything."

"I don't know what you mean."

"Things about Willow and the Terror, for example. I think I see what's maybe goin' on. I think that
ole Night Horse Swamp has some—what to call
'em?—doors maybe. Or like time portals. Places
where creatures like the Terror can slip out of the
real world into another world—and be invisible.
And take Willow with him. That make any sense?"

"Some, I guess. The swamp has got lots of mysteries."

There is another silence. During this one you
can't resist a glance over at Arietta and it swells your
heart until it's as big as a basketball and you're
afraid your dinkle doo might start its own kind of
swelling so you look away. You look at Willow's
mother, and you can see in her eyes that she's encouraging you to stay in contact with her aunt.

So you do.

You ask, "What else you got to say?"

And you are relieved when she speaks again.

"Joe Boy, I'm finding what life is really all about.
I'm finding what people need to do for each other."
You think about saying something, but you keep listening and Mushka keeps talking. "What people
need to do for each other is give blessings."

"Blessings?" you say.

"Yes, blessings, Joe Boy. They need to bless one
another."

"Yes'am."

"And I'm finding out what followers of the Old
Ways really need to do—what their *responsibility* is.
You know what a 'spy' is, Joe Boy?"

"No'am. Not really. A sneaky person maybe."

You hear her chuckle. It is a good sound.

Then she says, "A spy is somebody who uncovers

secrets, usually for somebody else. I see it now: what we're supposed to do, I mean. Our responsibility. We're supposed to be spies for the Goddess. And you know what kind of secrets we're supposed to uncover?"

"No'am."

"Well, I'll tell you. We're to seek out everything that's a mystery. That make sense?"

"Hmm," you say. Because you're not sure it does. Make sense, that is.

"It doesn't mean we have to *solve* the mystery. It's enough if we just . . . oh, I don't know, *experience* it. You see?"

"Yes'am," you say, but her words make your head hurt because you have been thinking too hard.

"Now, Joe Boy, I have one more thing to say to you. I want you to promise me something."

"Yes'am, I will."

"Promise. Promise this—and if you break this promise may you wake up with a rattlesnake in bed with you—promise me that if Tina and Gretta and Arietta go into the swamp to rescue Willow, promise me you'll shadow them, you know, go along behind in case they need help. Will you promise to do that?"

You hesitate quite a spell.

You aren't eager to return to the swamp.

You don't want to have to face the Terror.

But then you hear yourself say, "I promise."

And you can't take back those words.

THIRTY-EIGHT

Willow, we're coming for you.

On her deck as the evening warmth and humidity spread heavy droplets of mist up from and out over Night Horse Creek, Tina sat and waited—waited for what wanted to come—and thought about how good it felt to be firmly committed to an action.

She and her sisters would go into Night Horse Swamp and rescue her daughter.

But she wondered.

Willow, who are you now?

Would the six weeks her daughter had spent as a captive of the Terror have changed her? What would her physical and, perhaps more importantly, mental condition be?

Have I lost my Willow forever?

Answers to those questions seemed as distant as the twinkling of stars high above her. But not everything veered off in the direction of hopelessness. The Fossor witches were recapturing their magical abilities. Tina was casting spells again, albeit nothing very powerful—not yet. And Gretta claimed her "seeing" ability had largely returned; Artie was creating again, shaping potentially magical objects that could be taken into the swamp and used against the Terror.

And there was Aunt Mushka.

Through Joe Boy she had been able to commu-

nicate the need to destroy Anna Fossor's Book of
Shadows, and she had demonstrated that her healing powers had been reactivated. And it was evident
that she wanted very much to see Willow again.
Could that desire bring her out of the coma?

More questions.

Tina suddenly hugged herself, not because she
was cold but rather because being so distant from
so many answers made her feel a chill inside. It slithered through her like a cold snake.

"You mind some company?"

As usual, she had not heard him approach. He
was simply there, in the partial darkness at the end
of the deck, looking thinner than she recalled he
had, his eyes lacking some of the luster with which
she had become familiar. He was holding Rosebud
in his arms.

"Can't you ever just knock at the front door like
a regular person?" she said, her aggravation
feigned. She could tell he knew she wasn't upset
with him.

"Then I wouldn't be the mysterious stranger any
longer."

She got up and went to him and felt the love for
him she carried inside rise like water filling up a
glass.

"I see you have a friend," she said.

He smiled. "What on earth did you do to this
animal? Drug it?"

"Not exactly."

"Oh, wait, I think I know. You weren't practicing
your powers, were you?"

"I was. It just so happened that Rosebud was
nearby when the juices started to flow again."

"You're glad you have your magic back, aren't
you?" He set the cat down and took her in his arms.

"I have *some* of it back. Not all of it. It feels weak.
But, yes, I'm glad. I know I'm going to need it."

She nuzzled into his throat. She could smell the swamp on him—sweetness and decay and something elemental.

"So, you still have your mind set on rescuing Willow?"

She pulled back to look up into his eyes. There was just enough light on the deck to see a face half in shadow, half in the artificial illumination that showed a troubled expression.

"Yes, of course. My sisters and I are ready—I got them to agree to wait for you to go with us. Isn't that what . . . has something happened? Tell me, Shep—you'll help us, won't you?"

"Let's sit down," he said.

First, he told her of witnessing what happened at the sinkhole when the Terror frightened Mushka so badly that she became comatose.

"I acted like a coward," he admitted.

Tina shook her head. "I just can't really understand this—I can't understand you. How could you not help them? The Terror could have killed them. What is going on with you, Shep?"

She could see how regret was carving deep, dark lines in his face.

"The simple answer is that I'm weak—I'm trying to get strong, but it's . . . difficult. Like nothing else I've ever encountered. And yet, as powerful as the Terror is, I was shown a place in the swamp that may be even more powerful."

She listened intently, and then he told her of how he wandered in the swamp and seemed to be directed to the abode of the blind hermit, Brother Owen. And then he told her of experiencing the Pulse.

"It's a place the Terror is drawn to. It's terra incognita—and more. It's the heartbeat of the swamp, and being near it is like . . . it's like having pure mystery poured into you, and while it's happening

it scares you, but it also makes you feel—it exhila-
rates you. It made me feel as if I were climbing—
climbing up to where I needed to be. I've seen
strange places throughout the world: Stonehenge,
Easter Island, the great pyramids, and this one ranks
with them."

Tina found herself wanting to understand but
also wanting to rescue this man she loved from the
forces of dark magic that appeared to hold him captive. "I think I heard my mother speak of this place
once. She spoke of it as somewhere we should stay
away from. And you should, too; I want you to promise me you won't go there again. And I feel sick to
death that you've come under the spell of the Terror. I fear that the creature will kill you. Mostly, I
don't want you to face it alone. I want to be with
you."

He held her close and the night thickened. "I
think I've come to know something valuable about
the Terror. Entities like it don't wish to kill because
each time they do, they become weaker. The Terror
controls by controlling people. Its power over you
and your sisters lies in its control of Willow and its
weakening of your magic. But now it may be in danger of losing some of that control."

"But our magic returned because we burned our
mother's Book of Shadows. If we have any chance
against the Terror, it's through strength in numbers.
If all of us go into the swamp together, we can com-
bine our magical abilities—it's the only way, isn't it,
Shep? We'll be more powerful if we join forces?"

He pulled away from her arms, and she heard
him sigh as if he was doubtful.

"I don't know. You could be right. It makes sense,
and yet I'd like to be certain before you and your
sisters put yourself in that kind of danger. The Terror is a mysterious creature—the most mysterious
I've ever encountered. And it has gravitated to the

Pulse. The greatest fear I have is that we'll have to go there—we'll have to go there to get Willow back."

"If that's what it takes," said Tina. "I'm willing to do anything. I just don't want you to go after the Terror on your own. My sisters and I can help. Let us help. You said you would."

"I know, but . . . I need more time."

"How much? Shep, it's just a few more days until Midsummer's Eve. A new moon. The swamp at its darkest. You know what that means. We should go now."

"I can't, Tina. I'm not ready."

"But why? I don't understand."

"It's courage. I need more time to find the courage to do what we'll have to do."

"Don't you find it in my arms? In the love we have?"

She waited, and in his silence heard the answer she did not want to hear.

"Please, Tina. Two more days. Then we'll go—you and I and your sisters. You can count on it."

He reached for her and kissed her cheek, and then he left, and she could find no words. She had wanted their being together to lift her spirits: to give her, too, the sensation of climbing. But instead she felt that as he was disappearing into the humid night air, she was descending into a darkness from which she might not return.

THIRTY-NINE

Artie had asked Gladys to go home because she needed to be alone with her creation. With her magic. Another two days had passed. Midsummer's Eve was only a day away. She was concerned, but she would leave the planning of the venture into the swamp to Tina and Gretta.

Pleased with herself, Artie held the finished mask up in the candlelight.

Yes, the mask of the Terror: its haunting expression, the aura of it replete with several sets of razor-sharp grappling hooks attached to the middle and both sides of the forehead. She had softened the pine and curved it so that the piece could be worn as a mask with strips of leather to tie it on with.

If the chance presented itself—and she prayed to the Goddess that it would—she would use the mask as a mirror to attempt to trap the Terror, for she knew that if her magic worked, her creation would have the power to transform. In this case, possibly to change the Terror into a harmless entity.

She turned suddenly and caught a glimpse of a dark figure at one window.

Initially she was startled; then, after a moment or two, she smiled.

"You might as well come on in, Joe Boy," she said.

Shy as always, he came into the room, his eyes shifting from her to the mask and back to her.

"What do you think of it?" she said.

He hunkered down beside her and seemed apprehensive about touching the object.

"You make this?" he said.

"Yes. Most of my magic has come back, so I can create once again, and it feels wonderful."

She smiled and he returned her smile, and she was warmed by the innocent love he obviously felt for her.

"You goin' into the swamp with your sisters?"

She nodded. "Yes, very soon. To get Willow away from the creature."

"It'll be dangerous."

"I know. But I'm taking this mask to help defeat the creature."

"But how? What can it do?"

She leaned close to his face and in her most playfully frightening tone said, "Scare him!"

He started back, then caught himself, delighted momentarily, but she could see how that delight was shifting to concern.

"What if something goes wrong? What if the creature scares *you* more than you scare it? What's goin' to happen to you?"

Artie shrugged and giggled softly. "Guess I'll just have to hope somebody's around to save me."

The ghostly visitation had left her shaking badly. Webs of disbelief clung to her and she was having trouble breathing.

So real.

"Oh, Glen, why are you doing this?" Gretta whispered into the darkness of her cabin.

He was hovering just above her as she slept, and she had been awakened by his moaning and plaintive cries of anguish—sounds she recognized as that of a soul needing to be released from its own personal damnation.

But she couldn't reach him.

She was powerless to enter his realm, a deadrise world of lost beings.

Her thoughts had narrowed dramatically to a single call that was, in turn, connected to her single desire. The dark reality was that Glen had been damned to haunt her cabin on Pan Island, the very cabin that he had helped to build—the cabin in which they had fallen in love.

She had to do something to exorcize his spirit.

In her mind's eye, she saw flames.

She believed she had no choice. She knew what she must do.

Glen, forgive me.

You must stop. You must let go of me and this cabin.

As tears skated down her cheeks, she went about saving anything that she absolutely needed: some clothing, a few cooking utensils, her camera, a few books, including her Book of Shadows, the athame, and her firepot. She decided that any reminder of Glen must be left behind.

It would help make her revenge pure. That was now, more than ever before, her single desire.

Once she had safely removed the more indispensable items, she went about her task methodically, wadding up sheets of newspaper she had used as shelf paper, and soaking with gasoline.

She needed only one match.

It hissed. And the predawn world of Night Horse Creek brightened.

The flames danced along the foundation of the cabin. The small building itself was not close enough to any trees or dry grass to pose a threat beyond the island. She would stand and watch her world collapse upon itself.

Because it had to be. Her firepot vision had been on target.

And as she looked on, she thought about how the evolution of man's consciousness could not have taken place without fire—fire had transformed man. Fire was destructive. Yet, fire was also cleansing and annealing.

Fire was magic.

In those flames she saw a symbol of how her quiet life had been transformed.

A woman without intimacy had found intimacy. Then lost it.

Then had turned her energy not to peace of mind and wholeness, but to revenge.

Good-bye, Pan Island.

Good-bye, Glen.

The Terror had been victorious.

For the moment.

Her jaw stiffened and she cried quietly.

In the distance, she could hear the voices of Tina and Artie. They would think she was in danger. And so she knew she must load her life into her small boat and go share the truth with them.

In her boat, prepared to pole away from the island, she turned to take one last look at the cabin, the flames by then leaping their highest, and there, in the yellow-hot center she saw the vacuous face of the Terror, animated and vital and indifferent to all things human including every breath of her secret self.

Miss Billie Ruth has given you a bouquet of red roses to take to your friend's room. It is a hot, dry June afternoon, and you get to thinking that in summer it is usually hotter when there's a new moon. But you don't know why.

You don't know why Gretta Fossor burned her cabin on Pan Island to the ground.

Miss Billie Ruth and Mr. Buck don't know either.

Maybe Gretta Fossor has gone round the bend. That's Mr. Buck's way of saying that maybe she's gone crazy. You think that maybe the Terror could drive somebody crazy. Maybe even you. Maybe it's not so much that you are sinful—maybe you are a little bit crazy.

Maybe everyone who lives by the swamp is.

You are standing by your friend's bed and holding the bouquet of red roses, and the nurse helps you put them in a vase with some water in the bottom of it. The nurse says the flowers are pretty; the nurse is pretty, too. But you don't think she's as pretty as Arietta.

You think about the mask she made.

And you worry about Arietta.

You wish she wouldn't go into the swamp after the Terror.

But you cannot stop her.

As you stand by the bed, the Fossor sisters file in: Tina and Gretta and Arietta—beautiful Arietta, who smiles at you and her smile turns your tongue into chewing gum. You duck your head, and Tina asks you how your patient is today.

"I think she's still in Vasaria," you say, your words slurred because of what Arietta has done to your tongue.

"Will you tell her that the three of us are going into the swamp? Tomorrow morning, if not sooner. We want her to know."

"All right then," you say. "I'll tell her."

Your tongue is getting back to normal.

You hold Mushka's hand and look at her face. A nurse, or someone, has fixed her hair and smeared some red stuff on her cheeks and wrapped a blue scarf around her neck. Blue is her color. You squeeze her fingers to let her know you want to communicate with her, and when you do you feel ice-cold—and somehow you know that in the coming days you will feel ice-cold again. You try not to shiver, but you do. You are confused by the sensation and start to pull away, but then, in your head, your friend says:

"You're not backing out on your promise, are you? You know the one—you promised you would follow my nieces into the swamp. They might need your help."

"I'm not backing out," you say.

And you glance at the three women who are looking at you and hanging on the moment. You feel funny talking out loud when nobody else in the room can hear what the person you're talking to is saying.

"Good," says your friend.

"You goin' to stay in Vasaria forever?" you say.

"It's a nice place. I'd like to."

"What about Willow?"

There is a long pause.

"You're not goin' to let me forget about Willow, are you? You scamp."

"No."

"Well, I haven't forgotten. I want to see her again."

"But you can't if you stay in Vasaria."

"I know that. Thing is, Joe Boy, if you were here, you wouldn't want to leave either."

Suddenly you hear something else in your head: it's Willow's music. Throbbing, screaming music. And then the cold really hits you—and you hear Willow's voice, and she is telling you something you can barely hear.

"Quiet," you say.

Mushka hushes, and the silence in the hospital room deepens.

And Willow tells you that she is sending something to Mushka, and you don't know what that means, but before you can ask, Willow—or her voice at least—is gone.

You take a big breath and you say to your friend, "Willow is sending something to you, so be ready."

Tina stands up and says, "Joe Boy, what is it? What's going on? Can you hear Willow?"

And you turn her way. "Yes'am. I don't know what it means."

But things begin to happen.

Mushka's breathing is more animated. Her lips are moving. And her right hand is making a fist, then unclenching and clenching. The Fossor sisters huddle at the foot of the bed. And Tina says, "Joe Boy?"

And you shake your head and shrug.

Something very strange is occurring. You can feel it.

You can smell honeysuckle and kudzu all of a sudden.

And the smell makes you shiver again.

Then Mushka's body is shaking and her right hand is jerking and now everyone can see that she is about to wake up. Into your head, she says, "Joe Boy, here I come. I'm comin' back so I can see Willow again one day."

She blinks her eyes, and you hear a nervous shuffle of joy and surprise from the women.

And just before Mushka comes fully awake she says to you, "Look in my right hand."

When it's all over and you are riding back home with Miss Billie Ruth and Mr. Buck, you think about things. About what happened at the hospital.

About some things your friend said.

And about the amulet.

And magic.

You saw it with your own eyes. The Fossor sisters saw it, too. There's no doubt about what Mushka had in her hand—it was Willow's amulet. But how did she get it? How was Willow able to send it to her?

Magic.

When Tina saw the amulet, she gasped. The metal disk was tricked out on one side with a rayed sun enclosing an eye rimmed in flames. On the other side the words:

SOL OMNIPOTENS
TECUM LUCESCO

"It's Willow's," she exclaimed.

There was no doubt about it. You recalled Willow telling you about the all-seeing sun and the spirit of light within everyone. Light and heat, and you knew that Willow would always be fire and you would always be water.

After her doctor had been called in to check on Mushka, she sat up in bed and talked, and you handed her a single red rose and she just about broke down and bawled about it. She said she'd been thinking about roses and fire and about all things red because red was Willow's color—the color of the living spirit inside.

Then she said something, and you think maybe you can remember it word for word:

"Life," she said, "is a mysterious, terrifying, powerful, and wondrous experience. You can't ask why of it any more than you can ask the rose why it blooms. It just does."

You were sure glad she had come back to your world.

Everybody else was, too.

FORTY

Artie painted a red rose on the side of the john boat.

For good luck.

And Gretta said, "It feels like we're all virgins again."

Tina smiled at the remark.

It was a warm, moist dawn as she watched her sisters loading supplies into the boat. She had awakened them during the night, having decided that they could wait no longer. Shepherd wasn't coming—Tina could feel it. She had lost him: to the swamp, to the Pulse, to the Terror. It made no difference. The bottom line remained the same. She had put her faith in him, she had committed herself to him, and he had failed her.

Gretta had been staying with her since she burned her cabin, a ritualistic act that Tina understood implicitly. It was the kind of necessary burning, a natural burning, that would lead, ironically, to growth. She did not know what that growth entailed for Gretta, though she could assume it somehow involved the memory of Glen Favors and Gretta's intense desire for revenge against the Terror.

If only I could put my relationship with Shep to the flames.

But she knew she couldn't. She loved him. She wanted him with her.

He hadn't returned from the swamp, and so the issue at hand was rescuing Willow without him. She had gathered her sisters, and they had gone to Night Horse Oak where they had burned cedar branches and Tina had cast a protective spell over the three of them, and Gretta had breathed the cedar smoke and she had seen where they must go. During their ritual, heat lightning had danced at the edges of the intensely dry swamp.

And the panther had watched them.

And now it was time to launch this voyage for blood.

For her daughter.

"Yes," said Tina, "virgins. But not sacrificial ones, I hope."

"Doing what we must do," said Gretta.

"And we're together again," said Artie. "It feels right. It's dangerous—I know that. But I feel strong. Don't you?"

Tina could feel the tension as Artie searched the expressions of her sisters for signs of agreement.

"We have on our colors," said Gretta. "That should help."

And they did. Gretta in a long green dress, Artie in white, and Tina in purple. They were cool, everyday summer dresses—inappropriate in some ways for such a venture, and yet wearing them made each feel that her faith in the Old Ways was firm and resolute. They were dressing the part. They believed they were ready to face the forces of dark magic.

At the boat they joined hands.

"Blessed be," said Tina, then smiled in turn at Gretta and Artie. "Where to?" she said to Gretta, who had a vision of where they should pitch their camp later in the day.

"Baptism Island," she said.

"Gretta's right. This is what we must do, and we must do it," said Tina.

"I feel the presence of Mother," said Artie.

"Good," said Tina. "We'll need to have her along."

You think about the word "promise."

Such a big word. A heavy word. Almost as heavy as "love" or "sin."

You swim along behind the john boat that is carrying Arietta and her sisters into the swamp to rescue Willow and do battle with the Terror. You are following them because of the promise you made to your friend, Mushka, who is still at the hospital, but no longer in a coma.

She is thinking about you—you can tell.

In the water, you feel, as always, the rise of another creature—a water thing that wants to be you and you want to be it, only both are you—Joe Boy—and you are who you are. As you swim you can see the panther gliding gracefully along, keeping pace with the john boat.

You think that Willow is right: the panther is the guardian spirit of the swamp.

The Fossor sisters may need such a spirit.

It is hot and dry. You have never seen the swamp this low on water. Pools around the knees of cypress are almost gone. You notice again that all the swamp creatures are edgy, especially the gators and snakes—cooters or snapping turtles, too. For a moment you are chilled by the sight of a large piney rooter boar. This particularly magnificent specimen must weigh over 200 pounds. Its ivory-colored tusks look as sharp as butcher knives.

Mean and edgy.

The swamp is not a good place on this day. And there will be no moon tonight.

You have followed the john boat nearly a mile into the swamp when you catch a glimpse of her: Willow—naked, faceless, sneaking along the thicket that reaches out to the run. And then, as you continue to swim and feel your water creature within take over your body, you begin to follow the fleshly, yet ghostly presence of Willow.

You call out to her.

But she does not return your call. She keeps moving.

You follow down a deep run for how long you are not sure.

You sense the Terror is near. You stop swimming. You have lost sight of Willow.

You are not sure where you are. The john boat took a different run, and you realize that you have been led astray, and so you search for anything familiar—feeder creeks, cypress trail markers, whatever, and then, finally, you see something.

Brother Owen's cabin.

Your heart is glad.

Brother Owen will get you back on the right track.

You see him out beside his cabin, and the scene is so pleasant to view that it pumps up your heart as if it were a balloon. The old, blind man is standing among three white-tailed deer. His hand is extended. He is feeding one of the deer—a very young buck—some corn, and he is talking to the deer, and you wonder if the deer understands him.

You think it probably does.

When you see Brother Owen, you think of the word "saint."

A good word.

You momentarily forget about your fleeting vision of Willow.

She makes you think of fire and roses, but you don't know why.

You forget about the Fossor sisters, too.

You watch.

You are absorbed.

Old man and deer and swamp.

Everything belongs.

You are in a trance, and you are not even aware of how long you have watched from the swamp run, your body underwater except for your head, and you feel good. You feel so good that you think you might just float right up out of the water into the sky.

All the way to heaven.

The good moments don't last forever.

A shout fills your head.

There is red-hot fear in the voice, and you thrash and splash with your hands because you are so startled.

"Go! Get out!" the voice cries, and it slaps your brain and explodes in your ears and makes your teeth hurt, and you focus again on Brother Owen and you see horror gripping his face. He is surprised beyond words.

And you see the Terror rip up through the surface of the earth, right there in the middle of the blissful scene. There are animal shrieks of pain. The deer, slashed and bloodied by the antlers of the Terror, fall away, not expecting the unseen, unknown invader. And the old man is reaching out, not, it appears, to protect himself, but rather to touch the invader—to know his enemy.

You cry out a strangled warning to him.

But it is too late.

And you cannot believe your eyes.

You are gulping and you can't breathe and you feel that you are being punished for your sins.

You are compelled to watch as the gentle, old, blind man's body is torn by the many antlers, and you hear a death gurgle in his throat and he is knocked onto his back—and gutted like a fish.

You watch as the Terror stands over its victim, trembling.

And then it slowly swings its head around, and eyes from a realm beyond death stare at you, and the voice inside your head—the voice of your friend, Mushka—is screaming again. Screaming for you to save yourself.

FORTY-ONE

Twilight approached on Baptism Island deep in Night Horse Swamp.

The Fossor sisters had built a fire and were about to brew some tea and fix a modest supper. They had fashioned a workable campsite. They had pitched a white tent plenty large enough to sleep the three of them, though they would have liked to complete their business before the night is over.

It was Midsummer's Eve.

There would be no moon.

Being in the swamp on such an evening is foolish.

But they had a lantern, and they had the strength of their bond as sisters—they were hearts in darkness, and yet they were determined to wage a personal war with the forces of dark magic. They had brought cedar branches and cuttings of wild bamboo to burn for the protective spell their smoke cast, and Gretta would breathe from that smoke and attempt to see into what awaited them.

They were matter out of place.

Baptism Island. The island received its name from the fact that years ago swampers—mostly members of the charismatic Holiness Church with Signs Following—used the island and the deep run swinging into it for baptismal purposes. Sins by the hundreds had been washed away in this spot—or so those God-fearing swampers believed. And some of them

believed that their faith protected them from all
manner of threats: some took up serpents, testing
the scriptural pronouncement that believers could
not be harmed by poisonous reptiles or even from
the drinking of deadly concoctions.

Just beyond the island, the main fork angled off
as Cooter Run.

The old swampers kept their distance from it—
only the Bushyeye entered there.

But the Fossor sisters had locked themselves behind the doors of their own individual concerns,
and there was virtual silence as they sipped tea and
ate slices of cornbread. And after supper they fed
the fire until it roared, and they felt safer.

They tried to ignore the distant, albeit approaching strokes of lightning.

Each woman in her own way acknowledged that
a good bonfire is one of the most magical and trans-
porting of spectacles. They sank comfortably into
the primitive reverie the fire created, and then as
the texture of the night grew heavier around them
and the flames flickered lower, it was Gretta who
spoke.

"Do you hear the piney rooters?"

"Yes," said Tina.

And Artie nodded as well, and the unnerving
grunts of the wild pigs neared and gained volume.
Gretta fingered the blade of the athame as if she
expected to use it momentarily. Artie was admiring
the handiwork of the mask she had fashioned, and
Tina thought about Shepherd and wondered where
he was.

"Gretta, see what the smoke tells you," she said,
perhaps hoping that Shepherd might appear in
whatever vision she received.

"Are you ready for this?" Gretta asked, glancing
from Tina to Artie. And then she stood and lowered
her face into the escaping smoke.

She breathed and concentrated.

She surrendered to her magic.

And seconds later her scream tore the fabric of the night.

You swim as fast as you can.

Something is guiding you—the voice of your friend? Perhaps. You are putting distance between you and the scene of horror, and you feel guilty that you may have done something to cause the death of Brother Owen. You had been following Willow. But you can see that she has been under the control of the Terror, and you sense that the Terror did not want to kill. Killing is not its way.

But now you must find the Fossor sisters.

They must leave the swamp. Or risk losing their lives.

"Baptism Island," says the voice in your head.

And that is where you must go. Not a safe area of the swamp. Not one you like to go to. And as you swim—the water creature in you taking over—the voice says, "Mistletoe!" It says it again and again, and so in a wide run bordered by tall cypresses you slow and search the upper branches of the ancient trees for the parasitic plant your friend insists will protect you from your enemies.

Up you go. Knees squeezing hard against the venerable trees.

Up where all the rest of the world is below.

Where no evil can exist. Up so close to heaven you cannot help but smile.

You gather clumps of mistletoe and drape them around your neck. And down, down, down you go. It is getting dark, and off to the west you see lightning. The swamp is so dry you can taste the dryness. You can taste fire and roses.

And you become aware that the primitive realm

you are swimming through is unusually quiet as
night thickens. Where are the insects and birds?
Where are the frogs and gators? You wonder if the
mistletoe can really protect you on such a night.
You question why you are here.

Then you think of Willow.

And you head for Baptism Island.

They calmed Gretta as best they could. She dry-
retched, and Tina pushed her head between her
legs and told Artie to wet a cloth so they could press
it to Gretta's forehead. Time dissolved as Tina and
Artie hovered close to their sister and waited for
her to recover enough to share her vision. Minutes
passed. The heat and humidity were stifling. There
wasn't a breath of air, and jagged strokes of lightning were dancing ever closer to the great swamp.

At last, Gretta took a deep breath and said:

"There was so much blood."

And then she began to narrate what she had witnessed, things not *of* Willow and the Terror, but
rather things *from* them: the slaughter of the deer
and the murder of the old, blind man.

It was Artie who responded first. "This is all a
mistake. We have to go back—before it's too late."

And with those words she scurried away, out into
the border of darkness. Tina called for her to stay,
but realized that she needed to be by herself. Gretta
caught Tina's arm and looked into her face and
said, "It's already too late."

Tina held her by the shoulders and shook her
gently.

"Gretta, listen to me—*we have to do this. We have
to.*"

Her expression drained of energy, Gretta nodded,
and Tina embraced her and they held the embrace
until the eager, menacing grunting of wild pigs

erupted from beyond the nimbus of their fire. And they heard the terrified whimpering of Artie.

You are being drawn by the scent of kudzu and honeysuckle.

The essence of Willow. And yet you sense, as before, that she is not free. The Terror—the prince of dark magic—has her, is using her, to coax you ever deeper into the swamp, and you swim, careful not to lose your necklace of mistletoe, into waters you are not familiar with. Curiously cold waters. You swim until beyond you the swamp flickers with a ghostly light. You feel the air beating. It's like the sound of a beating heart.

Your friend is whispering to you: "Joe Boy, it's the Pulse. You gotta have courage. Willow's there, but the Terror has her."

You swim within view of the emanating light.

This, you feel, is the world that Willow has stepped into.

A gray, shadowy world of phantoms and unrealities.

The water is icy, so cold that it frightens you.

You are determined not to turn back when your friend suddenly cries into your ear: "Arietta! Arietta's in trouble on the island!"

"Stay right there, Artie. Whatever you do, don't make any sudden moves."

Tina held the lantern higher so that she could see her sister's face and know whether she had heard her words of caution. At Tina's side was Gretta, holding the athame as if certain she would have to use it.

Artie, thirty yards away, was hugging herself in fear. And not ten yards from her a sow and two

piglets were foraging, but another few feet beyond
them a huge boar, its tusks gleaming when the lantern light captured them, was sniffing the air.

Smelling fear.

Out of the corner of her eye Tina saw Gretta edging forward, the athame raised.

"No," Tina whispered. "Gretta, no."

And then she knew what she must try—her spell-
casting powers would have to be exercised, and they
would have to work or both of her sisters would be
at the mercy of the wild boar. With each approaching flash of lightning, the animal flinched, then recovered itself to eye Artie and the advance of Gretta.

Tina concentrated. And over and over again to
herself she repeated the word "Coda."

She shut her eyes tightly and held them that way.

Until she heard Artie cry out softly.

Suddenly, there, standing between Artie and the
wild boar, dripping with swamp water and trembling
with fear, was Joe Boy.

"Oh, Goddess, please help us," murmured
Gretta.

Tina continued attempting to cast a spell on the
wild boar, but she could see no indication that it
was working. The animal, in fact, had lowered its
massive head and was pawing the ground as if about
to charge.

Joe Boy did not move.

It was as if everyone had become a mannequin,
incapable of action, frozen by fear and balanced between cowardice and bravery. The tension held for
a score of heartbeats, an impossible-to-bear span of
time in which the swamp appeared to hold its
breath.

And then the night roared.

The high-pitched scream was not human—Tina
knew that immediately—and the movement from

the dense sedge grass was so quick that it almost seemed preternatural.

The panther, growling in anger, charged the wild boar.

There was a loud thud of animal crashing into animal and then the screeching roar of the panther mixed with the thunderous grunts of the boar, and a swirling motion as if the hand of God had reached down and spun the two creatures like tops. The volume of the battle rose to such a level that the island seemed to quake.

And then, just as suddenly, they bolted into the darkness, panther giving chase, wild boar turning every few feet to thrust at the big cat with its tusks. The roars and grunts continued into the distance, trailing off at last, punctuated by splashing.

And then silence.

You are shivering by the fire.

But you are happy inside.

The mistletoe around your neck is scratchy, so you take if off and toss it into the fire. Perhaps it helped keep you from being harmed by the wild boar—you do not know.

You think about the word "sacrifice" as you exchange glances with Arietta. She has brought you a cup of tea. She kisses you on the cheek and thanks you for your bravery. And you tell her that Mushka warned you of danger on the island.

Gretta asks you about the Terror.

Tina asks you about Willow.

And you tell them about the Pulse.

"We can't wait any longer," said Tina. "Midnight is approaching. It's time."

The four of them had been sitting by the fire.

each inwardly musing about the panther's intervention with the wild boar—the work of the Goddess?

"I sense that Mother is here with us," said Artie.

The others agreed.

"I'm ready," said Gretta. "I'm ready to face the Terror."

"Let's join hands," said Tina. "Let's pool our magic and Joe Boy's bravery—and let's get our Willow back."

She was fighting a welling of tears as the four of them stood and held hands. She forced a smile at Joe Boy, who looked small and out of place. And then he spoke, and what he said surprised and mystified each of them.

"Mushka says the music will save us."

They poled down Cooter's Run, their lantern barely effectual against the darkest night any of them had ever experienced.

"Has the swamp ever been this silent?" whispered Artie.

"I wish I had looked into the smoke one more time," said Gretta.

But Tina reached out and touched her arm and said, "We know what's ahead. We don't have to see it first."

"Up there," said Joe Boy. He was standing in the boat, fighting to maintain his balance, and when they followed the direction in which he was pointing, they began to see the ghostly light.

"Blessed be," Tina whispered to herself. "Goddess, help us."

And then Joe Boy turned toward her and said, "Mushka's sayin' words I don't understand. And she wants y'all to say them and keep sayin' them right up into the Pulse."

"What are they?" said Tina. "Can't you say them for us?"

He hesitated, and they could tell that he was listening to an inner voice.

"All right then," he said. "Here they are: *Nunc ex tenebris te educo*. I don't know what they mean."

And suddenly Tina began to laugh softly.

"Oh, Aunt Mushka, yes—the magic words."

And then the Fossor witches began to repeat them.

"Nunc ex tenebris te educo."

Now I bring thee out of darkness.

FORTY-TWO

Those words are ringing in your ears as Cooter Run widens and the fear in your throat is as thick as glue. And then you hear one of the women call out, "Look behind us!" And you hold your breath and watch as the derelict houseboat appears from nowhere and glides by, and at its rails are the ghosts of John Scarpia and Glen Favors and Brother Owen, and you know that they have been damned to an endless journey in the dark realm of Night Horse Swamp.

The Pulse draws.

A dead light generated by something unseen appears to pull the boat and to anchor it so that it is directly opposite this place that is older than the swamp itself—older than the world, older than God. You stare at its death hue and you think that in such a place it is always winter. Forever winter.

You shiver and your teeth begin to shatter and you almost forget it is June.

This is a place of harm.

It feels more deadly and threatening than any wild boar or gator.

And you know you don't belong here.

No one can.

And you want to leave immediately.

You suddenly smell ozone and you feel something like static electricity at your fingertips and close by a jagged stroke of lightning jabs at a line of tall cypresses and in a manner of seconds the treacherously dry swamp is ablaze.

You can no longer hear your friend, Mushka, and you feel little pinpricks of panic, but then you begin to smell honeysuckle and kudzu blossoms. Then your whole body goes numb because there, on a sandbar in the midst of the Pulse you see something incredible: Willow, naked, has stepped from another world into this one, and she sits down and rucks her knees up in front of some of her nakedness. She has no face.

"Willow!"

Tina clambers out of the boat, splashing and crying with joy.

At first her daughter gives no signal that she knows her mother is close. But Tina continues wading in the waist-deep water, tears flowing down her cheeks as she repeats Willow's name. And then she is rewarded: Willow's facial features magically return.

She is smiling. Her eyes are bright and winning.

But not for long.

Rising behind her, large and ominous, its nest of sharp antlers generating flickers of light as they rake through the humid air, is the Terror. At the sight of the creature, the women and the boy are as immobile as stones. Cold air roils up from the swamp water like mist.

It is Gretta who breaks the spell that has been cast upon them.

"You bastard!" she screams. "You took my love!"

Athame raised to strike, she scrambles into the water and rushes toward the Pulse, all her energies of revenge directed at the Terror standing protectively behind Willow. The creature looks upon Gretta

with hatred in its eyes, and when its vision locks onto
the dagger, tiny spiderwebs of blue-white heat and
light flow out from the tips of its antlers and strike
the blade.

Instantly it explodes in a shower of blue-white
sparks.

Gretta drops it, cries out in pain and frustration,
and sinks back toward the boat.

But Artie is there immediately to follow with her
attempt to defeat the dark magic of the Terror. She
is wearing the mask she has fashioned, and she is
herself a ghostly symbol of transformation as she
wades toward the Pulse in her white dress.

And momentarily her creative touch of magic
works.

The Terror appears mesmerized by the mask.

Powers somewhat weakened, it seems to stagger
before it rights itself and issues a primitive, animal-
istic grunt. Its eyes burn fire, and as it lifts its head
to the moonless sky something horrifying to witness
occurs.

Artie, bathed in a blue-white shower of light, is
levitated up from the swamp water, rising slowly,
spinning lazily as if held by an invisible hook at her
throat. Her head is thrown back and her arms fall
to her sides. And the mask, bearing its remarkable
similarity to the head of the Terror, roars into flames
and falls away from Artie's face and splashes into
the run.

She hangs there in the blue-white shaft of light.

She looks all-and-all a corpse.

"No-o-o!"

The shout seems to fill the world.

Tina steps aside as Joe Boy thrashes through the
water headed straight for the Terror. But he does
not get close. Tina and Gretta gasp at what they see,
and Joe Boy's next cry is one of pain rather than
anger.

Around his body the water of the swamp run ices over, trapping him in a waist-deep pool, and though he struggles with all his might, he cannot free himself.

Tina does not believe her eyes.

But she knows she must act—she knows she must try her magic. Willow is waiting. The Terror is in control, and the swamp is burning fiercely. She concentrates upon casting a spell that will diminish the Terror and send it back to some dark corner of the Otherworld.

Coda.

The word hammers in her thoughts as she concentrates.

Nearly a minute passes before she begins to feel that she has lost.

They have lost—her sisters and Joe Boy and Willow.

Gretta is sobbing. Artie is helplessly suspended twenty feet in the air. Joe Boy is frozen like the dead limb of a tree extending up from the bottom of a pond in winter. And Willow's smile has disappeared.

Tina lowers her head and is on the edge of giving up hope.

The music is faint at first.

It seems to come from the darkness beyond the tops of the trees.

It seems to come from the stars.

Or from someone descending stairs from the attic of the night.

It is the sound of a guitar.

Tina looks up. "Shep!"

She watches as the man she loves lowers into the scene like a triumphant angel.

The guitar he has been holding morphs suddenly into a large bird—like a hawk or an eagle—and it

swoops down from him toward the Terror. Aware
that it has become prey rather than predator, the
creature readies its antlers to meet the attack, but
the bird dives and somehow magically enters the
chest of the beast.

The Terror shrieks in pain, a primitive, ancient
emotion that is palpable.

And the creature is weakened.

And Shepherd descends like a parachutist landing. Lower and lower until he drops down and into
the creature, disappearing like snow melting on
flames.

Watching the spectacle, Tina cries out because it
appears, momentarily at least, that Shepherd has
been absorbed into the body of the Terror and defeated. Then she sees the scarred hands of the man
she loves push out from the creature's chest and
lightning flashes from up out of the Pulse.

And the swamp erupts in a blinding shower of
white-hot light and trembles as if being rocked by
an earthquake.

Only Tina looks back.

She does not know what has happened beyond
one fact: her daughter, Willow, is with them, in the
boat, and Gretta and Artie have pulled Joe Boy free
of the ice-encrusted pool and they are trying to revive him.

Tina begins to pole furiously.

"Which way?" she cries.

And the flames of the raging swamp fire are
blocking the run with thick smoke. For Tina, it is
like her nightmare of being in a fiery furnace.
Gretta joins her, and with both of them poling they
make progress. A doubling back, then an instinctive
turning down a more narrow run, and within minutes they follow the meander until Gretta exclaims:

"Tina, there's no way out!"

In front of them a dark curtain of smoke whispers open and a great stage of fire seems to shout at them from all sides.

FORTY-THREE

"We have to get help for Joe Boy!"

Artie and Willow are hovering near the boy. Artie is pleading with Tina, but it appears that the boat and its occupants are trapped by the flames. Fiery branches from tall pines and cypresses crash around, striking the water and generating ugly hisses.

"We'll never make it!" cries Gretta.

Tina looks on helplessly. The fire is everywhere.

Then she glances down at her daughter, who is on her knees, her eyes closed, her lips moving as if in prayer.

"Willow?" says Tina, hunkering close to her. "Willow, sweetheart?"

But the girl continues her small ritual.

She is whispering something.

A single word.

Coda.

Over and over.

The fire rages ever closer, and the smoke is suffocating.

Tina is dizzied. And for just an instant she believes that Gretta may be right: they won't make it. Night Horse Swamp has become an earthly hell from which there is no escape.

"It's the panther!"

Gretta's words jolt Tina back to her senses. And

then she sees the big cat, too, peering at them from
a hummock. Suddenly Willow stands.

"Follow her! Follow the panther!" she calls out.
And they do.

Thirty minutes later they look back upon a world
choked with smoke, a world from which they have
been delivered—by the panther.

"Where did she go?" asks Gretta.

"Back into the everywhere," Willow explains.

"Let's go home," says Tina.

"We need to hurry," says Artie. "Joe Boy is con-
scious, but his breathing is labored. He's got to have
some medical help as soon as possible."

Willow kneels by him once again.

She holds his hand.

And the boat rides low and sleek upon the water
and everyone tries to remain hopeful.

But Gretta has stared into the smoke and has seen
something that tracks her face with lines of apprehension.

"What is it?" Tina asks her.

Gretta meets her sister's eyes, but cannot respond.

"He's dying!"

They had not quite reached Night Horse Creek.
Artie was holding Joe Boy's face in her hands, and
she was looking up at the others, pleading with
them as if certain they could do something to save
him.

Though the conflagration was a quarter of a mile
behind them, they could feel the heat from it. Seeing the expression of alarm on Artie's face, Tina
directed Gretta to start poling toward a cypress backwater. But she did not know how they would be able
to help the boy.

It was Willow who, once again, came to the rescue.

"Mother," she said, pressing her fingertips against the side of her head, "I can hear Aunt Mushka. I can hear her."

"What is she saying?"

"She says . . . she says, I can heal Joe Boy. If she can stay in my head, then maybe I'll be able to heal him."

Tina heard Artie whisper the word "Maybe" as if disappointed.

"Okay," said Tina. "What do we need to do?"

"Stop at the next hummock. I have to get him back in the water. It's his element—it's the only way we can save him."

You feel a wet warmth spread over you and through you.

Someone is holding you. Holding your body and pushing you underwater. Someone is pressing your hand hard, squeezing it as if trying to get the blood circulating.

You have never felt so cold in your life.

You feel as if you have swallowed ice cubes.

You feel as if you have frost on your tongue.

Your teeth are chattering, but the warm swamp water and the touch of the other person—is it Willow?—are pulling you out of a frozen dream. That's where you've been—in a frozen dream. And every word that comes into your mind is cold and icy. Thinking makes you shiver.

But you are returning from that world.

And you know that you are returning because even underwater you can smell something familiar: kudzu and honeysuckle.

And you begin to hear voices as you hold your breath and you are pushed deeper under the water.

One voice is Willow's. One is Mushka's. You do not comprehend what they are saying, but you sense that their words are meant to save your life.

Beneath the water you are a cold creature waking up or being born.

Below you a bright, white light appears.

A wonderful light. You want to swim down into that light and embrace it.

But the voices won't let you. The voices tell you that if you go to the light you won't ever return.

Return.

The word is a light unto itself. You are pulled both ways: down to the light and up toward the voices, and the struggle continues for as long as you can hold your breath.

You know who has won when you break the surface of the water, gasping and crying out, blood pumping once again through your veins, and the first thing your eyes focus upon is something you haven't seen in a long time.

Willow's smile.

FORTY-FOUR

"It's a beautiful fire," said Willow.

And she meant it more deeply than if she had tossed off a remark about a beautiful sunset or a beautiful day—*beautiful fire* resonated from her secret self.

"Yes, a magnificent one," said her mother. "They say, of course, that it's what the swamp needs. It has a healing, restoring function—I guess rather the way you restored Joe Boy. With Aunt Mushka's help."

From the deck where they were sitting, she looked beyond Pan Island at the low flames spreading out in front of the larger, more impressive ones at the heart of the conflagration. Several days of smoke had leeched the brightness out of the sunlight. She glanced from the burning swamp to Willow and said, "Are you glad to be home? You've been very quiet these past two days. I still wish you'd let me take you to a doctor for a checkup."

Willow smiled and shook her head. "I'm fine. And I'm glad to be here. It was a strange experience. I've told you everything I can remember. It was like, I don't know, suspended animation or something. So unreal. It's going to take time to . . . you know . . . be who I was again."

"Of course," said her mother. "You know we'll all do what we can to help. I'm sorry about your father—sorry about how magic turned dark and . . ."

Willow went to her and stood behind her mother's chair and hugged her to show that she understood and that there was no need to finish the thought. So much of what had occurred was in the realm of the unsayable.

"I want to hear about Willis Shepherd," she said.

Then she swung around and sat in her mother's lap and listened to a woman in love.

"But he's trapped there, isn't he?" said her mother almost as an afterthought to her narrative of falling in love with a Cunning Man who seemed to want to become fully human again and to love and be with her.

"Yes," said Willow. "The Terror no longer has power in the swamp, and the Pulse will remain indifferent to all that humans do. But this man you love sacrificed himself for us."

Her mother nodded soberly. "And there's no way . . . is there?"

Willow said nothing.

But her secret self whispered that, yes, there was a way—a way to give her mother a chance at the love she deserved.

You listen to the words of your friend.

"Joe Boy, that's what you've got to do: Let the mud of yourself settle so you can see in the clear water who you are. Dark magic has knocked you around some—knocked around all of us. But we goin' to be good 'n fine. Cavatina, she's so happy to have her daughter back, and Allegretta, she's goin' to live with me now. Not goin' back to Pan Island. Arietta, she's goin' to be with Miss Michaels. There's love there. And you—you, my friend, are goin' to keep runnin' the rope-pull ferry and ringin' that plowshare and bein' a fine young man for Miss Billie Ruth and Mr. Buck."

Your friend is at home now in her own bed, still recovering, but there is a sparkle in her eyes, and when she talks about the future it all sounds good. Except, of course, the part about your Arietta going away with that woman.

But you get to thinking that maybe you'll meet another Arietta one day—maybe not as beautiful and sexy—but close.

So you stand and talk with your friend.

In the days ahead, the swamp fire continues, burning fiercely, yet slowly, edging closer to the spit as the moon changes, swelling to half its light, and during hot afternoons you swim with Willow and the two of you enjoy each other's company.

There is something, though, in Willow's faraway look that troubles you.

Often you catch her staring at the big blaze as it inches closer.

You do not know what she sees there in the flames.

Then one evening as a bone-white half-moon shines down through the smoke of twilight you see her swim off by herself. And you follow.

Like a spy for the Goddess.

The approaching night is on fire.

Willow doesn't know that you are following, or if she does, she doesn't let on that she does. She never stops to turn and shout for you to go back, so you continue at a distance, your concern growing as she nears the heart of the fire raging on a hummock off the main run.

When you finally realize what she is about to do, it is too late.

Too late certainly to change her mind.

When she is standing on the hummock, dripping with swamp water, and facing the waves of heat throbbing out from the fire, you think of Brother Owen and a single word.

"Sacrifice."

You want to join Willow. You see now by the way she walks into the flames that she is doing so joyfully, selflessly, and you think that you would like to feel that same kind of joy. You catch a whiff of honeysuckle and kudzu.

And then another fragrance.

Roses.

You look into the huge blossom of fire that dwarfs Willow even as she merges with it, and you no longer see flames—you see a gigantic bouquet of roses.

You have tears in your eyes, but you do not call after your friend.

You cannot join her. The sacrifice is not yours to make.

And as she disappears into the conflagration you hear music.

Nirvana and Danzig.

Witchy music.

Willow's music.

FORTY-FIVE

"She did it for us."

A late afternoon thundershower had put out much of the fire, and as that same storm had hurried across the great swamp it seemed to have reached down and swept the man she loved up into its winds and its darkness, intent upon delivering him to her arms.

That was the romantic view.

Tina needed Shepherd now more than ever before. Willow had gone back. Her action had stunned Tina, who believed her daughter had shaken off many of the effects of being the Terror's captive and was ready to evolve into a young woman and faithful adherent to the Old Ways.

"How do you know that?" said Tina, responding to Shepherd's comment.

They were sitting on the couch, and she was struck by how alive, how vibrant Shepherd looked—how free.

"It was the only way," he said, "that I could have been released from the swamp, from the residue of dark magic that continued to hold me there and to keep me from returning to you. There had to be a sacrifice. You might say that the rules of the Otherworld demanded it."

"But why must you leave again?"

"Because I've recovered the courage I need. I

mean, the courage to be a Cunning Man again and to perform the holy tasks required of me. Please understand that."

Tina shook her head.

She could feel the inevitable rushing into her life, rushing into the moment, an elemental something over which she had no control.

"When will you come back?"

He took her into his arms and kissed her ear and the corner of her eye.

"I love you," was all he said.

She sighed, and they held each other, silence filling in around him, and their embrace held as darkness spread over the swamp.

When at last she pulled away from him she said, "Be who you need to be. I have no right to ask you to be someone else. Be who you are meant to be."

"Thanks to you and your family, I can be."

She looked deep into his eyes and then reached for his scarred hands.

"Go now," she said. "Before I beg you to stay."

FORTY-SIX

In the end mystery dominated.

The Terror. The Pulse. Night Horse Swamp.

Even the word "Coda" remained stubbornly in the realm of mystery.

But no one can live sanely with mystery without asking questions, and for the survivors of the reign of dark magic there could be no answers.

"Live the questions," Aunt Mushka wisely told all who would listen.

And so, in the end, you must imagine Joe Boy standing by his rope-pull ferry signal beneath a bright and heavy full moon. He misses Willow. He misses Arietta. Every so often he will visit his friend, Mushka, who is a bit feeble, though she is being tended to lovingly by Allegretta. And less frequently, he visits Willow's mother, who has put her spellscast Web site back on-line.

If you are picturing Joe Boy awash there in the moonlight, imagine along with him that you suddenly hear music—Willow's music, soul-rocking music—but that you hear another kind of music as well.

A distant, ghostly guitar playing.

And maybe if you close your eyes along with Joe Boy you can imagine something else ghostly: a giant, phantom horse—the Night Horse—thundering through the ancient swamp—with Willow on its back.

Imagine Joe Boy opening his eyes and smiling. He's smiling because he *belongs* in this strange world. His secret self knows it. He has his small hammer raised, ready to signal that the ferry is about to cross. But before he does, he hears the whisper of the man whom he once saw walk upon the moonlight.

Here is what the moonlight man says:

"The world is sometimes darkness,
but when the great light of the day
strikes the swamp, it is finished
in beauty."

Imagine Joe Boy swinging hard, ball-peen hammer against the single plowshare hanging by a chain. Hear the unmistakable clang, clang, clang. Anyone who knows how to listen can.

You could have heard it on the dark side of the moon.

EPILOGUE

If you have a secret self—you know the truth of this tale.

ABOUT THE AUTHOR

Stephen Gresham lives in Alabama. He loves to hear from readers; you may write to him c/o Pinnacle Books. Please include a self-addressed, stamped envelope if you wish to receive a response.

BOOK YOUR PLACE ON OUR WEBSITE AND MAKE THE READING CONNECTION!

We've created a customized website just for our very special readers, where you can get the inside scoop on everything that's going on with Zebra, Pinnacle and Kensington books.

When you come online, you'll have the exciting opportunity to:

- View covers of upcoming books
- Read sample chapters
- Learn about our future publishing schedule (listed by publication month *and author*)
- Find out when your favorite authors will be visiting a city near you
- Search for and order backlist books from our online catalog
- Check out author bios and background information
- Send e-mail to your favorite authors
- Meet the Kensington staff online
- Join us in weekly chats with authors, readers and other guests
- Get writing guidelines
- AND MUCH MORE!

**Visit our website at
http://www.kensingtonbooks.com**

When Darkness Falls
Grab One of These
Pinnacle Horrors

Scare Up One of These Pinnacle Horrors

Feel the Seduction of
Pinnacle Horror